# Readers love the Stonebridge Mysteries
## by MAGGIE KAVANAGH

### *Double Indemnity*

"*Double Indemnity* is a fast paced murder/mystery with a well developed plot that twists and turns from start to finish."
—Carly's Book Reviews

"This book is one wild ride!"
—MM Good Book Revews

"*Double Indemnity* grabbed me from the first page, and I didn't let go of the story even when I finished the last page"
—The Novel Approach

### *Inner Sanctum*

"The first paragraph of the story leaves you intrigued. At the end of the first chapter, I was hooked and could not wait to finish the story."
—Hearts on Fire

"The beauty of this novel lies in its simplicity. It was easy to sink into the story and forget about reality."
—Scattered Thoughts and Rogue Words

"…Maggie Kavanagh writes an intriguing mystery."
—Divine Magazine

By MAGGIE KAVANAGH

Taking Flight

THE STONEBRIDGE MYSTERIES
Double Indemnity
Inner Sanctum
Blind Spot

Published by DREAMSPINNER PRESS
www.dreamspinnerpress.com

# Blind Spot

## Maggie Kavanagh

Published by
DREAMSPINNER PRESS

5032 Capital Circle SW, Suite 2, PMB# 279, Tallahassee, FL 32305-7886 USA
www.dreamspinnerpress.com

Blind Spot
© 2016 Maggie Kavanagh.

Cover Art
© 2016 Maria Fanning.
Cover content is for illustrative purposes only and any person depicted on the cover is a model.

ISBN: 978-1-63476-745-3
Digital ISBN: 978-1-63476-746-0
Library of Congress Control Number: 2015950523
Published January 2016
v. 1.0

Printed in the United States of America
∞
This paper meets the requirements of
ANSI/NISO Z39.48-1992 (Permanence of Paper).

*To my partner in crime. Always.*

# Acknowledgments

HERE WE are at the end of a long road. I am so grateful for the help I've received along the way. Thank you to the entire Dreamspinner production team for always being ready to answer questions and lend a hand. A special thanks to Maria Fanning, who has created some gorgeous cover designs for this series. I would also like to extend my gratitude to Liz Fitzgerald, my Dreamspinner editor, for her observations, insights, and her swift red pen. Last and certainly not least, much love and thanks to Olivia Mandell, who edited presubmission drafts of this novel, and Michela and Justyna, dear friends who read this book at all stages of the drafting process and offered their feedback and support. I'm extremely lucky to have such wonderful people in my corner.

# Chapter 1

THE LUCKY Star resembled a prom set from an eighties movie. Streamers hung from the ceiling and a disco ball spun in the middle of the room, flashing tiny beams of light. In the corner a DJ played "Born to Run" from bass-heavy speakers, but the small crowd was even louder, screaming and blowing noisemakers as Sam Flynn stood holding his boyfriend Nathan's hand. He blinked in surprise.

A banner reading HAPPY 29TH BIRTHDAY, SAM hung behind the bar, where everyone was hiding when Sam and Nathan entered.

"So this is why you wanted to hurry down here so fast," Sam yelled in Nathan's ear over the music.

Nathan chuckled and grabbed him around the waist. "Maybe."

"You sneaky bastard." Even though he'd stopped drinking, Sam loved the Star, not least because one of his best friends, Rachel Mayer, tended bar. She stood behind it, clapping and looking very self-satisfied. To her left her girlfriend Alex wore a glittery birthday hat over her short white-blonde bob. Further guests included Sam's other best friend, Yuri Manella, and Damon Blake, who Sam hadn't expected to see, since he'd recently moved from Stonebridge, Connecticut to Hartford. He gave Sam a smile and a nod.

"I wondered what you all were planning." Sam tried to hide his grin and mostly failed. Some guys from Manella's Landscaping whooped and raised beers to toast in the corner. Even Antonio Rivera, one of Nathan's FBI buddies, was there.

"Are you surprised?" Nathan leaned down and kissed Sam on the cheek. His new beard scratched lightly against Sam's skin.

"Hell yeah, but you shouldn't have done all this."

1

"Why not?" Nathan's dark eyes glinted in the flashing lights of the disco ball. Sam hadn't been sure about the beard at first, but it was growing on him—pun intended. Nathan looked hotter than ever. After six months of living together and over a year of dating, Sam still thought Nathan was the most attractive man he'd ever seen.

"Because you know I hate surprise parties."

"I know you say you do, but I also know when you're lying. Don't I?" Nathan arched an eyebrow, and Sam flushed all over. He wondered what Nathan had planned for them later, after the party. In fact, he'd been tingling with anticipation since Nathan mentioned it over breakfast.

"Yes, sir." He urged Nathan's head down and whispered into his ear, grateful for the loud music. If any of his friends overheard him addressing Nathan in that way, he'd never live it down. They had no idea what he and his boyfriend got up to in the bedroom, and they didn't need to know. Nathan responded with a devious smile.

After the song ended, the DJ spoke into the mic. "Welcome to the guest of honor, *Sa-a-aaam Flynnnnn*." He played some annoying sound effects—fart noises and whistles—and Sam wondered where the hell Rachel had picked him up.

Everyone erupted into an off-key rendition of "Happy Birthday." Sam rolled his eyes and leaned back into Nathan's embrace. He didn't mind being a year older, but for a long time he'd dreaded birthdays. They always reminded him of his parents, who had made a big deal over every milestone for both of their sons. This year he'd spent a quiet morning with Nathan and then gone to visit his little brother, Tim, at Shady Brook, the facility he'd lived in since a car accident had killed their parents and left him comatose over seven years before. Sam's throat tightened. He wished Tim could be here.

The singing fizzled out into more shouts and whistles, and then the music started up at a more conversational volume. Sam and Nathan crossed the room toward the bar and greeted their friends.

"Hey, you," said Rachel. "Happy birthday." She slid him a Coke sans rum. "You should have seen the look on your face when you walked through the door." She grinned and put both hands to her cheeks, making a silly "surprised" face.

"You're all conniving and can't be trusted," said Sam. "But thank you." He leaned over the bar and kissed her cheek. "You look great."

"You like it?" Ever since high school, Rachel had worn her hair Afro-style and liked to streak it with color. Instead of her usual purple, however, this time she used silver.

"Yeah. It's very dystopian future."

"That's what I was going for."

Alex took advantage of his distraction to wrangle a party hat onto him from behind. He grunted with protest and went to remove it, but Rachel shook her head at him. "Don't you dare. She's so excited about those damn hats."

They chatted for a while about the party, until Sam realized Nathan had disappeared to talk with Rivera on the opposite side of the room. Nathan was smiling and laughing at something the older man said. Instead of the pang of jealousy Sam felt months before when he suspected Nathan might be attracted to Rivera, now he was simply pleased Nathan was enjoying himself. He only hoped Nathan wouldn't be disappointed when his friend headed back to New York.

A slap on his arm made him turn. "Hey, stranger." Yuri grinned at him, cheeks dimpling. "Happy birthday."

"Thanks. Great to see you, man." Sam hugged his friend. They'd been partners in Yuri's family landscaping business for years, but recently Sam had sold back his share in order to pursue his journalism career. He still worked part-time during the week, but it had been a while since he'd been on a project with Yuri. "How're you? Had any hot dates?" Sam waggled his eyebrows.

"Oh, you know. A few here and there. Nothing serious."

"Good for you." Lord knows his friend deserved a little R & R after the breakup he'd gone through in December. Yuri had an amazing body, a sweet personality, and a sexy Greek accent to boot.

Yuri took a sip of beer and licked the foam off his top lip. "So, the big two-nine."

"Yep."

"Almost thirty."

"Shut up." Sam gave him a light punch. "And anyway, you'll be here soon, my friend."

"Attention." Rachel started dinging a spoon against a glass. "Thank you all for coming. We're here to celebrate Sam's birthday. I wanted to plan a roast, but Nathan talked me out of it." There were a couple of good-natured boos from the crowd and scattered laughter. Nathan shrugged sheepishly. "It's a shame, because I have some really good material," Rachel continued. "Sam, you're a pain in the ass, but you're our pain in the ass. I've known you for fifteen years, and I love the hell out of you. We've been through a lot together. I know this last year hasn't been easy." People nodded and murmured. Stonebridge was still recovering from a spree of arsons that had culminated in a Halloween-night explosion at the Episcopal Church, leaving a total of twelve people dead and many more injured.

Sam met Damon's eyes from across the room. The teenager had been the lead suspect in the case until Sam and Nathan apprehended the real culprits, who were now safely behind bars. Damon gave him a half smile of commiseration.

"But our city is strong," Rachel continued. "Our community is strong. We won't be defeated when we have people like Sam in our corner. Not when we have people like Damon Blake, who's here tonight and starting college in the fall. Let's raise our glasses to Sam and Damon, and to Nathan, Sam's sugar daddy, who you can thank for the open bar."

Another cheer erupted, and Sam laughed and clapped. He made his way toward Damon.

"Hey man," said Sam. "I'm glad you could make it. Thanks for coming."

"I wouldn't have missed it." Damon thrust out a gift, looking slightly embarrassed. He ran his hand over his closely shaved head. "It's not much."

Sam was touched. He took the package, which felt decidedly like a paperback book, and then pulled Damon into a one-armed hug. "You didn't have to. Things are going well?"

"Yeah. It's weird to be out of town, but it's a nice change of pace."

Sam smiled. "Good to hear." They chatted for a couple of minutes, until other partygoers started to interrupt. Sam put them off to say good-bye to Damon, who was getting ready to leave. As a rule, the bar didn't allow minors after nine.

"Anyway, if you're ever in Hartford." Damon put out his hand.

"I've got your number."

Sam scanned the crowd to find Nathan. Well-wishers and friends stopped him for hugs along the way. By the time he managed to get to his boyfriend, the music had switched from rock to club music with a sultry beat.

"Dance with me?" Sam asked.

"Of course."

Nathan was a great dancer. He moved his hips in a seductive rhythm, staying close to Sam and guiding him onto the impromptu dance floor. Though Nathan was five inches taller, Sam never felt dwarfed by his height, but rather complemented by it, just as Nathan's dark looks balanced his light. Sam wrapped his arms around Nathan's back and felt his strong muscles working as they moved.

All eyes were on them. Sam caught a glimpse of Rachel, who gave him the two thumbs-up signal. They were showing off a little, but Sam figured it was his right. He was the birthday boy, after all, and he was dancing with the hottest guy in the room. Nathan leaned down to whisper in his ear. "Do your friends really call me your sugar daddy?"

Sam laughed at the unexpected question. He'd almost forgotten what Rachel had called Nathan.

"Yup." Not only did Nathan pay for Tim's health care, he always objected whenever Sam reached for his wallet on other occasions. At least he allowed Sam to front his share of the rent for their apartment. It was one of the reasons he'd stayed on part-time at Manella's. While he preferred writing to the landscaping work, it didn't quite pay the bills.

Nathan frowned. "I'm not old enough to be a daddy." His recent birthday—thirty-seven—had given him a taste of midlife crisis. Sam kept expecting him to show up at home with a new sports car and a babe in the passenger seat.

It made him consider his answer. "You're so smoking hot, they have to call you something when they describe you, or they'll embarrass themselves."

"Nice save, but you're lying. Your pulse picks up. Here." Nathan put his hand to Sam's racing jugular, sweeping his fingertip down the arch of Sam's exposed neck.

"That's not the only thing that makes my pulse race." In fact the dirty dancing was creating a problematic situation for polite company. At least others had joined them on the dance floor. Rachel and Alex were swaying together a few feet away, staring at each other with grins on their faces.

"I've got plans for later. Can you wait?"

"I don't know…. I might need a reminder in self-control."

"Hmm. Just wait till you open your present." Nathan leaned down to give Sam a brief, openmouthed kiss. Sam didn't detect any booze, which meant Nathan was abstaining—he usually did as moral support for Sam when they went out, but it also meant they'd be playing later. Early on Nathan had made it clear each of them had to be sober when they scened. No booze, no drugs—which was fine with Sam. Being with Nathan was enough.

"So, what are we doing later?" Sam asked.

"You'll have to be patient."

They continued dancing for a couple more songs and then grabbed a few snacks from one of the side tables. Rachel announced it was time for presents.

"I told you guys, no presents," he protested.

"Sit down and shut up."

Most of them were inexpensive, which was fine with Sam—a few books and Blu-rays he wanted, a couple gag gifts from his work friends— but when it came time for Nathan's gift, Sam paused and weighed the small package in his hands.

On Christmas Nathan had given him a new laptop computer, an ultrathin silver model he'd secretly drooled over for months. He hadn't exactly been able to reject the gift sitting in Nathan's parents' living room, but it was an extravagance he felt a little ridiculous accepting, seeing as his own gifts to Nathan—the new Murakami novel and a sweater Rachel had helped him pick out in a desperate dash to the mall—were worth barely a fraction of what Nathan had paid. Of course Nathan hadn't seen the problem, but later, after Sam explained his embarrassment, he promised no more expensive gifts unless they agreed beforehand. He hoped Nathan had taken their talk seriously and that, when he opened this present, he wouldn't be confronted with a gold watch or something equally lavish.

When he opened the package, he frowned down at a simple silver keychain. It gleamed in his fingers. The initials on it read S+N.

A few guests muttered things like "oh how nice," but Sam could tell they weren't impressed.

"Do you like it?" Nathan asked. He was fighting a smile. There was obviously more to this present than met the eye.

Sam nodded. "I love it."

The DJ stopped the music again, and Sam looked around, waiting for someone else to stand up and make an embarrassing speech.

"You guys. You guys," Rachel said, grabbing the microphone from the front of the room. "Shut up and listen. The mayor is dead."

"Oh, come on, Rach," Sam called out. "It may be my birthday, but murder's taking it a little far." A few laughs from people nearby slowly faded as Rachel shook her head and held up her phone.

"I'm not joking. It's all over Twitter. Looks like he was found unresponsive in his home a couple hours ago."

Sam exchanged a glance with Nathan. It was huge news. He grabbed his phone and started scrolling through the #RIPMayorWhite hashtag. There was no more information than what Rachel had announced, but Sam felt his blood fire up. Things had been quiet the last few weeks, and he'd been waiting for a big story.

"Looks like I've got to take off," said Rivera, slapping Nathan on the shoulder.

"Of course. Let us know what's going on, Tony."

"You bet."

Once Rivera was gone, the room erupted in conversation. At Sam's prompting, Rachel turned on the bar TV and flicked to the news channels. It hadn't yet reached the national level, but the local ten o'clock was reporting from St. Mary's hospital.

The reporter talking to the studio newscaster cocked his head as he listened into his earpiece. "That's right, Ted. Mayor White was apparently found in his bedroom by his wife earlier this evening."

"Any word on cause of death yet, Brian?" the newscaster asked.

"No word yet, but there are rumors the mayor was suffering from angina over the past few months. It may have been a heart attack."

"Very true," said Ted the newscaster. "We know he was trying to get in shape and lose some weight under doctor's orders. It's been slow going because of his age."

The mayor was sixty-three—a large man with a well-known passion for greasy double cheeseburgers. Heart attack did seem the most likely scenario. After a few more questions with not much detail provided from the on-ground reporter, Rachel turned the TV off and the music started back up. No one in the bar had much love for the mayor, whose policies had always favored the rich suburbs of West Stonebridge over the grittier downtown. While Sam wasn't exactly fond of his deputy either, surely the guy couldn't be worse than White. And then, during the next election cycle, maybe some new blood would have a chance.

"So, what do you think? You want to get out of here?" Nathan asked as the party started to break up.

"Hell, yeah." Sam was itching to get back to his computer.

He said good-bye to everyone and followed Nathan into the pleasant May night. It would be another month or so before things heated up for the summer, and Sam enjoyed the temperate spring.

"I can't believe the mayor's dead," he said, falling into step beside Nathan as they walked the seven blocks back to their place.

"You couldn't have asked for a better gift." Nathan elbowed his side.

"Oh, come on. I'm not heartless. But after what happened on Halloween, the guy was clearly unfit for office. He should have resigned months ago."

"True."

After the bombing of the Episcopal Church, Mayor White had received a ton of criticism from all sides. Sam had written a scathing piece on his blog, and even the normally pro-White *Gazette* had published some op-ed pieces condemning his decision to hold the Halloween block party, even though the arsonist terrorizing the city was still on the loose.

"Well, I'll tell you what," said Sam, "I'm not happy the guy's dead, but maybe this is a blessing in disguise for the city."

"Maybe so."

"I wonder if Judy White's down at the hospital. Maybe we can pop by quickly, see if she needs a shoulder to cry on?" If he could get the scoop straight from the mayor's wife, leave the *Gazette* in the dust….

"No. Not tonight. You're going to let it go for tonight."

"But—"

Nathan shook his head. "It can wait. But I can't." He opened his hand. There, on the flat of his palm, was a small key. A frisson of excitement ran up Sam's spine. He thought of the silver keychain.

"Is that for—"

"Yes."

"Well, I suppose the mayor will still be dead in the morning." Sam was buzzing with anticipation by the time they entered the building and hit the button for the elevator. He still got a kick out of living in a place that actually had one.

Upstairs their white cat, Shadow, was lounging sleepily on the rug near the door. She immediately sprang to her feet and began meowing for her dinner. Then she narrowed her blue eyes accusingly when neither paid her any attention.

"All right. All right," Nathan said, picking her up. Then he looked at Sam. "I'm going to feed the cat first. You, go get into position and stay quiet. I don't want to hear a sound."

"With or without the blindfold?"

"With. Hold this key in your lips."

"Okay."

"Okay, sir."

Sam's belly swooped at Nathan's dominant tone. "Okay, sir." He quickly entered the bedroom, kicked off his shoes, and yanked his shirt over his head. The blindfold was in the black box they kept under the bed, along with the other equipment they used for play. Sam ran his fingers over the flat paddle Nathan gave him several months before. The smooth wood was cool to the touch, and he shivered remembering the first time they used it. He hoped they'd use it tonight.

After he grabbed the blindfold and undressed, he kneeled at the foot of the bed with his hands behind his head, cock already hard. The metallic taste of the key wasn't pleasant, but Sam wasn't about to disobey Nathan—he was too eager to see what it would unlock.

# Chapter 2

THE FIRST thing Sam noticed the next morning was the pain in his muscles as he stretched. His ass was sore—in a good way. The next was the thin metal and leather band around his neck. They hadn't taken it off after the session. Sam wanted to wear it as he slept, a reminder he belonged to Nathan, though Nathan had allowed him to keep the key as a gesture of good faith. It was the best gift he'd ever received and definitely the best birthday he could remember.

Feeling lonely on his side of the bed, Sam wriggled under the covers to get closer to Nathan. The sheets were empty and cold. He blinked and sat up. It was still early, and a vague light filtered in from beneath the blackout curtains. Otherwise, the room was dark and hummed with the sound of the air conditioner. Shadow was sleeping on Nathan's pillow.

Figuring Nathan would be back to bed soon, Sam pulled the covers around him and let the previous night replay in his mind. A delicious heat ran through him when he remembered how Nathan had brought him to orgasm twice. How the collar felt when Nathan held it from behind as they fucked.

His morning erection pulsed with desire, and he squeezed it to relieve some of the pressure. He wanted Nathan to find him with his hand wrapped around his cock. Would he want to punish Sam for starting without him? Or would he enjoy the view and get his own cock out so they could watch each other jerk off? Sam loved seeing Nathan touch himself with those long, capable fingers.

But the anticipated toilet flush never came, and eventually Sam figured Nathan had gotten up for good. The distant smell of coffee percolating finally got him out of bed.

He grabbed a fresh pair of boxer briefs from the dresser and pulled them up over his hips, noting how enticing his boner looked—rock hard and tucked snugly up and to the right. With any luck, Nathan would want to get his mouth around it. Today was Sam's official birthday, after all. He deserved a morning BJ.

Before he exited the bedroom, he caught a glimpse of himself in the full-length mirror. He paused. His eyes were feverish—a brighter green then their usual hazel—and his lips were swollen. When he turned, he noticed some red marks on his back. They were fading and likely wouldn't bruise, but he wouldn't be taking his shirt off around anyone but Nathan for the next couple days.

He brought his fingers to the silver and black leather collar. It was about a half-inch wide, resting just beneath his Adam's apple, and the leather was smooth and supple. On the front it held a small embossed plate with their initials, like the keychain. At the back was a loop that Sam suspected was for a leash. Nathan had finally confessed he'd had it custom made. Sam smiled. Twenty-nine was going to be a good year.

Nathan was on the phone in the living room. He didn't look up when Sam entered, but from his body language, Sam could tell something was wrong. His first thought was something had happened to Nathan's parents. But even though Nathan was frowning, he didn't look devastated, as he certainly would if he'd heard bad news about his folks. He noticed Sam and held up a finger. Obviously he wanted privacy.

Sam went into the kitchen to grab a cup of coffee and try not to eavesdrop. Though, if Nathan was talking to Rivera about the mayor's death, he wanted to know about it. The conversation continued for another couple of minutes, barely audible. If it wasn't about the mayor, it had to be work—a new case, perhaps. Otherwise Nathan's boss would never call on a Sunday. A bag of fresh chocolate croissants from Franco's was set on the marble countertop, and Sam pulled one out and started to munch the flaky awesomeness. He made himself focus on the sweet gesture and not on whatever Nathan was saying. If it was important, they'd talk about it.

Nathan joined him a couple minutes later, looking tired. When he saw Sam eating, he smiled and came forward, using his thumb to swipe a bit of chocolate from the corner of Sam's mouth.

"Tasty?" Nathan asked.

"Yeah. They're awesome. Thanks. When did you get up?"

"Oh, about an hour ago. I thought you might want to sleep in after last night." His eyes went right to the collar. He seemed pleased Sam was still wearing it.

Sam set down the rest of his pastry, grabbed Nathan by the hips, pulled him closer, and nudged his semi against Nathan's pelvis. "I'd rather go for round two. Maybe you'll let me fuck you this time."

Though Nathan smiled, the expression didn't reach his eyes. He was stiff in Sam's embrace. And not in the good way.

"What's going on, Nathan?"

A line creased the skin between Nathan's eyebrows. Nathan poured himself a cup of coffee and sat down at the kitchen table. "We need to talk."

"I hate when you say that. It's never good news."

"I've got a case."

Sam's stomach dropped three stories and was crushed under the weight of a cement truck. He held his breath. "Oh?"

"They want me to go undercover again."

"I see." The thing he'd worried about for months was finally happening. He had told himself he would deal with it, but it was easier to be brave when contemplating hypotheticals. "What's the case?" he asked, trying for nonchalant as the blood drained out of his face. So this was what it felt like to be yanked out of complacency.

"I don't know many details yet, but there's a 'gentlemen only' pop-up club in southern Jersey, and the local cops suspect illegal activity. Probably prostitution, but more than likely underage sex. Don't know if it's child trafficking, but they want me to scope it out." He paused and swallowed. "With a partner."

For a crazy moment, Sam wondered if Nathan was going to ask him, and his heart leapt with relief and excitement. But the grim set of Nathan's mouth stopped the thought in its tracks.

"I see." Sam gripped the counter with both hands, digging his fingers into the sharp corner to stop himself from thinking. A partner. Nathan touching someone else. Doing the things Sam and Nathan did together—the things that were *theirs*.

"Aren't you going to say anything?"

"What is there to say?" Sam's mouth was dry and sickly sweet from the pastry. "You've got a job to do." It wouldn't matter. It couldn't matter.

Nathan loved him. Nothing would change it, not even sex with someone else. He gritted his teeth at the lie while his gut threatened to regurgitate the now-hated croissant.

"And you're not angry?" Nathan arched a skeptical brow.

"I knew this might happen when we got started." And it had been titillating at first, when Nathan told Sam all about his undercover work. How he learned to dominate his partners. Hearing about his training with a dominatrix on the West Coast. Imagining all the people Nathan had slept with in order to get deeper into the organization and discover the rotten secret at its core. Children. Children who were stolen from—and sometimes even sold by—their families, forced into sex work with little chance of escape.

How could Sam tell Nathan no, he couldn't do his job?

"Who's the partner?" he asked instead.

"Name's Eric. I've known him for years, but he usually works in the Midwest. He's a character. Not my type, by the way."

"Huh." Sam didn't know how he felt hearing Nathan would be working with a man, rather than a woman. Then again, it was a "gentlemen only" club.

"Sam, talk to me. Tell me you're angry. Tell me to go fuck myself."

"Do you want to do it?" Sam tried to keep his voice neutral. Half of him wanted to tell Nathan to fuck himself, but the other half was scared of losing him for good—which was exactly what would happen if he gave Nathan an ultimatum.

Months before, Nathan risked his job to trust Sam's instincts. He told Sam he was more important than his position at the FBI. But there were children involved. He knew Nathan wouldn't back down from his duty if it meant saving innocent lives.

"Of course not. You know I don't." Nathan grabbed Sam's arms, not quite pulling him into an embrace.

Sam resisted. "Do I?"

"God, I hope so." And even though he was gratified to see the truth in Nathan's eyes, Sam had to look away. He was afraid of what he'd see if he searched deeper.

"All right. Well. I don't want to hear about it. Any of the details. Okay?" He pushed off the counter and sidestepped Nathan. "You do what you need to do, but I don't want to know."

SAM POUNDED the pavement as the music boomed in his ears. Sweat ran in his eyes, but he didn't bother to swipe it away while he focused on the uneven sidewalk under his feet. Occasionally he dodged a pile of dog shit or piece of garbage. But even with all the distractions, he couldn't escape his thoughts.

It had been over a week since Nathan got word about his new case, and it would be another before Eric arrived and the two of them headed for New Jersey. Seven days, and Nathan would be gone. Sam meant what he said about not wanting to hear the details. Ignorance wasn't bliss, but it was a hell of a lot better than knowing what Nathan would have to do. At least that way, he could fool himself, safe in the comfort of his own denial.

It was only sex, after all. Sam had never been a possessive lover. He never thought very far into the future either.

He hopped over an overturned garbage can and turned down the alley behind their apartment building. At least the exercise kept his mind off the tempting oblivion of the bottle. Since Nathan was home each day, doing research for his case, Sam started going on longer and longer runs and then heading to the coffee shop to work on his writing. He hadn't produced much, aside from a couple short, freelance pieces.

By the time he reached the back stairwell, his lungs felt like they might burst, and his legs were jelly. He checked the running app on his phone and wasn't surprised to see he'd logged over eight miles. His shorts and T-shirt were soaked through.

Upstairs, Nathan was on the phone, pacing around the living room. He laughed at something the person on the end of the line said, but when he noticed Sam, he made his excuses.

"All right. I've gotta go. See you soon, Eric."

*Eric.* What a hilarious guy. Sam grimaced as he kicked off his running shoes and reached for the water bottle he'd left on the coffee table.

"Good run?" Nathan asked.

"Yeah. Pretty good." Sam knocked his head back and let the water flow into his mouth. He swallowed it greedily, not meeting Nathan's eyes.

"I was thinking of heading to the pool in a bit." Since Nathan moved to the city, he did laps at the local Y at least three times a week. The man was a seal in the water.

"Cool."

Nathan frowned at him. "What are you up to later? I thought we could grab dinner."

"Sounds good, but I'm seeing a movie with Rach and Yuri. Sorry. No significant others allowed." Sam tried to smile, but the expression felt as foreign as snow in July. And maybe he drank too much water too quickly. It sloshed in his gut. He slapped Nathan's arm. "Actually I better get cleaned up or I'll be late. I'll see you? Have a good swim." The stupid fake smile hurt his cheeks.

"Right," said Nathan.

Even though Sam tried to ignore it, their relationship had become strained, almost polite—a far cry from the fun, passionate connection they shared until recently. He hadn't worn the collar Nathan gave him since the morning he heard the news.

He hated it. And although he knew it was mainly his fault, he didn't see any other way. Shadow pronounced her judgment with a yawn from the couch as Sam retreated to the shower.

A FEW hours later, Sam sat across from his friends at a Greek diner for a postmovie bite. Rachel and Yuri were chatting about the film as Sam picked at his fries. The burger was still half-eaten on his plate, but he couldn't force the rest of it down. During the movie he'd gotten a text from Nathan.

*Heading to bed early. I love you.*

"So, did you like the giant talking penis, or did you think it was a little over the top?" Rachel asked him.

Sam nodded, surprised at being addressed. "What? Uh. Yeah."

"Dude, did you even watch the movie?" Yuri grabbed one of Sam's fries and popped it in his mouth. "You were the one who picked it."

"Sorry." Sam grimaced. He couldn't have commented on the plot under waterboard torture. "I guess I'm distracted."

"Oh? Trouble in paradise?" Yuri raised an eyebrow.

"No. It's nothing." Nathan had asked him never to broadcast the details of his work. Sam would be overstepping boundaries to share his concerns with his friends, no matter how much he might want to vent. And though they'd likely respond with support, he didn't want them shit talking Nathan. It wouldn't make him feel any better.

Rachel saved the day. "The mayor's autopsy results are nuts. Are you writing about it?"

Sam dropped the fry he'd been dragging through ketchup and straightened up in the booth. "Wait a minute, what autopsy results?" He'd been waiting all week, but the investigation seemed to be taking its sweetass time.

Rachel frowned. "It was all over the news this afternoon. You didn't see? They found crack in his blood, along with alcohol and some sort of poison. Ritalin? No. That's not it."

"Ricin," Yuri supplied.

"Are you sure it was ricin?" Sam asked. Ricin was one of the most potent and easily synthesized poisons out there. And it only took a small amount to do the job. It was also renowned for delayed onset, as any casual *Breaking Bad* watcher knew—meaning it could be administered hours or even an entire day before the onset of symptoms.

"That's what they said on the news. Trace amounts."

"I can't believe the mayor was doing crack," said Yuri. "With the amount of money the guy had, you'd think he'd be into the pure stuff."

Sam was already grabbing his phone and googling. Sure enough the top hit from an online rag read *Mayor's Shocking Autopsy Results Reveal Heavy Drug Use, Poisoning*. Other, more reputable news outlets followed with less-salacious headlines. Sam clicked on one link and started to read.

"*According to a source close to the mayor's family, who requested anonymity, the mayor had begun using illicit drugs as early as his first term... refused to seek help... personal behavior becoming more erratic... trace amounts of deadly poison....*"

"Jesus," said Sam. As he scrolled through the rest of the article, his pulse picked up. "It says here there likely wasn't enough crack in his bloodstream to kill him."

"Yep," said Rachel. "Someone poisoned him."

"But who?" Sam's mind started to spin. The list of people who disliked the mayor was incredibly long.

Rachel shrugged. "I don't know. Why don't you figure it out?"

Sam reached for his wallet and threw down a twenty to pay for his food. "I've got to go." His friends teased him good-naturedly as he slid out of the booth and slipped his phone into his back pocket. "I'll see you later."

WHO KILLED *Mayor White?*

The cursor blinked on the blank Word document as he considered the possibilities. Shadow nudged her way under his arm and took an inconvenient seat on his lap, digging her claws into his hip. She'd grown, but she was never going to be a very large cat. Sam started typing.

*Deputy Mayor?* Out of everyone, Deputy Mayor Rick Morgan seemed to have the most to gain from getting rid of his boss. Perhaps he knew about White's drug use and counted on the autopsy to reveal drugs as cause of death. If so, he overestimated the amount of poison to use. The mayor hadn't metabolized it all.

*His wife?* Maybe she got fed up with his drug use and generally repellant behavior. She was in her early forties and would live a long, wealthy life as a widow. And she had discovered him at home in bed— maybe to rid herself of suspicion. She could have easily slipped poison into his food, or even dosed him as he slept.

*His dealer?* It didn't make much sense. Why kill the hand that proverbially fed you? Unless the mayor had done something stupid, like not pay for his dope, which seemed unlikely. White wouldn't have wanted to risk the chance of exposure. But blackmail was a definite possibility.

*Someone with a personal vendetta?* Another long list. The mayor favored the rich suburbs of West Stonebridge over the poorer downtown. Over the years his policies had infuriated a lot of people—Sam included. The mayor's incredibly ironic "Streets Clean" program was designed to nab small-time dealers. It had received its share of positive attention, but the church bombing had turned the public tide against him once again. Maybe a family member of one of the victims who'd been killed in that bombing? Sam made a mental note to do some research the following day, since he was already yawning. He snapped his laptop shut—frightening Shadow off his lap—and made his way to the bedroom, where Nathan had fallen asleep with the lights on.

His chest clenched painfully as he noticed the phone near Nathan's lax hand, the book at his side.

Trying to be quiet, Sam set both of the objects on the nightstand, disrobed, and slipped under the covers. The king-size mattress dipped slightly with his weight. He breathed out and stared up at the darkened ceiling.

White's murder was a welcome, exciting distraction, but with Nathan sleeping beside him, Sam's mind gravitated back to more personal worries.

He wondered what this Eric looked like—whether he was attractive, whether he was gay. Probably yes to both. The last time Nathan went undercover for a sex-trafficking case, he wound up fucking his partner in addition to the men and women he'd been trying to mine for information. Nathan admitted they'd done it off the clock too. He said Eric wasn't his type, but he could have said that to spare Sam jealousy. And there was the laughter earlier.

Sam kept telling himself it was only sex. He could live with it as long as he didn't know the facts. Maybe. But what if it turned into more? Two men working together under high-stress circumstances were bound to get close. They needed to rely on one another, to trust one another completely. All of those long hours on the job, forced to make small talk, which could easily turn into deeper conversation. Would Nathan develop feelings for his new partner, as Sam suspected he had the last?

Sam turned onto his side and tried to make out Nathan's profile in the shadows. He hated feeling the poison in his blood. They hadn't made love since Nathan broke the news.

He needed that connection more than anything. Sam reached for him in the darkness, found the warm flesh of Nathan's arm, and ran his fingers under the sleeve of his T-shirt. Nathan shifted and murmured in his sleep. Sam moved closer to press against him, hooking his leg over Nathan's thighs. His naked cock poked Nathan's hip.

"Are you awake?" he whispered.

"Am now," Nathan said with a sleepy sigh. He rubbed up and down Sam's arm. "How was the movie?"

"I couldn't concentrate on it. I…. God, I need you. Please." His cock ached as he urged his hips forward again, so Nathan could feel it.

"Really?"

The surprise in Nathan's voice made Sam's throat close up with emotion, and he rolled on top of him without another word, fitting himself between Nathan's spread thighs. Sam kissed Nathan hard, thrusting his tongue possessively into his mouth, and groaned when Nathan reciprocated with vigor. Nathan held him tighter, his cock firming underneath Sam as they continued to kiss and rub against each other. Even though his body was fired up, Sam couldn't quiet the thousand doubts and questions running through his mind. The last six months had been nearly perfect, but maybe he'd been mistaken to trust that it would last. He'd let his guard down, given in, let Nathan into his heart with no reservations. He knew better.

"Need you," he whispered into Nathan's ear between kisses.

Nathan surged up and flipped them over, trapping Sam's body underneath his. "Oh yeah? How?"

"So hard. Just… fuck." He couldn't think when Nathan bit at his neck and licked and sucked kisses into the sensitive skin. He took Nathan's head in his hands and pulled him tighter, urging Nathan to leave marks. He wanted it to hurt. Maybe he whimpered. Nathan stilled, and even in the darkness, Sam could see his concerned expression.

"Are you okay?"

Grunting with frustration, Sam writhed under the firm mass of Nathan's body, his trapped cock seeking friction. "I'm fine. But I won't be if you don't fuck me. I want you to fill me up." Who knew if they'd be able to go bare again anytime soon? Not if Nathan was going to be sleeping with other people.

He kissed Nathan again, savagely, using his teeth and biting into the kiss. Instead of responding, Nathan held his hands down and forced their mouths apart. "Maybe this isn't a good idea. We need to talk—"

"Screw talking. I swear to God, if you don't fuck me now, I'll go find someone who will."

The sound Nathan made could have been a growl. "No you won't."

"Oh, yeah? What makes you think you get to have all the fun?"

"Fun? Do you think this is fun?" Nathan nearly spat the words. "You think I enjoy having you not speak to me for over a week? Not being able to touch you?"

"So touch me now." He was so worked up, he didn't know what he would do if Nathan didn't give in. Maybe he would go insane. "Please." He begged sweetly, the way Nathan liked most. Then he swiveled his hips and was gratified to feel Nathan's sizeable erection nudge him in return.

"You can be a manipulative bastard, Sam Flynn."

"Yeah. Well, you already knew that much."

"You want me to fuck you hard?" Nathan kissed him again, without tenderness. His beard scratched roughly against Sam's chin.

"Yes. Please. Please, sir." Sam held his breath.

"Get on your knees." Nathan's voice was dark. "Hands on the headboard."

Heart pounding with excitement and a tinge of foreboding, Sam did as Nathan instructed. It was dark in the room, but he could hear Nathan rustling in the drawer next to their bed and a bottle of lube clicking open.

"You don't like to talk. Hmm?" Nathan asked. Without preamble, he dipped two slicked fingers into Sam's hole and started to work him open. Sam grunted and pushed back. "You want to keep all your feelings bottled up? You want to make me miserable?" He rubbed deeper, expertly finding Sam's prostate and lighting him up from the inside. Sam whined and arched his back, unable to stop himself from responding. "Answer me." Nathan leaned forward and bit Sam's earlobe. "Or am I going to have to repeat the question?"

Sam shuddered and closed his eyes as Nathan withdrew his hand. A stinging slap to his ass made Sam hiss with pleasure. He wanted Nathan to work him over, even if he didn't deserve it.

"I'm going to make your ass so red," Nathan whispered. "And then I'm going to fuck it for my pleasure. Not yours. Do you understand?"

"Yes. Please."

Another hard slap, this time to the left cheek. Sam's cock twitched and leaked below him. The first time Nathan ever spanked him, it was playful—but Sam wanted more. Eventually there was the paddle, but he still loved Nathan's hands on him. He looked forward to spanking sessions more than almost anything else they did, especially afterward, when Nathan cared for him. Though at first Sam found it difficult to give in, Nathan always insisted. He was careful to make sure Sam was okay, but he wasn't only concerned with Sam's physical comfort. He tended Sam when Hoff hurt him, took him in after his apartment burned down. He paid for Tim's care, and he understood when Sam wanted to talk about his parents. And when he didn't. He made it feel natural and safe to be vulnerable. He was everything Sam had never known he needed.

A startling clarity came with the next stinging slap. Sam couldn't share Nathan—not with anyone, not for any reason. He tucked away the thought and closed his eyes as the next volley began.

Nathan didn't hold back. Sam started to rock into the rhythm as his ass went numb and his mind followed suit, drifting pleasantly as each sting abated and then echoed in a different spot. Loud sounds of slapping skin filled the room like strange music. Nathan was breathing harshly, and Sam wished he'd left on the lights so he could see his face—the dark expression of desire written there, the powerful lust. Occasionally Nathan's erection grazed Sam's sore ass, evidence he was enjoying himself as much as Sam. He spanked lower, lightly, and tapped Sam's tight balls with the flat of his palm. "Do you want me to stop?"

"No," Sam whispered. "No, sir."

"Then thank me. Thank me for this gift."

He spanked Sam again across a particularly sore area, and Sam winced. "Thank you. Thank you, sir."

"That's more like it."

Sam's head hung between his shoulders as his body tensed and relaxed, tensed and relaxed. He was getting close to coming simply from being spanked. Every impact tightened his groin, made his cock throb with the building release.

"Nice and hot." Nathan leaned over Sam's body and covered it with his own. He gripped Sam's ass. "I'm going to fuck you now. So hold on."

Another uncapping of the lube, and then Sam yelped as Nathan impaled him with one long slide. He started fucking Sam hard, pistoning his cock in and out in a punishing rhythm.

"You think anyone else is going to fuck you like this?" Nathan asked, panting through his thrusts.

"N-no. Oh God."

"You're damn right. This ass is mine, and don't you forget it." He slapped Sam again, as if to emphasize his claim. An electric current sizzled through Sam with each brutal penetration. He tried to brace himself even though his arms were shaking. Nathan held his hips and drove home again and again, filling Sam up like he wanted.

He realized he was chanting "Yes, yes."

"You want to come?" Nathan asked. This time his voice was softer.

"Yes. Please. Please."

"Are you going to stop running away from me and talk?" Nathan reached under the bowl of his hips and grasped Sam's erection.

"T-talk about being m-manipulative." Sam could barely speak as his balls tingled and ached with the need to come. Every twist and pull of Nathan's fist made his toes curl.

"Well, you don't make it easy. Now fuck my hand like you mean it."

Sam did. He thrust shakily forward and shot his load right onto the comforter. Seconds later his arm muscles finally gave out, and he collapsed onto the bed with Nathan's heavy weight on top of him. Nathan pumped his hips erratically as he climaxed deep inside and then came to rest flush against Sam's back and sore ass. Their breathing gradually slowed, and Nathan pressed a kiss against the side of Sam's face. Even though their bodies were slick with sweat, Sam didn't ever want to move.

"You never answered me," Nathan whispered in his ear. "Don't think I'm going to let it go."

Sam's mind was a jumble of pleasure and returning anxiety as Nathan withdrew and went to the bathroom to get his supplies. He blinked against the light and buried his head into a pillow, then spread his legs as Nathan urged. A warm, wet cloth pressed against his hole. He let it happen, motionless, afraid to speak. Nathan didn't break the silence either. He worked methodically, rubbing the fresh-scented aloe onto Sam's ass with slow, tender circles. It wouldn't be bad after a day or so. The spanking didn't leave marks or bruises beyond redness. Sam was more concerned about the conversation they were about to have. He wondered if he could delay it for another few hours.

Moving with care, he turned onto his back and grabbed Nathan's arm. He could already feel the tension and regret radiating from Nathan's body.

"I needed that," he said, to preempt any guilt. After another tug Nathan came willingly and wrapped his arms around Sam's bare torso. He was still uneasy, though.

"Sam—"

"I know we have to talk." Sam kissed Nathan's cheek, missing his lips by a millimeter. "But can it wait until tomorrow?"

Nathan sighed. "I suppose."

Sam pressed another kiss to his temple. Nathan's rigid body started to relax, but neither of them slept right away. Sam couldn't help wondering what would happen when Nathan returned. He'd have to be tested. They hadn't used condoms in so long, and being free with each other was an important part of their intimacy. He knew how much Nathan loved coming inside of him, and he loved it too. The renewed caution would be a continuing reminder of the sacrifices Nathan had to make for his job, and Sam feared it would drive an even larger wedge between them.

Nathan had to be equally worried. He'd already made it known how much he disliked Sam's silence.

He had to be hurting. Sam tightened his hold. "I love you," he whispered.

"I love you too. So much." There was sadness in Nathan's voice. Sam didn't like it, but he still couldn't face the reality their inevitable conversation would bring. He wasn't sure he could face it the next day either.

# Chapter 3

THE NEXT morning he found Nathan drinking a cup of coffee on the couch, looking better rested than he had the day before. His dark hair was sticking up in the back, which Sam always found endearing. A shade of wariness crept into his expression when he saw Sam standing in the doorway.

"Morning. How're you feeling?"

Sam was wearing boxer briefs. He brought his hand automatically to his ass. It was still a little sore, but he liked it.

"Not bad," Sam said. "But I definitely need some coffee."

He poured himself a cup and reentered the living room, where Nathan was waiting for him. His laptop was open on the coffee table displaying an article about the mayor's suspected murder.

Sam sat down and gestured to it. "Crazy, isn't it?"

"Considering the last couple of years in this town, I honestly can't say I'm surprised." Nathan took a sip of his coffee and quirked an eyebrow. "You didn't kill him, did you, Sam?"

"Ha-ha. Would you turn me in if I did?"

"Never." Nathan was dead serious.

"That's good to know." Sam set his coffee mug down on a coaster. He'd never even owned a coaster until he moved in with Nathan. "There's a pretty long list of suspects, though." He rattled off his list from the night before, glad for the distraction, though he knew he was only delaying the inevitable conversation.

Nathan nodded thoughtfully when Sam mentioned the possibility of someone taking retribution for the October bombing. "Makes sense."

"It's shitty of me," said Sam between sips of coffee, "but I almost hope, if it is someone who lost a family member, they're never caught. White never should have gone ahead with the Halloween party. His bad judgment caused needless deaths."

"Does that mean you're going to let this one slide?" Nathan asked.

"Nope. This is the biggest story in months. I'm thinking of heading down to the station later to talk to the chief."

Nathan frowned and rubbed the bridge of his nose. "I know you're not going to listen to me, but be careful. I don't like the thought of you getting involved in something like this while I'm… while I'm gone."

An uncomfortable silence settled between them, and the clock on the wall tick-tick-ticked. Eric would arrive in six days.

After the previous night, Sam had almost allowed himself to believe Nathan wouldn't take the case after all. It was wishful thinking. The achy, sick feeling in his stomach returned, and he set down his coffee.

"I hate this."

"I know." Nathan put his hand on Sam's shoulder, and even though he wanted to lean into the touch, he flinched away. A torrent of words flooded out.

"I know it's selfish of me, but I can't stand the thought of you sleeping with anyone else, even for your job. It makes me sick. I know I've said I'm okay with it and I don't want to know the details, but I don't think it's going to work for me. I've been fooling myself, and not very well." He clenched his jaw and tried to control the beating of his heart.

Nathan looked stricken. "I know. Do you think I feel any differently? That I'd feel any differently if the situation were reversed?"

Sam remembered Nathan's possessive words from the previous night, how jealous he'd been at the idea of someone else giving Sam what he needed. He'd wanted to give Nathan a taste of his own medicine, but he regretted it. It wasn't a game.

He swallowed and took a deep breath. "I've never had this with anyone else, and I can see it… I don't know. Festering inside me. I don't want to resent you, but I keep thinking about how much you liked it… before. Emma wasn't enough for you. What if that happens to us too?" He could imagine it now—their relationship dissolving into anger and mistrust, the love that meant so much to him turning to ashes.

"I never got to have this conversation with Emma, but I can be candid with you. What we do together is so much better than anything I did undercover because we love each other. I don't want to give that up. And I don't want to hurt you."

"What are we going to do, then?" He stared glumly at his hands and swallowed. "I don't want to share you with anyone else." Sam knew he wasn't strong enough to walk away completely. He would take whatever Nathan offered him.

"All right." Nathan moved closer, and Sam didn't push him away. "What would you say about a compromise?"

"What do you mean?" The surge of hope mingled with anxiety.

"Well, this club is different from the last one I worked. For one thing, it's a pop-up, which means it moves place-to-place and city-to-city to avoid the cops. The clientele varies, so it's less likely I'll run into the same people regularly. It's more like a network, and if the local PD's right, and the mob's in charge—"

"What? You didn't say anything about the mob before." Sam frowned as concern for Nathan's safety overruled his jealousy.

"You told me you didn't want any details."

"But the mob…. Won't it be dangerous?"

Nathan gave him a crooked smile. "Now look at who's using double standards."

"I just don't want you to get hurt."

"I know. I won't. Eric's a good agent, and he'll have my back. But what I was saying is, if the mob is involved, they're staying on the down low, which means all we have to do is convince people we belong there. Last time I was too nervous, and my hesitation drew suspicion. I went a little overboard to compensate, as you know."

Sam nodded slowly. Nathan had participated enthusiastically rather than blow his cover during his last case. It was one of the main reasons he'd felt so guilty after Emma's death. He had to live with the knowledge that he'd willingly slept with other people, liked it, and justified it to himself as part of the job.

"Okay." Sam hesitated. "I still don't understand what will be different this time."

Nathan turned to Sam and took his hand. "Well, Eric is single. He's told me he doesn't have a problem getting close to suspects if he needs to. And since we're posing as a couple, people won't ask questions if we explain I'm only interested in him. I can come up with a list of mutually agreed upon allowances—"

"What kind of allowances?"

"For instance, would you mind if I scened with Eric without having sex? It's not always about penetration, as you know. What if I tied him up? Maybe did a little pain play or light bondage to get him ready for someone else?"

Sam thought about it. He didn't like the idea of Nathan getting too close to Eric, but he supposed it was better than screwing anyone he could get his hands on.

"I guess that would be okay. But no sex."

"No sex."

"And no kissing." Sam felt pretty passionately about that one.

"Definitely no kissing."

"I want to meet him."

Nathan bit his lip. "You will. I was going to tell him he could crash here in the spare room while we prep for the case next week, but I wanted to clear it with you first. Is that all right?"

Sam certainly hadn't planned on sharing Nathan during his last few days of freedom, but at least he'd be able to scope the guy out and see if he was really so damn funny. "I guess so," he said, not bothering to conceal his begrudging tone.

"This is all an act. It's not for real. And we'll only be working this one case. What I need to know is, can you live with this?"

Sam looked at the lines creasing Nathan's forehead. He'd lost so much, and he was making an effort, in spite of the dangerous situation he'd soon be negotiating. Sam needed to meet him halfway. "I think I can. As long as you're honest with me."

"I will be." Nathan leaned forward and kissed him. "I promise."

"I trust you," Sam said before he deepened the kiss.

"You'd better," Nathan replied breathlessly. He broke the kiss to say "It goes without saying you won't be seeking what you need elsewhere while I'm gone."

"I only said that to make you jealous."

"You're nothing but trouble, Sam Flynn."

"But you love me."

"God help me, I do."

"The feeling is mutual, Sid." Sam whispered Nathan's middle name. Nathan had once used it to secretly communicate when he was on a case, and it had been an intimate joke between them ever since. He took the opportunity to push Nathan onto his back and straddle his thighs. Nathan's mouth was slack with surprise and pleasure as Sam leaned down. "Let me show you how much."

A FEW hours later, armed with a nonfat, sugar-free vanilla latte, Sam loitered on the steps of the Stonebridge Police Department. The place was busily preparing for Chief Donna Howard's press conference later that day. A few news vans idled across the street, their reporters getting preened and powdered before they went live. People in business casual entered and exited the stone building, not sparing Sam a second glance. A panhandler approached him, and Sam ferreted around in his pockets for some loose change. He had nothing but a couple quarters, meant to be used for parking.

"Thanks buddy," said the guy, who was missing most of his teeth and reeked of booze and urine.

"No problem."

Sam almost sipped the beverage in his hands before remembering it wasn't for him. He checked his phone again and tapped his foot. Noon. And just like clockwork, only thirty seconds later Donna Howard exited the building flanked by another officer. She wore a steel-gray suit to match her short, straight bob, and her black heels clacked on the steps as she descended.

"Wait up a sec, Chief," Sam called out. She glanced up from behind her trendy tortoise frames.

"Well look what the cat dragged in," said the chief, though her Brooklyn accent held a trace of a smile.

Sam walk-jogged to her, careful not to spill the brew. He greeted the officer next to her and held out the coffee. "How're you doing? I thought you could use this."

Chief Howard took the cup and sniffed, then sipped. The flash of surprised pleasure on her face confirmed he'd chosen correctly. "How did you know this is how I like it?"

"I had a feeling."

"Assuming you didn't lace it with ricin." She arched a manicured brow at him, and Sam eyebrowed her right back.

"Gotta gain your trust first, before I escalate to poison," Sam said with a chuckle. "You're no good to me dead."

She continued walking, gesturing with her head for Sam and the flanking cop to follow. "I know you're not down here to bring me a coffee. Though it is appreciated, I can tell a bribe when I see one."

"Guilty as charged, Chief. I was sort of hoping for an exclusive before the conference," said Sam. "You know, for old times' sake?"

Though he and Donna Howard were far from besties, a sort of respect had grown between them since she stepped into Chief Sheldon's old position. Sam knew she liked him. She'd turned a blind eye to his obstruction during the arson case, when he'd kept the main suspect's whereabouts a secret. Of course Damon hadn't been guilty, or else she wouldn't have been so lenient.

As they turned the corner to the deli where she lunched almost every day, Sam kept pace beside her. She hadn't told him to get lost yet, which meant she was thinking about it. The backup cop didn't seem as pleased. He gave Sam a suspicious look, and Sam could see the guy was fully armed and at the ready.

"What's with the escort?" Sam asked.

"Can't be too careful," said Chief Howard, opening the door to the deli with her free hand. Delicious smells of pastrami and grilled onions greeted them, and Sam's stomach rumbled. He could already taste the grease.

"You think someone might target you?"

"Never know. White appointed me, after all. I figure his enemy is my enemy." The PD had gotten flack for failing to stop the Halloween party on the night of the bombing, though, due to their quick response time and efficient crisis intervention strategy, they'd fared better than the mayor in the court of public opinion. And Chief Howard was on record saying she had approved the cancellation of the party before the bombing.

"Unless it was personal," said Sam.

"Unless." She dragged out the *s* on the end of the word and lowered her voice just a little. Whether it was a hint remained to be seen. They made small talk until it was their turn. Chief Howard eyed the backboard menu and then stepped forward and cleared her throat. "The usual," she said to the cashier.

The teenaged girl smiled. "All right. Chicken salad on rye with a half-sour pickle, coming right up."

Sam gave his order and fumbled for his wallet in his back pocket. "I've got this, Chief."

Chief Howard smirked at him, one corner of her mouth lifting. "I feel positively spoiled."

They collected their food and found a table in the back of the bustling restaurant. Sam sat across from the chief while her escort scanned the room. He hadn't ordered lunch and didn't appear very interested in their conversation.

"All right. So you bought me a sandwich and a coffee. Now what do you want? I'm assuming this isn't a date." She took a giant bite and munched loudly.

Sam grinned. "I wanted to get a couple quotes from you for the article I'm writing, if you don't mind. Is there anything you can tell me about the case? What kind of leads you're looking into?"

"I can't say more than I'll say at the conference. But we're giving this investigation top priority. I've got a whole team on it."

Sam leaned forward. The escort cop eyed him like he might want to take a bite out of Donna's sandwich. "Where does Rivera fit in?"

"He doesn't. He's heading back to New York. Soon," she said. "This case is under local jurisdiction, and this time I'm keeping it that way."

As Sam indulged in his delicious pastrami, he wondered how Rivera felt about leaving town. He had personal history with the chief, and it obviously wasn't an easy relationship. Whether they were still sleeping together was yet to be determined. Nathan thought not, and the way Donna was aggressively biting into her sandwich at the mention of Rivera, maybe he was right. "So do you know how the poison was administered?"

"Looks like through food or drink," said the chief. "Probably the day before he died. But he could have been dosed any time during the previous twenty-four hours."

"Hmm," said Sam. "So it had to be someone who handled his food. Someone who had easy access to the house and the kitchen?" The mayor's wife, Judy, sprang to mind again, though the Whites had a live-in cook and housekeeper. *Hmm.* Now there was a thought.

The chief didn't seem convinced. "Not necessarily. He had several events the day before he died—a lunch meeting with the city council and then an evening benefit for the Streets Clean project. There were two hundred people present, at least."

"Invite only?"

"Yes. But there wasn't much security. It was at the Hyatt, downtown. Staff going in and out. Open doors. Then again, no one was expecting a murder to take place. Should have known better, considering what town we live in."

Sam jotted down a few notes and decided to take a little trip there after the press conference. The Hyatt was probably the nicest hotel in the area. "That means it could have been practically anyone. Though, if the murderer dosed the hors d'oeuvres, others would have gotten sick. The mayor's food or drink was specifically targeted."

"Exactly."

Sam tsked and shook his head. He took another bite of his sandwich, which he'd almost forgotten, and chased it with a sip of iced tea. He still couldn't get over the hypocrisy. White made such a big deal about getting drugs off the streets after his would-be democratic competitor, the philanthropist Stephen Feldman, was found dead in his tub nearly two years before. Of course back then no one knew about Feldman's ties to the mob. He had profited from bringing drugs into the city, and used his charitable foundation to launder the money and give the dirty cops a cut to look the other way. Until recently, Mayor White's hands had been clean from any association with the Voronkovs.

But what if he'd been involved all along?

"Hey, kid, is your sandwich all right?" Chief Howard asked.

"Yeah. Why?"

"You look like you just took a bite of sludge from the East River."

"Maybe I did." Sam wiped his mouth with his napkin. Then he leveled a serious look at Chief Howard. He needed to know the truth. "Did you know about the mayor's drug use?"

"Absolutely not." She fixed him with a glare. "How dare you accuse me of something like that."

"Sorry, Chief." He threw his hands up. "I was only curious. It's pretty crazy it went on so long with no one speaking out. I mean, his aide must have known. But I guess it was the guy's job to keep the mayor out of trouble. You've probably already questioned him." Barney Collins was a semicloseted gay man Sam had bumped into once or twice at New York clubs. Sam always wrote him off as someone who voted against his own interests in favor of power and privilege. He was the mayor's right-hand man, and Sam wondered why he hadn't added the guy to his list of suspects. If anyone had access to White, it was Collins.

Chief Howard made a noise of disgust. "Of course we did. And let me tell you, the guy was about as useful as a bag of broken nails." The dismissive way she spoke of Collins confirmed him as a major suspect. Clearly she didn't want to answer any more questions. She checked her watch and started to rise. "I've got to head back to the station to get ready. Thanks for the lunch. You coming with?"

Sam's fingers tingled with anticipation. Forget the Hyatt. Collins was next on his list. "Actually, something's come up. I'll catch it on TV later. Thanks a bunch, Chief."

Without waiting for a good-bye, he threw down a couple dollars for a tip, grabbed his notepad, and headed for the door.

# Chapter 4

BARNEY COLLINS'S city hall suite was on the third floor of the building, at the end of a corridor of otherwise-tiny administrative offices. Sam pushed the frosted-glass door open and confronted a woman sitting at a desk and talking on her cell phone. She seemed startled at Sam's sudden appearance and begrudgingly told whoever was on the other end of the line that she had to go. Sam waited. Other than the assistant, there didn't seem to be anyone in the office. Maybe the staff were at a meeting?

"I don't have an appointment," he explained. She put down her phone. "But I was hoping I could see Mr. Collins."

"He's gone for the day." It was only a little after one.

"Gone where?"

"I don't know." She shrugged. Then she leaned forward, her blue eyes lightening with mischief. "But off the record, it probably involves a liquid lunch."

"Thanks."

Sam scoured the nearby watering holes looking for a thin, blond man. There were several bars that catered almost exclusively to city employees, but after a few unsuccessful attempts, Sam realized Collins was probably trying to fly under the radar.

He finally found him several streets away from downtown, seated at a shabby bar with New York prices. A couple flies buzzed around Sam's head, and he swatted them away. The whole place had a "seen better days" vibe. Collins had seen better days too. His thinning hair was swept to the side, and he stared hollowly at the bottles lining the back of the bar. Sam sat several stools to the left of him and nodded at the bartender, who was reading the sports pages.

"What can I get ya?" he asked when he saw Sam.

"Whatever light beer you've got. Don't much care."

"Coming up."

Sam figured that, by ordering a beer he detested, he'd be less tempted to drink it. He hadn't touched a drop in a year. Over the last few months, he'd started to wonder whether he was an alcoholic or alcohol dependent. It was a spectrum. He couldn't deny it had been hard to stay functional, and he'd done some pretty stupid shit. The cravings were bad for a while. But even so, he quit almost cold turkey, and he was proud he had the willpower to kick the habit without any help. Maybe putting a name on it didn't matter. Now, as the bartender flipped the top of the crappy beer and slid it over, Sam hardly gave it a second glance. He wasn't about to start drinking again, anyway. His life was better without it, and it felt good to be philosophical. He was in total control.

He mock-nursed the beer and scoped out Collins from the side of his eye. He was drinking a martini—from the looks of the empty glass in front of him, at least his second. Liquid lunch, indeed. Sam smiled at him noncommittally, wanting the spark of recognition to start with Collins. He'd already decided that a questioning-reporter approach wasn't the best strategy, especially if the guy was as edgy as he seemed.

Sam gave him a half smile and pretended to check something on his phone. It worked.

"Don't I know you from somewhere?" Collins asked.

Sam glanced up at him, feigning confusion. "What? Oh, you do look familiar."

"You're Sam Flynn. Right?"

"Guilty as charged." Sam grinned, and Collins's doe-like eyes widened slightly with interest. He took the bait and moved two seats closer to Sam.

"I haven't seen you out much lately," said Collins.

"Yeah. Well, you know. Keeping busy." If Collins didn't know about his relationship, Sam could use it to his advantage. Getting him to talk might be the most important thing Sam could do for the case, and harmless flirting never hurt anyone.

"Oh? Doing what?" There was an edge of interest to Collins's voice.

"Writing. I've got a blog."

"Right. That's you. *Under the Bridge.*" Collins wrinkled his nose and polished off his martini. Sam gestured to the bartender for another one.

"Don't care for it, I imagine."

"Well, you haven't exactly been friendly to the local government. Bet you're gearing up for a scintillating indictment of the mayor. Right? Is that why you came here?"

Collins was a little savvier than Sam expected. He shook his head emphatically. "No. Not at all. I feel bad about what happened." It wasn't a complete lie, after all. He put his hand on Collins's thin shoulder—a brief gesture intended to put him at ease. "How are you holding up?"

The answer was obvious in the way Collins's hand trembled as he held the stem of his fresh martini. A bit of liquid sloshed out of the glass and onto the bar, and the smell of gin filled Sam's nostrils. It was little more appetizing than the crappy light beer sitting untouched in front of him.

"Oh. You know." Collins let out a nervous laugh. "Not great, I guess. The cops questioned me yesterday. They think I had something to do with it. I know it."

"Really?" Sam asked, feeling worse for him by the minute.

Collins took another gulp. "It's ridiculous. I never would have…. Rodger wasn't perfect, but he was a good boss. Generous to a fault."

Sam cocked his head and tried not to laugh. While he'd been infamous for his tight control over the city coffers, White likely paid Collins very handsomely to do whatever fetching and carrying he required. Losing that income would be quite a blow for someone used to living well—as the expensive watch flashing on Collins's wrist suggested. He was on his third fifteen-dollar martini.

Sam offered a sympathetic grimace. "I'm sorry. It must be hard."

"It is," said Collins, obviously excited to have someone to talk to. "It really is. I don't know what I'm going to do."

"Maybe you need a vacation. A little R & R."

"Maybe so."

"A trip down to Fire Island, perhaps." Sam raised an eyebrow, and Collins smirked back.

"Unfortunately I'm stuck here until the police no longer require me."

So they'd obviously told him not to leave town. Very interesting. It was possible Collins knew the identity of the killer, even if he wasn't directly involved. Now that they'd established a rapport, Sam wasn't sure he should mention it or press the issue. He fished out his wallet and grabbed one of his cards, then slid it over to Collins. It disappeared under his hand.

"Call me if you ever want to talk. You'll find I'm a very good listener. And I don't give up my sources—to anyone." He injected a bit of seriousness into his statement and then stood and pushed himself away from the bar.

Collins's hand trembled as he held the card. "Do you… maybe want to get together sometime? Socially?" he added as though he needed to clarify.

Sam felt a pang of guilt. He didn't want to mislead the guy. "Thanks, but I'm seeing someone."

The disappointment on Collins's face was obvious but faded quickly. He picked up the martini again.

Sam slid his stool back into place. "But I meant what I said. I'm not out for your blood, but I would like to help, if I can. Anytime day or night."

"Thank you." He sounded grateful—almost pathetic. Sam left the bar doubting he'd ever hear from him and also wondering who had Barney Collins so worked up that he could barely hold himself together.


"So you think Collins knows who killed the mayor?" Nathan asked as they watched the evening news.

"Yeah. He was obviously scared out of his mind. But it could have been because the cops are keeping an eye on him. Hard to tell." Of course Collins could have done the deed, but Sam suspected he wouldn't have willingly put an end to the cushy job and prestige of being the mayor's aide. It didn't gel with what he knew about the guy.

"And he asked you out." Nathan stared glumly at the TV.

"Ahh. So *that's* what's bothering you." Sam had almost been gleeful when he told Nathan. "But I don't think you want to get into another conversation about double standards, do you?"

"I guess not," Nathan muttered.

"And anyway, he's not my type." Sam parroted back the words Nathan had used when describing Eric.

"Hmm." The news program ended, and Nathan flicked through the channels at record speed, not settling on any one long enough to even determine content.

"You can relax, by the way. I told him I was seeing someone."

"You left out that bit."

"Yeah. Well, making you jealous is my new favorite hobby."

Without another word Nathan set down the remote, turned, and tackled Sam to the couch. His dark eyes flashed dangerously. "Oh really?"

"Yeah." Sam's cock hardened instantly as Nathan ground down on him. His heart started pounding like he'd sprinted a mile. Giving Nathan a taste of his own medicine was sweet, and Sam wanted to indulge. He licked his lips. "But to be honest, he's not a bad-looking guy."

"Oh, *really?*"

"Nice body." Truth was the guy was a bit on the thin side for Sam, and he'd never liked blonds. But he wasn't about to admit it.

"Yeah? Did you want to fuck him?" Nathan's high cheekbones flushed.

Sam didn't answer. He arched his back to rub his hard cock against Nathan's. His jeans were too tight, constricting his almost painful arousal.

"That's it. Get naked and face the wall. Spread your legs and don't look at me. You don't get to come tonight."

Sam held back the whine building in his throat. He'd pushed Nathan too far, and he was going to be punished. He deserved it. And what a painfully sweet punishment it would be.

But first he needed his collar.


THE DAYS ticked down. In some twisted, yet effective effort to keep Sam's mind off his looming departure, Nathan kept denying him his orgasms, and Sam's frustration was building to volcanic levels. He could hardly think. His dick hardened up at the sight of Nathan fully clothed. It got so bad he couldn't even take a piss without getting a hard-on. He was tempted—oh so tempted—to beat off in the shower. But he resisted. Until Nathan gave him permission to come, he was determined to hold back. Even though Nathan would understand, he would know, and Sam wanted to please him. He wanted to prove no one else could please him like Sam could—certainly not *Eric*.

Even so the need for release was becoming intolerable. He was a walking erection—and of course Nathan loved every minute. He was evil.

One morning Nathan stood behind Sam as he sat at the kitchen table, trying to do research. He ran his hands up and down Sam's chest and tweaked his nipples over his T-shirt. Voila, instant boner.

"Jesus, I'm trying to work here," Sam grumbled. After so many days of similar teasing, his dick should know better, but it was hopelessly optimistic. *Down, buddy.*

"Am I distracting you?"

"Yes. You're distracting me. Quit it." Sam was poring over the Streets Clean Gala guest list, which he'd managed to finagle from the events manager at the Hyatt. He could already tell the thing wasn't going to help narrow down the suspect pool. Anyone who was anyone in Stonebridge and the surrounding towns had attended, and many of them had personal or political vendettas against the mayor. Sam wondered if the entire event was designed as a malfunctioning olive branch.

"Hmm." Nathan ignored him and kept up the torture. Until Nathan had started showing them attention, nips hadn't been in Sam's top erogenous zones. But once they came online, sensation seemed to travel directly from them to his cock via electric wiring. His erection pressed solidly against his fly.

"Do you want me to stop?" Nathan bit his earlobe, and Sam shivered involuntarily. He tilted his head so Nathan could kiss his neck. The collar shifted when Nathan pressed his lips to it, and Sam started to breathe faster. He'd been wearing it around the apartment, and he knew Nathan was pleased.

He also knew why Nathan was seeking his attention. With Eric due the next day, they didn't have much alone time left.

"I… mmmh." Sam gave up, flipped his laptop closed, and turned the chair around to face Nathan. The bastard had an obvious hard-on too, but he'd been getting off at least once a day.

Sam squeezed it, but he wanted it in his mouth.

"You want to suck my cock?" Nathan asked huskily.

"Yeah." Sucking Nathan's dick was pretty much the best thing in life. Sam loved it—the musky taste, the salty precome coating his tongue. He got down on his knees. His heart fluttered as Nathan unzipped his fly and pulled out his uncut cock. It stood at attention, a gleam of wetness at the tip. Sam looked up from under his eyelashes. The floor was hard, but he didn't mind the discomfort. "May I taste you, sir?"

Nathan ran his hands through Sam's hair and drew him closer. "You may. And since you've been such a good boy and you've asked so nicely, you get to suck me however you want and swallow all my come."

Sam's cock twitched in his jeans as he leaned forward to swipe the head with his tongue. It tasted almost sweet, and Sam mouthed at it, using his lips to push back the tight foreskin. Nathan held him indulgently, not putting any pressure on him to go further.

"Mmm," Sam said. "Tastes good." He slipped one hand into his waistband to tuck his cock tightly against his belly. The touch made him groan, and even though he knew he was tempting fate, he left his hand there.

"You must be so hard with my dick in your mouth. How many days since you came?"

"Five," Sam panted. "Five, sir."

"Is that the longest you've ever gone?"

Sam mouthed along the length of Nathan's cock, making it nice and wet. "Yes, sir." Since he was at least thirteen, probably.

"Do you think you deserve to come today?"

"Yes. Please. Please." Sam nuzzled at Nathan's fly, trying to get at his balls, which were still trapped inside. The wiry hair ticked his nose. To oblige him, Nathan reached in and revealed himself, and Sam closed his eyes and ran his tongue over the tightening skin. He heard Nathan's breath hitch.

"Do a good job, and I'll think about it."

Sam looked up to watch. Nathan closed his eyes, and his mouth fell open as Sam went to town. He used one hand to guide Nathan's cock deep and nearly choked as he took it down to the root. Instead of rearing back, he fought his gag reflex and let his muscles work around the intrusion. He began to move slowly, bobbing his head as he held Nathan's balls firmly in his grip. On the off slide, he swirled his tongue under the thin, suede-soft foreskin, and Nathan gasped. Sam was always envious of how sensitive he was there.

It didn't take much longer for Nathan's dick to harden even further and start to pulse—and Sam swallowed every bit, loving the way Nathan shuddered and groaned as his flesh became too tender to touch.

After one last lick to the slit, Sam sat back on his haunches with his head bowed and his hands behind his back.

"Stand up," Nathan ordered.

Sam did, his stomach twisting with desire.

"Now get your cock out."

Sam fumbled with the zip fly of his jeans, almost scarring himself for life in the process. His angry, dark red cock jutted from his groin. Nathan gently lifted his chin, encouraging Sam to meet his gaze. He looked sated and, Sam hoped, altruistic.

"Kiss me," said Nathan, leaning down to capture Sam's mouth. "You can use your arms."

The kiss rocked Sam from head to toe, and he stumbled into Nathan gratefully, sliding his tongue deep into Nathan's mouth. He clung on as Nathan stroked his cock in a slow, steady rhythm, unable to stop thrusting his hips. His balls tightened, and his belly quivered with the impending release.

The doorbell rang.

"Shit," Sam panted out. He was so close he felt ready to cry with the ruined orgasm. "Please, please, please, no."

"Shh, it's okay."

With one swift movement, Nathan sank to his knees and took Sam's cock into his mouth. His full lips stretched, and he started sucking Sam with vigor, bringing him right back to the edge. It was a gorgeous sight. His beard made him look even more masculine and sexy as he swallowed. The doorbell rang again.

"I... I... can't." He needed to come so badly.

Nathan pulled off him with an obscene pop. "Yes you can, baby. Give it to me." And then he was down again, ruthlessly working Sam's erection.

Legs trembling, Sam held Nathan's head. He wasn't even in control of his own movements and he couldn't think about anything but coming. His orgasm crested and rolled over him with incredible force, shocking him with its violence. It seemed to go on forever, and Nathan sputtered as he tried to swallow it all.

Sam collapsed half on Nathan, half on the floor as the doorbell rang a third time. He was pretty sure his bones had dissolved.

Nathan glared at the sound and wiped his mouth with the back of his hand. "Who the hell is here?" He stood and buttoned up his jeans with a "do not fuck with me" look on his face. Then he swooped down and planted a kiss on Sam's forehead. "I'll be right back."

Not even moving to zip himself up, Sam stared up at the ceiling as his pulse started to slow and postcoital lethargy threatened to pull him under. He closed his eyes and willed the stupid solicitor away.

"I know I'm not supposed to get in until tomorrow" came an unfamiliar voice from the living room. "But I caught an earlier flight. Figured we could use the prep time."

*Eric.* Sam's eyes popped open, and he tucked his softening dick into his boxer briefs and did a quick check to make sure there wasn't any come on his jeans. Dignity restored, he found himself incredibly grateful for the wall dividing the kitchen from the living room.

"Yeah. Well you ever hear of texting or calling first?" Nathan grumbled.

Eric laughed. "I did, my man, but you didn't answer. What did I do, interrupt something? You do have a well-fucked look on your face."

Sam rounded the corner and took in the scene.

The guy stood around six foot two, Nathan's height, though he probably outweighed Nathan in muscle mass. He wore a sleeveless shirt to show off sculpted, tattooed arms, and his dark hair was cropped military style. The overall effect didn't exactly scream submissive, but Sam knew better than to typecast. He was definitely not the kind of guy you wanted to get into a bar fight with—probably why Nathan selected him as a partner in the first place. On the safety front, at least, Sam felt a little more at ease.

"Hello there," said Eric in a deep, drawling voice, the origin of which Sam couldn't quite place. He extended his hand, and Sam took it, offering a firm shake. "You must be Sam. Nathan's told me so much about you. Eric Duquesne at your service. But my best friends call me Duke."

Sam nodded. "Good to meet you."

Eric whistled. He didn't let go of Sam's hand right away. "I should have known it'd take a pretty thing like you to bring him 'round to the right side." He pronounced "thing" like "thang." When Eric's eyes latched on to his throat, Sam realized he was looking at the collar. He flushed and pulled his hand back as a mixture of pleasure and nervousness rushed through him. It was the first time anyone else had seen it.

"Careful, Eric," said Nathan.

"Understood. Understood." Eric winked and grinned devilishly. In spite of himself, Sam smiled back. This guy was trouble. He swung down the army green rucksack off his back and dropped it on the floor, and Sam noticed a worn US Marine Corps patch on the side. "What's a guy need to do to get a drink around these parts?"

It was only 11:00 a.m.

Nathan crossed his arms. "We don't keep alcohol in the house."

"Ahh." Eric seemed to get the message. "Well, I guess I'll survive. Coffee?"

Nathan went to grab a cup while Eric sat on the couch and stretched his long legs in front of him. He raised his arms and rested his head back against his interlaced palms. A few crisscrossed scars marred the brown skin on one of his arms, and two letters—*FP*—were tattooed on his bicep.

"Nice digs," said Eric.

Sam followed his gaze. The apartment was furnished in a tasteful, masculine style, thanks to Nathan's more sophisticated aesthetic. But bits and pieces of Sam had crept in over the last few month—books on new media and changing journalism practices, favorite '80s DVDs, a crappy painting of a hot naked guy that he found at a garage sale. Nathan didn't want to hang it at first, but Sam insisted they display it as a conversation piece. After all, he'd spent ten bucks on the thing, and it was terrible *art*. Generally Nathan let him do whatever he wanted. He offered to give Sam money to buy some new things, but Sam refused it. He already relied on Nathan far too much.

It sometimes bothered Sam that he didn't have more stuff. He lost most of his possessions in the fire, save some childhood things stored along with old family possessions in a small rental unit. He had never cared for material goods, but sometimes he wished they could get a new place and start fresh as equal adults. It was a moot point, since there was no way he could afford it on his salary.

Maybe one day, if his hard work paid off. If they were still together.

"Thanks," he said simply.

"So, how long have you two known each other?" Eric gave him another appreciative up-and-down, and Sam finally placed his accent. Louisiana Creole.

"A while, but we've only been together a little over a year," Sam said. "I used to do landscaping for Nathan and Emma."

"You don't say? Damn shame what happened to that gal. She was a real sweetheart."

"Yeah. She was." Sam glanced toward the kitchen. He didn't want Nathan to overhear them talking about Emma, but Eric seemed happy to change the topic on his own.

"Gotta say it's strange being up north again. But it'll be good to work with Nate."

Sam smiled tightly. Maybe they should talk about the weather. "How long have *you* known Nathan?"

Nathan reentered the room with the coffee and a glass of water, and Eric leaned forward and took both drinks with a smile.

"Thanks, bud." Eric raised his occupied hands and waggled his eyebrows. "Double fisting, my favorite. So you never told your boy here about how we met?"

Nathan grimaced, obviously not fond of the story.

"Well, I'll tell you—first time I met Nate at the academy, he'd never even fired a gun. When was that now? Eleven years ago? I was a new recruit too, but I'd been through hell and half of Georgia already. This guy, he was so proper, almost like royalty. We thought there was something huge lodged up his ass—"

Nathan raised one mildly irritated eyebrow. "Ah, come off it, Eric. I wasn't that bad."

Sam was still trying to process the information. "Wait a second. You trained together?"

"Yep." Eric polished off the glass of water with a few large gulps. "Soon as I left the corps, the Feds swept me up. Been with 'em ever since."

The conversation continued, and Sam learned about a Nathan he'd never known. Eric was filled with stories about the academy—including pranks the new agent trainees used to play on one another, like stealing each other's clothes during shower time.

"And Nate," Eric said as he wrapped up another story. "He ran the last five miles with his head held up, even with his sprained ankle. Nope. He wouldn't let it get him down. He was a real trooper. But he had class. You know? Looks like he still does."

There was nothing ironic about the statement. In spite of the joking, he seemed like a genuine guy. Sam was starting to like Eric Duquesne.

"After training we went our separate ways. My field office was in Texas, and Nate was just married."

"So, what have you been doing since?" Sam asked—maybe too abruptly.

"I was down on the border for the last five years. Messy business. Lots of people dying out in the desert." He shook his head and made a noise of disgust. "Such a waste. I'm looking forward to the change of pace, to tell you the truth." He arched an eyebrow at Nathan.

Sam cleared his throat. "So, have you been... uh, trained, like Nathan has?"

"You mean in BDSM? Hell no. I've been in the community for about eight years now."

"Oh." So he was experienced. Very experienced.

"And I'm a switch, if you're curious." He aimed his amused gaze at Sam. "That's an offer. You wanna maybe do something together? Get rid of the tension?"

"I think we better focus on the case for now," Nathan said darkly. Sam hid a smile behind his hand.

Eric seemed bemused. He shrugged. "Well, if you boys decide you want to play sometime, once this is all over, you give me a call. The more the merrier, I always say. Life's too short for monogamy."

Sam snorted, and Nathan glanced up at the ceiling, like he was waiting for some higher power to give him strength. Eric's general lightheartedness had rubbed off on Sam, and he started to feel better about the prospect of Nathan and Eric working together. Even though Eric would probably fuck Nathan gladly, he wasn't the type to get involved with another man's boyfriend—unless asked, of course. And he certainly didn't seem interested in settling down.

"The man is a menace," Nathan groused once they'd shown Eric the extra room, and he said he was going to take a shower. "I can't believe he was flirting with you in front of me."

"I like him."

Nathan's eyes glinted. "Oh, you're so in trouble now."

# Chapter 5

SAM PRESSED a kiss to his brother's smooth, cool forehead. He smelled clean—like the baby shampoo the Shady Brook staff used on patients. But Tim was almost twenty-three years old.

"How's everything going in here?"

Sam smiled as he turned to find his brother's nurse, Lisa, wearing scrubs covered with bears juggling tiny oranges and apples. He almost never saw her in a repeat pair. She wheeled in the new bag of IV fluid and started to unhook the depleted one with efficient movements.

"Oh, not too bad," Sam said, watching her.

"Whatcha reading today?"

Sam glanced at the book in his hands. Every time he visited his little brother, he spent some time reading out loud to him. Lisa suggested it would help keep Tim's brain active, and it provided the additional bonus of giving Sam something to do. That day he'd chosen an old Sherlock Holmes mystery, *The Hound of the Baskervilles*. Sam had liked reading Arthur Conan Doyle when he was younger.

"Oh, neat," said Lisa, swiping her bangs back from her forehead. "Don't mind me. I'll just be a minute." She checked Tim's blood pressure and wrote a couple things down on her chart. "Holler if you need anything in here. All right?"

Sam thanked her. After she left, he settled down in the chair next to Tim's bed and opened the book. About fifteen minutes later, he sighed and closed it again.

"Nathan's leaving tomorrow," he said.

45

The doctors didn't know if Tim was aware of his surroundings, but Sam imagined his brother could hear him. He wondered what he might say in response.

*Sorry, bro. That sucks.*

But Tim never used to call him "bro." He'd called him a jerk on several occasions. Sam realized with a pang that he didn't know what his brother might say, and he probably never would. Still, it helped to talk about it. For the sake of secrecy, he wasn't able to share his fears with Rachel and Yuri. But Tim was a good listener.

"I'm sure everything will be fine. I'm worrying for nothing. Eric doesn't seem like a bad guy." In any case he still had the mayor's murder to occupy him, among other projects, so he'd have plenty to distract him while Nathan was away. As long as he didn't think too hard about what his boyfriend would be doing there, he'd be fine. He had to trust in Nathan.

He squeezed Tim's hand again, and just for a second, he imagined Tim squeezed back.

WHEN HE got back to the apartment, he discovered Nathan and Eric in the living room, trying on bondage gear. Or rather Eric was trying on bondage gear. Nathan was dressed in his regular clothes, but Eric sported a rubber collar that fit snugly around his thick neck. He also wore a pair of nipple clamps, connected together by a thin metal chain dangling between his tattooed pecs.

"Uh." Sam blinked as he came into the living room. "Am I interrupting something?"

Eric grinned and held his arms wide. "Whaddya think?" His nipples were pinched into tight beads by the clamps, and Sam couldn't help staring.

"What did you guys do? Raid a sex shop?"

"Nope," Eric said, bending over to rummage through a large cardboard box. "This is all my stuff. Had it shipped." He pulled out a black latex mask with a zippered mouth closure. "I've been wondering where this was. This thing is great." With some difficulty he pulled the tight-fitting material over his head, then unzipped the mouth, stuck his tongue out, and waggled it suggestively. "Easy access. See? But then, if you want to shut me up—" He zipped it again.

"Impressive," Sam said with a snort. He looked at Nathan, and the two of them shared a tolerant, amused glance.

"I've got all sorts of stuff in here," Eric said, holding up a couple bottles. "You guys need any leather or latex cleaner, just let me know."

Eric was still pawing through his loot as Sam went into the kitchen to see about food. He thought of whipping up some pasta and jarred sauce—not exactly a gourmet feast, but not take-out lazy either. Maybe they even had some stuff for salad lying around.

"You guys hungry?" he called over his shoulder.

"Starving, darling," drawled Eric.

"What do you want to order for dinner?" Nathan asked. "Chinese?"

Sam laughed to himself. Nathan would probably order out every night, if he could. Sam grabbed a couple boxes of spaghetti from the cupboard and filled their largest, rarely used pot with water. He was adding sauce to heat in a small pan when Nathan approached from behind and put his arms around Sam's waist.

"You're cooking?" Nathan rested his chin on Sam's shoulder.

"Didn't you know? Boiling water is my specialty. You guys having fun in there?" It wasn't meant to sound snarky, but Nathan was instantly all apologies.

"Eric's a bit of a ham, if you hadn't noticed. He just tore open the box and started taking off his clothes. I hope you don't think anything was going on."

"Of course not," Sam said, though he could have done without the defensiveness in Nathan's tone. He wasn't sure he was going to forget the nipple clamps anytime soon either. "But I might as well get used to it. Do you... uh... what are you going to wear?"

"I've never been into dressing up. But you, on the other hand—"

"I'm not wearing one of those gimp masks," Sam said. "That was way too *Pulp Fiction* for me. No latex bodysuits either."

Nathan huffed a laugh against Sam's neck. "I was thinking something more basic. Something to highlight your fabulous ass—like a jockstrap." He cupped the attribute in question with both hands.

The idea wasn't unappealing. In fact Sam thought it would be hot. He hadn't worn a jock since college. "As long as it's not leopard print, I'm game. And I want to see you in some leather pants."

"That can definitely be arranged."

Sam stirred the sauce as it started to bubble. "And I was thinking…. I'd like to try something like those clamps Eric had on."

Nathan leaned into him and ran his hands up Sam's chest to pinch his nipples. "Sounds like a great idea."

When the water started to boil, Sam kicked Nathan out of the kitchen and asked him to set the table. Eric popped in to model a thong-and-assless-chaps combo, and Sam found himself actually giving thoughtful criticisms. "Yes. The magenta is too much," and "Sure. A couple studded wrist cuffs would be the perfect complement." How had this become his life?

He managed to not overcook the spaghetti too badly, and the three of them watched *Jeopardy* and ate from steaming, heaping bowls on the couch—just Sam, his boyfriend, and his boyfriend's BDSM work partner. A regular Hallmark-family moment.

SAM GOT up early the next morning. He found Eric awake and puttering around in the kitchen, butt naked.

"Oh," Sam said as he rounded the corner and eyeballed Eric's low hangers. The guy had a full, untrimmed bush, which contrasted with his closely cropped hair up top. "I didn't know you were… uh." He flushed and looked away.

"Hope this doesn't bother you?" Eric asked. He used his muscular ass to hip-check one of the lower cupboards shut. "I'm a firm believer in nudity. It's good for the soul. Freeing. I'll cover up if you want me to."

"It's fine." Sam carefully skirted the periphery of the kitchen to grab a mug. "I'm just not used to waking up to find random naked men in my kitchen."

Eric frowned. "What a shame."

Sam helped himself to a cup of coffee and tried to work out how he was feeling. In less than three hours, Nathan and Eric would be gone and Sam would have to live with it. There was no denying Eric was attractive. He would probably be tempted if he were in Nathan's place, but he didn't have Nathan's history with him. There wasn't anything between them, and he doubted there would be in the future. It was all for show. An act. He could live with that.

He grabbed his laptop from the kitchen counter, where it was charging, and headed for the living room.

There were still no arrests in the mayor's murder investigation. Sam wondered whether there had been any developments since the last time he spoke to Chief Howard. He figured he might as well head to the station to poke around—maybe follow up with Barney Collins too.

"I want you to know I have no intention of moving in on Nate." The statement distracted Sam, and he looked up from his laptop. Sometime in the last five minutes, Eric had located his underwear and put on a wife beater. He'd also apparently fallen under Shadow's spell. She lounged belly-up in his massive tattooed arms, purring like a motorboat as he scratched under her chin. "The guy worships the ground you walk on, anyway. You don't have nothin' to worry about."

Sam flushed. "The feeling's mutual. And I'm not worried."

"Oh no?" Eric raised an eyebrow in his direction.

"Well, you have to admit, this whole thing is weird."

Eric shrugged. "It's all relative. If you saw some of the things I've seen, you'd be thanking your lucky stars Nate's got a case like this. Don't you trust him?"

"Of course I trust him." But... once Nathan was in the field, who knew what might happen? It wasn't impossible that he might meet someone who interested him. Worry twisted Sam's stomach even though he tamped it down.

"Listen. I get it, man. I had a guy I was crazy for once. We were together in Iraq. Had a threesome with another buddy, and it was strange. I didn't like it." He stared off into the vacant space behind Sam's head.

"So what happened with the guy?" Sam asked. Was this mysterious lover the referent of the *FP* tattoo? He was surprised at the revelation that Eric had served in Iraq, though he didn't know why he should be. The timeline made sense.

Eric shrugged, his nonchalant grin firmly back in place. There was a hollowness behind his eyes, though. "It's not important. Love isn't for me. It's too much... everything." He shook his head and went back to petting Shadow.

Before Sam could ask him to clarify, Nathan stumbled, bleary-eyed, out of the bedroom.

"Morning," he said, smiling at Sam. Once he saw Eric in his underwear, he closed his eyes and muttered something to himself. At least he had put some clothes on.

"Hi, lazy bones," said Sam.

Nathan approached him and gave him a quick kiss. "What're you two talking about?"

"Oh, nothing." Sam didn't want Nathan to know about his continuing concerns, because it would suggest he didn't trust him. He did. But he hated not knowing what might happen. Unforeseen circumstances couldn't be prevented.

"I'm gonna take off for an hour or two. See the town and give you some time alone," Eric said. He was already walking toward the guest room. "Be back at ten. And then we head out. Right?"

Nathan nodded. The two of them would be met by their handler and receive their final briefing later that day, and then they'd be off to someplace in New Jersey. The specific location hadn't been disclosed. Nathan couldn't even tell Sam the alias he'd be using, but Sam did know that he and Eric would be posing as a newly married couple. The two of them had already gotten matching rings, but Nathan hadn't put his on yet.

Once Eric was dressed and gone, Sam closed his eyes and rubbed them. He chastised himself for being so damn emotional.

"I'll be home before you know it," Nathan said softly. "And I'll only be a few hours away. Yeah?"

Sam steeled himself, opened his eyes, and took a deep breath. He turned to Nathan with a seductive smile. "Well, we still have some time. Let me give you something to remember. What do you want? You want to fuck me out here? Maybe use some toys? I'll get the blindfold—"

Nathan grabbed his hand before he could get up. "No."

"Don't tell me you want to cuddle?" Sam teased. The serious expression on Nathan's face made his heart clench along with his stomach—like all of his essential organs were connected to Nathan, and his departure was twisting them up.

"No. I want you to fuck me." Nathan's eyes were a little watery, and Sam wasn't sure if he should acknowledge it or pretend he didn't notice. He cupped Nathan's neck from behind and drew him forward.

"Okay," Sam whispered, leaning his forehead against Nathan's. "Okay. Let's go back to bed."

They undressed slowly, taking their time to feel each other's bodies as they kissed. Nathan seemed to want Sam to lead, so he did. He ran his hands over Nathan's chest and down to his hips. Nathan's cock lay thick and hard on his belly, and Sam leaned down to kiss it, but didn't take it into his mouth.

"Turn over."

Nathan grunted something unintelligible, flipped onto his belly, then ground against the soft duvet. His hips canted back, as though in anticipation.

Sam leaned down and kissed a trail to Nathan's fabulous ass, which was toned and firm from all the swimming. He urged Nathan's legs apart to kneel between them. Splayed out like that, Nathan was a sight to behold. Sam drank in the long lines of his body—his defined, sleek muscles and narrow hips. Nathan's hole twitched under the inspection, and Sam ran one finger over the tight furl, smiling as Nathan shuddered.

While Nathan might excel at taking control in bed, Sam knew exactly what to do to make him lose it. He thought he knew what Nathan needed.

Not wasting any more of the precious time they had left, Sam spread Nathan's cheeks and kissed him right above the clench of skin and then dragged his tongue along a wet, slow path downward. Nathan moaned and pushed back at the contact, and Sam flicked his tongue around his entrance, not lingering long enough for any real satisfaction. He blew softly, letting the warm air tease and tantalize. Then he placed a full kiss right where Nathan needed it. A jolt ran through Nathan's body, and Sam felt it everywhere they were connected. He nuzzled in deeper, probing with his tongue to open up the tight passage, breathing in the male scent he loved so much. Gradually Nathan started to respond. His muscles quivered and relaxed. Sam gave his ass a playful bite and then added a finger to stretch Nathan's rim.

The first time Sam had kissed him there, Nathan was unsure, but it hadn't taken him long to give himself over to the sensation. Sam loved knowing he was the only one who had ever made Nathan come undone like that—the only one who had ever been inside him. And maybe Nathan wanted to remind him their relationship was a mutual, evolving dynamic. They belonged to each other.

Soon Sam's own need became overpowering. His cock pulsed between his thighs as he reached for the lube.

"No. Just you." Nathan looked over his shoulder. His eyes were dark with desire and another, more vulnerable emotion.

"It might hurt," Sam gritted through his teeth.

"I'll be fine." Nathan arched his back in defiance. "Do it."

Sam instinctively obeyed the commanding authority of his tone. With fingers shaking from arousal and emotion, he urged Nathan's hips up and guided his cock to the cleft of Nathan's ass, which was still wet from his mouth. He nudged the tip of his dick against Nathan's hole.

It always seemed impossible, but Nathan opened to him, and he fit himself in, inching deeper. The first full slide was excruciating pleasure. Sam watched himself disappear and bottom out, and he ran his hands up and down Nathan's lower back in a soothing motion. After so many sessions of orgasm delay and denial, he could come right that instant, simply from Nathan's velvety muscles clenching around him.

He started a slow rhythm, rocking into Nathan with each thrust. He angled for the best possible penetration, and when Nathan held on to the sheets with both hands and moaned loud and long, he knew he'd found it.

"Like that?" he asked, starting to pant with exertion.

"Shit." Nathan met him thrust for thrust, arching his back in a long, beautiful line. From the tension radiating from his body, Sam knew his orgasm was building. He also knew Nathan was having a hell of a time stopping himself from barking orders. While he appreciated the reversal of their usual power dynamics and what it meant, Sam wanted Nathan to let go. He slowed his stroke.

"How about this?"

"Mmm. Harder. Don't play with me. Not now." Nathan's voice sounded raw, and Sam bit his lip. He pulled out.

"What are you—"

"I want to see you," Sam said. "On your back."

Nathan switched position so Sam could kneel between his thighs again, but this time his mouth was accessible. Sam slid back into him and leaned up for a kiss.

It was even better with Nathan's face visible. His expressive mouth was soft with pleasure, not hard like it sometimes was when he dominated Sam. He was vulnerable and precious—the most precious thing in Sam's life. Nathan wrapped his arms around Sam and urged him on.

"Love you," Sam whispered, catching Nathan's lips clumsily as he started to come, and the words turned into a groan. With his heart pounding in his ears and his orgasm blotting out all other sensation, he missed the moment Nathan came. But after, when he collapsed on top of his lover and felt the cooling wetness sticking their skin together, he smiled.

"I love you," said Nathan softly. He brushed his fingers against Sam's lips. "Be careful while I'm gone. All right?" His eyebrows drew together in a look Sam knew all too well.

Sam reached for the tissues and grabbed a couple for Nathan. "I'll be fine. Focus on your case. Don't worry about me."

"That's what you always say." Nathan snorted. He wiped the smear of come from his belly, balled the tissues, then tossed them at the can near the side of the bed—and missed by a mile. Sam laughed, but his throw was no better. The alarm clock already read 9:40 a.m., and as much as he wanted to crawl back into bed and tuck against Nathan's side, Nathan was already in business mode.

"You know the combination to the safe," he said, striding to the closet and rifling through his clothes. The safe held enough weaponry to take down the Spanish Armada if they ever showed up in Stonebridge.

"Yes. Yes." While Sam didn't like having so many guns in the house, he knew it was important to at least appear willing to use them if trouble arose. He'd needed one to take down Randall Palmer, aka Benedict Anderson, on Halloween. But even though the asshole deserved it, Sam hadn't enjoyed shooting him in the leg.

"I'm serious," Nathan said, pausing to look back over his shoulder. "At the very least, you need protection. I don't want to worry about what you might be up to here."

"It only seems fair. Tit for tat."

Nathan furrowed his brow. "Tit for tat? Really?" He pulled on a crisp, black button-down and a pair of dark jeans. No suits on this venture. "Sam—"

"Okay. Okay." Sam sat up and hugged his knees to his chest. "I get your point. But I will be fine. And you take your own advice and stay out of trouble. I want you home in once piece."

Nathan leaned down for a kiss. His beard scratched Sam's smooth-shaven chin. "Understood."

# Chapter 6

SAM BREATHED in the humid country air and surveyed the muddy lot with his hands on his hips. A housing development had hired Manella's to seed and plant all of the new yards. They were building cookie-cutter houses for families and young professionals making the move from city to country. When Yuri called him to ask if he was interested in helping out, Sam immediately said yes. Sitting around the empty apartment with only Shadow and his laptop for company was starting to take a toll, and it had only been a couple days since Nathan's departure. He glanced at the sky, hoping the rain would hold off for at least a few hours. They couldn't afford to lose another day. Around him the other guys discussed the plan of action.

"Hey, bud," said Yuri, elbowing his side. "What do you think?"

"I think it's a helluva project. What's the turnaround on this one?" Sam swiped at a horsefly buzzing around his head.

"They want it done by Friday. Family arrives Monday. We better get our asses to work."

Sam rubbed his hands together, eager to get them dirty. "You're the boss." He enjoyed the work more since he didn't have to do it every day. It was clear that Juan, Yuri's new partner, had a lot more ambition for the business, anyway. He was the one who'd gotten the development contract.

The morning grew into a sunny, late-May afternoon. Sam shot the shit with the other guys, but in quiet moments, his mind wandered to Nathan. He wondered whether he and Eric had hit the club yet, and if so, what it was like. Of course he didn't really want to know, but he couldn't help thinking about it. He had only heard from Nathan once so far—a brief call on the night he arrived in Jersey. They planned to talk that night, though, so Sam pushed the negative thoughts out of his mind and focused on the work.

He was tired by the end of the day, but not terribly so. With all the running he'd been doing, he was in the best cardio shape of his life. He whipped off his shirt and used it to mop his sweaty forehead. The rain had held off, but it was only a matter of time. Thunder rumbled in the distance.

Yuri stopped Sam by his truck.

"Hey. What're you doing tonight? You want to see a movie with me, Alex, and Rach? Maybe go bowling or something?" He smiled and his right cheek dimpled. "I deserve a rematch after last time."

"It's not my fault your bowling score would make any golfer proud." In fact Yuri had gotten so mad the last time they played, he'd vowed never again.

Yuri punched his bare arm. "Ha-ha. So?"

"I'd like to, but… I can't. Sorry." Nathan was calling him at eight, and Sam wanted to make sure he'd be able to talk with no distractions. Still, he felt stupid admitting he was turning down plans with the gang to talk to his boyfriend.

Yuri saw through him immediately. He made kissy noises. "All right. Your loss. Tell Nathan we all miss him."


SAM'S CELL didn't ring until a quarter after eight, not that he was keeping time. He grabbed it up, heart beating fast, and grinned when he heard Nathan say his name.

"Hey, yourself," he said. "How's it going?"

"Oh. Not too bad so far. I miss you."

The evasive quality of the response gave Sam pause. "I miss you too. It's weird without you here." He was stretched out on the too-large bed, where he'd been playing sudoku on his computer until Nathan called. Shadow curled next to him, keeping his side warm.

"I'll be home before you know it."

"That's what they always say," Sam muttered. "So, have you been to the club yet?"

"We got our introduction from an insider last night. Eric put the moves on him at the hotel bar."

Sam forced a chuckle. "What was it like?"

"It's hard to tell from one visit. If there's trafficking going on, it's likely not well known. Everything seemed consensual, and everyone there last night was of age."

It wasn't exactly the type of answer Sam was looking for. Nathan obviously knew it, because he continued. "But if you're asking if I fucked anyone? No." Sam could hear the eye roll in his voice.

"Okay."

"So how was your day?"

Sam allowed the change of topic. He gave the short version, not wanting to bore Nathan with the details of landscaping work, but glad to have his full attention. The nervous feeling of anticipation started to dissipate as they talked. When Nathan chuckled and told Sam how much he missed him—how much he needed him—Sam's cock started to fill. He responded to Nathan's voice like one of Pavlov's dogs.

"I want you to talk to me," Sam said. "Can you? I... need you."

A sigh from the end of the line didn't sound promising. "I'm not exactly alone. Eric's in the shower, but he'll be out soon."

Sam stared blankly at the ceiling. His erection was going down like the *Titanic*. "Your shower?" he said, before he realized how ignorant it sounded. Of course they'd be sharing a hotel room. It made practical sense, and Sam didn't know why he hadn't considered it.

"Unfortunately, when it comes to agents bunking on a case, the bureau is cheap."

Silence. Why hadn't Nathan mentioned it before they left? He thought they were being candid with each other. "Ah."

"Does it bother you? We're not sharing a bed." Nathan sounded slightly annoyed. Sam didn't want to be the nagging, doubting boyfriend. If he were in Nathan's place, he'd probably be irritated too.

"Sorry. It's fine. I'm being stupid." After all, crashing in the same room wasn't any more intimate than tying up the guy and giving him a spanking.

"As soon as I come home, I'm going to give you what you need. I promise."

"You have to go?" Sam's voice echoed back at him. Stupid cell phones.

"Unfortunately yeah. I have to cut it short tonight. We're meeting someone at nine." The regret in Nathan's voice was clear, but it did little to alleviate Sam's disappointment.

"Ah. Okay. Can you talk tomorrow?"

Nathan hesitated, and it sounded like Eric was back in the room. "Probably not. It'll be a busy day. What about Thursday? Maybe we can Skype."

Sam perked up. "Okay. Thursday works for me."

"I'll try to get some privacy. Eight on the dot. I'll text you with instructions."

"Mmm," Sam murmured. "Sounds like fun."

"Oh, it will be." Nathan's voice held a dark promise. "Listen. Before I go I wanted to say I appreciate you being so understanding. I know this isn't easy for you, and I hope you know how much it means to me. I love you."

"I love you too. Be safe."

When they hung up, Sam stared at his cell and tried to sort out his conflicting emotions. It was only eight thirty, and he'd given up a night out with friends for a fifteen-minute conversation. At the same time, Nathan's parting words had affected him deeply, and he was filled with gratitude and love for him—and anticipation for Thursday.

They'd come so far from the days when Nathan was secretive about where he spent his time. And Sam had come a long way with his honesty. All the same Sam wondered about the second visit to the club. He wasn't going to sit in their empty apartment with his mind spinning like a hamster wheel.

The first thought that occurred to him—even after all his months sober—was beer. An ice-cold sixer would do. He grabbed his running shoes instead.

AT LUNCH the next day, in the middle of a heated Red Sox-Yankees debate with Yuri, Sam's phone rang. He didn't recognize the local number, and his heart skipped a beat. What if something had happened to Nathan? He answered with numb lips.

"Sam Flynn here."

"Hi, Sam. This is Barney Collins, from the bar the other week. You gave me your number?"

Sam gave Yuri an apologetic nod as he turned to take the call. "Hey there. Good to hear from you."

"Is it really?" The guy laughed nervously and a little too loudly. Sam wondered if he was at the bar.

"Yeah. Of course. What can I do for you?"

"I wanted to talk to you, if your offer is still on the table."

It didn't sound like Collins wanted a date. His voice trembled, even though he was obviously trying to maintain control. "Absolutely. Where and when?"

"Tonight. Nine o'clock. Same place as last time."

Sam answered quickly. His curiosity was piqued. "Sounds good."

"Oh. And… it will just be you. Right?"

"Yeah. Just me. See you then." Sam's pulse picked up. It sounded like the guy had something for him—maybe even dirt on White's murder.

The phone went dead. When Sam turned back to Yuri, his friend grinned slowly. "Who was that? Don't tell me you're cheating on Nathan."

"Of course not. It was a source."

"On the mayor?"

"Maybe." Sam frowned. He didn't like the way Collins sounded. Maybe meeting in public wasn't a good idea, especially if he had information about White's poisoning. Another voice—the result of the past two years of deception, betrayal, and violence—urged caution. He had no reason to trust Collins, and even though the guy didn't seem like a murderer, appearances could be deceiving.

Nathan would want him to bring a gun. He'd insisted Sam get a license to carry, in case they ended up in another dangerous situation. But Sam still didn't feel comfortable with a concealed weapon. He brushed the dirt off his work pants and stood up.

The rest of the day, he wavered back and forth trying to decide what to do. In the end he rationalized that they would be in public, and he could easily take Collins if it came down to it, so he left Nathan's gun cache alone. Before he left the apartment, he checked himself in the mirror. Even he had to admit his dirty blond hair looked good. He had started wearing it longer on top and parted and slicked to the side. Although he abhorred hipster snobbery, he liked their haircuts. He chose the brown blazer he wore for interviews and a pair of skinny jeans. At the last moment he wondered if he looked too nice—too much like a guy headed out on a date. He figured it probably didn't matter. Barney already knew where they stood, and it was a business meeting.

The bar was nearly as empty as it had been when Sam first found Barney turning his liver into a martini pickle. Unlike that day, soft jazz filled the air, and the few patrons sat spaced out at the long bar, each lost in silent thoughts. One couple chatted quietly at one of the small tables. The dim lighting muted the shabbiness of the place and made it look almost elegant.

Barney Collins gave him a wan smile as Sam approached the bar. He had almost polished off one of his signature drinks. "Thank you for coming," he said and waved the bartender over.

"What'll it be?" the bartender asked Sam.

"I'll take a seltzer with lime," he replied.

"Absolutely not," Collins exclaimed with a nervous laugh. "Get my friend here a gin martini, extra dirty, and I'll have another as well."

Before Sam could protest, the bartender went to make the drinks. Something like desire curled through Sam, but he pushed it out of his mind. He didn't have to drink the damn thing, and he wasn't going to. After another, Collins probably wouldn't notice anyway. His cheeks were already flushed, and his eyes were slightly glazed.

"So, how're you doing, Barney?" Sam asked as he slid into the empty seat next him. The barstool creaked as it settled.

"Not so great."

"I'm sorry to hear that."

"Thanks. It's a miracle I'm still alive," he mumbled.

Sam wasn't sure he heard correctly. "What do you mean?"

"Oh, nothing. Nothing." With thin, bony fingers, Collins plucked the green olive out of his glass and finished his martini with a flourish. The rattle of the cocktail shaker punctuated the silence between them.

"How are things with the cops? You get the all clear yet?" Sam stopped tracking the bartender's efficient movements and turned his attention to Collins.

"As if. They called me down there again today, but I'm not saying a word. Not a word."

Sam lowered his voice. "So you do know something about White's death."

The bartender brought them their drinks. Sam sucked in a breath as the gin martini was placed right under his nose. The piney, floral fragrance advertised it was top shelf. His mouth watered. He hadn't eaten dinner yet, and olives always seemed especially tempting on an empty stomach.

When he turned back to Collins, he was already slugging away.

"Are you going to answer my question?"

"Not if you want to stay alive. Do you?" Collins posed the question honestly, without passion. Some of the nervousness from their earlier phone conversation had gone out of him too. Probably an effect of the booze.

Sam's pulse ratcheted up. "I'm pretty fond of living. Yeah."

"You said I could trust you. Right?"

"Of course. I never give away my sources." This was it—his big chance to break the story of the mayor's murder. It was huge—the chance of a lifetime.

Collins's expression became sly. "How do I know you're telling me the truth?"

"You don't. But it's obvious you want to talk or you never would've called me down here. Something in you wants to trust me."

"I can't trust anyone."

"I know how that feels." Sam touched his slender forearm where it rested on the bar.

Collins seemed startled, but he didn't move away. He closed his eyes. "No. I don't know if you do. You see, I want to do the right thing, but I can't. I'm a coward."

Sam couldn't figure out what Collins was playing at with his hot and cold act. Either he had evidence or he didn't. "Something happened. You can tell me."

"I quit my job yesterday. Or maybe I was fired. I'm not really sure." He laughed mirthlessly.

"What are you going to do?" Had someone else on staff orchestrated the murder? It was possible. The deputy mayor, perhaps?

"This wasn't a good idea. Someone at this bar could be watching us right now." Collins glanced around nervously.

Sam did the same, but a cursory sweep of the room didn't indicate anyone taking an unnatural interest in them. No one could overhear their quiet conversation, especially with the music playing. But Sam knew better than to take their privacy for granted. He leaned closer. "You think someone's tailing you?"

Collins seemed like he might answer, but then he changed tacks. "You seem like a real ambitious guy, Sam. I get it. But you're honorable. I was never like that. I was out for myself, and I knew it. I didn't care. But if I'd known then…. Jesus." He scrubbed a shaking hand over his face.

Sam considered what to say. If he had any doubt before, it was gone. It had been a politically motivated assassination, and whoever Collins was running from scared the shit out of him. He figured he might as well be bold. "But you do have evidence."

"Shut up," Collins hissed under his breath. "Drink your martini and try to look like you're at least vaguely interested in me. That's why I asked you here, you know."

Without thinking Sam picked up the martini and took a small sip. The liquor washed over his tongue easily, and he tipped back a little more. It warmed his esophagus and burned a comforting trail down to his gut. He sipped it again for good measure, and then set the glass down.

*What the fuck are you doing, Flynn?*

A few sips didn't mean anything. He needed to stay focused. "You asked me here on a date?"

Collins plastered a seductive smile on his face and leaned toward Sam to whisper in his ear. "No. I got your message loud and clear. I asked you here so if anyone sees us they'll think we're on a date." His lips brushed softly over Sam's cheek. Though the touch wasn't unpleasant, it didn't stir a response. But anyone who saw them would think they were lovers. Was that how Nathan felt, doing his work?

"Who did it, Barney? Why are you so scared?" Sam whispered back to keep up the ruse. "Let me help you."

"You know, it's true. I do want to trust you. But I was right. This wasn't a good idea."

"I can help you," Sam repeated, though he wasn't sure it was true. *Dammit.* He wished Nathan were here. He would know what to do.

"No. You should stay away from me." Collins turned and finished the rest of his martini. He drew out a few twenties and left them on the bar, tucked discreetly under the base of the glass. "Good-bye, Sam."

"Wait." Sam grabbed Collins's wrist and leaned close again. The bartender was polishing stemware on the opposite end, but he cast them glances every few seconds. He didn't seem to be more than casually curious. "You're not going to do anything stupid. Are you? You're not going to try to hurt yourself?" He examined Collins's thin, pointy features. His chin jutted out haughtily, though his lips trembled.

"I'm a coward. Remember? If I were brave, maybe I would."

Once Collins left, Sam took stock of the situation. He didn't like being in a nearly empty bar with strangers. Maybe he should have brought a gun after all. The conversation with Collins replayed in his head. If it could be called a conversation. It was more like a series of enigmatic statements and riddles.

He still worried the guy might do something desperate. Whatever he'd said about being a coward, there was more to Barney Collins than met the eye.

Then there was the implied warning. Whatever Collins knew, if shared, might put Sam's life in danger. "Don't trust anyone" had become a motto to live by over the last couple of years, but Sam still trusted people. Nathan, of course. Yuri and Rachel. Chief Howard.

*Chief Howard.* White had appointed her, and yet Sam instinctively trusted her. That trust had only been reaffirmed through their interactions over the past year. Now she knew Sam was interested in White's murder. Collins obviously didn't trust her, or else he would have told the police what he knew—unless the evidence implicated him too.

"Would you like another?" the bartender asked.

Sam looked down. With a jolt of surprise, he realized he'd finished the martini. He hadn't even made a conscious decision to drink it, but he recognized the buzz warming him from the inside.

"No. Thanks. I'm… I'm good."

He pushed back from the bar and stood up, lightheaded. After so long without drinking, he'd completely lost his tolerance. He left the bar quickly, without meeting any of the other customers' eyes.

Instead of walking home as he might have under other circumstances, he hopped on the city bus and took a window seat. He doubted anyone from the bar had followed him, but it felt safer to be in public rather than walking dark city streets alone. The bus was filled with late-night commuters and a few college kids and smelled strongly of exhaust. It lurched around a corner, and Sam's stomach clenched. He hadn't eaten dinner. No wonder he was feeling the martini so strongly.

He decided it wasn't such a big deal. It had only been one drink, and he said no to a second, although he couldn't deny he'd been tempted. *"Do you want another?"* Yes. He did. But he'd resisted.

Maybe he could handle the occasional drink. In any case there were more important things to think about, and he needed to talk it over with

Nathan and get his take on the whole Barney Collins sitch. He grabbed his phone and then remembered Nathan was working. He would have to wait until their Skype date the following night.

It seemed very far away.

# Chapter 7

SAM'S PHONE buzzed in his back pocket. He grabbed it, read the message, and immediately flushed bright red. He hoped the other guys would think it an effect of the hot sun. It was a scorcher.

*I want you on the bed, legs spread so I can see all of you.*

It was the third such text he'd received in the past few hours—a list of instructions that had given him several inappropriate erections.

First there was, *After you get home, shower and use the medium plug. I need you nice and stretched.*

Check.

Then, *Wear the black leather cock ring. Get nice and hard for me.*

Double check.

And now the latest instruction, which provided a good visual for what was going to happen. He discreetly adjusted his half-hard dick and stowed his phone again. Hopefully the rest of the day would pass quickly.

They'd already laid new turf in the front and backyard of the new lot and had begun planting perennials and birch saplings to make the place look more natural. The trees formerly populating the development had been razed to make room for identical modular homes. Half the crew had gone with Juan to another job, so it was only Sam and Yuri and one of the college kids Manella's often hired for the summer. This one was a lot cuter than some, and he hung on to every word Yuri said and kept giving him flirtatious smiles.

"Better watch yourself with him," said Sam when they were out of earshot. "He's definitely cruising you."

Yuri shrugged, but he gave the new guy a glance out of the corner of his eye. "He's legal."

"Barely."

"But look at him." Yuri bit his lower lip.

Sam did. The kid smiled and waved, completely unself-conscious, and then went back to work. He reminded Sam of a golden retriever happy to be playing outside.

Yuri continued. "So sweet. All innocent and eager and—"

"Just waiting for an older man to corrupt," Sam said, cutting Yuri off before he threw up in his mouth. "How the mighty have fallen. I remember you once saying you wouldn't ever sleep with someone from work again."

Yuri grinned cheekily. "Well, if he makes the first move, maybe I can bend the rules a little."

"You're having an early midlife crisis."

"Maybe so." The smile on Yuri's face and his happy agreement made Sam snicker. Maybe it would be good for him to date someone younger. The kid certainly seemed to think Yuri was special. It would be uncomplicated—except for the whole boss/employee thing. Still, that was only temporary.

Uncomplicated would be nice for a change. Sam took a swig from his water bottle and thought again of Barney Collins. He had called him earlier in the morning to make sure he was okay, but he got no answer, which concerned him. He planned to drop by Collins's apartment on the way home to check on him. It wasn't hard to find his address.

His phone buzzed with another text.

*Watch this video at 7:50* it read, followed by a link. Considering the rest of the instructions, Sam didn't dare click on it in public. He chuckled and texted Nathan back. *Yes sir.*

COLLINS LIVED in a luxury-condo complex in West Stonebridge, not too far from the mayor's mansion. Sam noticed the police cruisers immediately— two of them, both with lights flashing. One was the chief of police.

*Shit.* Sam pulled his truck to the curb. Maybe something had happened to Barney after all. Sam should never have let him go home alone. He slid out of the cab and thrust his hands into his dusty pockets, guilt mingling with dread in his stomach.

Chief Howard stood with Antonio Rivera and another couple cops on the sidewalk.

"Hi," he said hesitantly, looking from one to the other.

"What are you doing here?" Rivera crossed his arms. His jawline was covered in rough stubble, and he wore his FBI jacket.

Sam was just as surprised to see him. "I thought you were going back to New York?"

"Not until next week."

Chief Howard looked exasperated. She ignored Rivera and turned to Sam. "What *are* you doing here?"

"I had an interview with Barney Collins for my blog. Is he…?" He gestured toward the building.

"He's gone." She seemed none too pleased.

"Gone?" Sam repeated.

She nodded. "Apartment's packed up. Car's been found abandoned at a rest stop down in Pennsylvania. He took off."

The wave of relief made Sam's shoulders sag, but he stopped himself from making a remark. The cops didn't need to know he'd seen Collins the previous night. After all he hadn't learned anything from him aside from what they already knew. Feeling relatively safe that he wasn't obstructing justice, but still unsure enough to be nervous, Sam looked for his exit and began shuffling backward.

"Well, then. I guess I'll be heading—"

"You don't have any idea where he went. Do you?" The chief arched an eyebrow at him.

"No idea," he said honestly. "I hardly knew the guy."

Luckily the chief and Rivera began to focus on each other. The tension radiating from the two of them piqued Sam's curiosity, but he figured he better get while the getting was good.


At 7:50 p.m., Sam settled on the bed with his laptop. Framed by the leather cock ring, his erection lay firmly on his belly, and the plug he'd inserted after his shower nudged against his prostate. He was pretty sure Nathan would be pleased with how he looked, since he'd so carefully followed the instructions. Now it was time for the link.

He waited while his browser loaded. It was an amateur video, slightly blurry, but when the lens focused, Sam's eyes widened.

There was a man hung suspended from ropes, which seemed to mold around his body, caressing him intimately between the thighs and around the chest, ankles, and arms. The ropes held him a few feet above the ground, facing downward. His stiff cock jutted from between his legs, which were held open at the ankles by a spreader bar. Another man, wearing only jeans and holding a riding crop, circled him with a pensive look on his face. He started tapping the man's bare buttocks—lightly at first, and then harder— until the sting of the crop made the submissive cry out in pain and desire. He struggled in his bonds but couldn't free himself, and he moaned when the Dom touched his bare skin with the palm of his free hand in a gentle caress that ended in a harsh slap to the inside of his thigh. Then the Dom reached between his sub's legs and started stroking his erection. The struggle ceased, and the sub moaned in unadulterated pleasure, at the mercy of gravity and his Dom's roaming hands.

Desire curled through Sam's belly as he imagined being suspended by those ropes. They pulled tightly but didn't seem to cut into the sub's skin. Just when he thought the sub might come, his Dom started up with the crop again.

The phone rang.

"Hey," Sam said, answering breathlessly. He was having a hard time not touching himself, and Nathan's voice on the end of the line was a relief. "Are you online yet?" He had booted up his chat account but hadn't heard the telltale ping. "I'm all ready for you."

"Actually no. Something's come up."

"What?" He almost made a joke about his dick, but stopped himself when he realized Nathan was serious.

"I just got a text from Eric. He's heading back to the club, and I've got to go with him."

"I thought you went last night." Disappointment cut through Sam's lust like a cold blade.

"We did. But I got word that one of the major persons of interest is going to be there tonight. This might be our only chance to make contact. I'm supposed to meet Eric in twenty minutes."

"Well, shit." Feeling a little like he'd been punked, Sam snapped his laptop shut and sat up on the bed. The plug shifted inside him, reminding him of his slow-burning arousal, but his erection had started to soften.

"I'm really sorry."

"It's okay. I understand. You've got a job to do." It was difficult to hold back his heavy sigh, but he managed—barely.

"I'll make it up to you, I promise. I'll bet you look gorgeous right now. Did you follow my instructions?"

Sam snorted. "What do you think?"

"I know you did." Nathan's voice was husky. "Watch the video again and imagine it's me doing those things to you. You can come whenever you want. Okay?"

Sam swallowed. "Okay."

They said their good-byes and Sam tossed the phone down on his bed and then stared down at his cock, which was still half-hard. His balls ached from the long-distance foreplay, but he didn't much feel like watching the video again.

Had Nathan sounded eager to go to the club, or was Sam imagining things? He tried to banish the thought, but his mind was like a Venus flytrap, latching on to it and not letting go.

A messed up mixture of adrenaline, horniness, and jealousy warmed his blood again, and his dick hardened. He took it in his hand and started jerking himself without any finesse. He closed his eyes, but every time he did he saw Nathan with someone else—some faceless man or woman. His orgasm happened quickly, but the release left him feeling empty and slightly disgusted. He wiped his hand on a dirty T-shirt and went to the bathroom to remove the plug.

At least his evening was probably going better than Collins's. He wondered what had happened to him.


THE LUCKY Star was packed for Thursday karaoke night, and Sam slid into his favorite barstool. An off-key singer belted out the chorus to "More Than a Feeling," while his friends looked on, clapping and laughing. Sam turned his attention to the taps beyond the bar, and his mouth watered.

Rachel was working, just as he'd expected. He waved a greeting, and she saw him and approached with a curious look on her face. She snapped a bar towel at him. "Hey, stranger. What are you doing down here?"

"Oh, I needed to get out of the apartment for a while."

"You must be lonely without Nathan, huh?"

Sam nodded rather than admit it out loud. Rachel smirked. Not knowing the details of Nathan's case, she probably thought Sam was a big baby for missing him. "You want a soda?"

His throat closed around the word "sure," and he tried not to stare at the gleaming bottles of liquor winking back at him from the high shelves behind the bar. He knew Rachel would never pour for him, but another martini would be just the thing.

She brought back a soda with a twist of lime, and he sipped it, wishing for the stronger burn of alcohol. Another karaoke standard began, sung by a woman with a smooth, velvety voice. Rachel leaned over the bar.

"I have the craziest news."

"What?" He raised an eyebrow. She was grinning madly, like a cat who'd eaten an entire cageful of canaries.

"Me and Alex are getting married."

"Shut the fuck up. No way."

"I can't. It's true." She stuck out her left hand, and there on her ring finger, was a small gold band with a little ruby in the center. It didn't seem like Rachel's taste, but then she explained that Alex had picked it out.

"It was a joke at first. Her parents are coming to visit next week, and she wanted to freak them out. But then, after she gave it to me, well… we got talking." Her skin glowed as she spoke. Rachel wasn't naturally one to gush. "It's crazy because my first reaction was yes. Just yes. I didn't even have to think about it. It feels right. So what do you think?"

Her contagious emotions made Sam smile. "I think it's great, Rach. I'm so happy for you."

"I mean, I'm twenty-nine. It seems like a perfectly respectable time to get married."

"Absolutely respectable. So when's the big day?"

Rachel stared down at her hand and flexed her fingers. "Haven't set it yet. I figure there's no rush, but we'll probably do it down at city hall. Sam—" She paused dramatically. "Will you be my maid of honor?"

"Always a bridesmaid." He rested his head on his hand and feigned a sigh. "Of course. I'd love to. Just remember, my best color is peach, and yellow washes me out."

"I was thinking purple."

"Purple works. Have you told the 'rents yet?" Sam sipped his soda again and keenly missed the alcohol.

"Nope. We're waiting to tell both sets together. We figure that way they'll be peer-pressured into acting socially acceptable. I'm not worried about my mom and dad, but Al's folks are still weird about the whole interracial-girlfriend thing. At least I'm Jewish." She frowned down at the ring.

"You're perfect. And if they don't see it, then fuck 'em."

"That's exactly what Alex said."

Sam leaned forward and kissed her cheek. For some reason the news choked him up. It seemed like both an end and a beginning. They were still young, but they weren't kids anymore. How had time passed so quickly?

An irritated customer called out, "Can I get some service, *please?*" and Rachel gave Sam an exasperated look.

"Gotta run. Let's talk later. Okay?"

"Sounds good. Congratulations, Rach. And tell Alex congrats for me too."

She beamed again and turned to serve the impatient guy. The place was getting crowded. Maybe the new karaoke night was a good call for business. Sam left a few bucks on the bar and went out into the night.


HE ENTERED another bar, a few blocks away. Without thinking too much about it, he strolled up to the bartender, ordered a whiskey on the rocks, and paid for it in cash. He needed to quiet his mind a little. Going back to the empty apartment seemed a guaranteed recipe for a sleepless night, and he had to work in the morning.

He ignored the twinge of guilt and shame he felt on the first sip. It wasn't illegal. One drink wouldn't hurt. It hadn't when he finished the martini.

Collins had apparently decided to cut and run. Sam wondered if he was fleeing from the cops, or if someone else was breathing down his neck. Sam couldn't blame him for taking off, but he was still curious about what Collins wanted to tell him. In any case he was probably halfway across the world or hiding out in a Podunk town, somewhere off the beaten path. Sam didn't care anymore, though he supposed he should. If the wrong person saw them together, he could be in danger. Nathan would be so disappointed if Sam got himself into trouble while he was away.

The whiskey went down so smoothly he regretted ordering a single. It had been a small pour, and the ice watered it down. He motioned to the bartender for one more—a double. Just enough to take the edge off. Just enough for him to go home and sleep soundly, without any bad dreams.

He sipped his second drink. He didn't want to be a disappointment, though he feared he wasn't doing much to impede the process. But was he the only one to blame? What about Nathan? The missed calls and the quick chats were starting to grate on Sam's nerves. Nathan was probably out doing who knew what. Or whom. Maybe he wouldn't even tell Sam the truth.

The bar door opened with a jangle, and Sam turned around and was startled when he noticed a familiar face. He set down his glass—empty again.

Antonio Rivera was smooth-shaven, and he wore casual clothes. His smile took on a sardonic edge when he noticed the empty drink.

"Hello, Rivera," said Sam, staring right back. He wasn't about to hide from him, even if he was Nathan's friend.

"Fancy seeing you here," said Rivera as he took a seat next to Sam.

"I popped in for a nightcap. You come here often?"

"I've been renting a room in the building across the street." Rivera gestured toward the window, and Sam recalled seeing a couple of nondescript brownstones when he came in.

"Oh."

The conversation continued in stilted fits and starts until the bartender approached.

"I'll have another," said Sam.

"And I'll have what he's having," said Rivera. Sam remembered what Rivera once said about trying to quit drinking when he was Sam's age. Obviously it hadn't worked, but Rivera seemed like a functional guy. He could handle his booze. And if he could, so could Sam. It didn't have to be a big deal.

Sam closed his eyes and took a substantial sip. The whiskey warmed his insides predictably. It felt nice.

"What brings you to my neck of the woods?" asked Rivera.

Sam paused. They'd never met privately without Nathan, and they'd never socialized. He couldn't tell Rivera the truth. "Just took a walk and found myself down here."

"It's a little out of the way for you."

"I like to try new things," Sam said with a shrug.

They were silent for a while, both nursing their drinks. The pleasant fuzz of inebriation softened Sam's worries. He felt at ease again. Bolder. He didn't have to answer to anyone. He turned to Rivera. "So, when are you heading back to New York?"

"A few days. I've got a new case. So that's it. Good-bye, Stonebridge." He lifted his glass. "You've been a real pain in the ass."

"Hey," said Sam. "She's a pain in the ass, but she's my pain in the ass."

"You can keep her. So, any luck on your story?"

Sam was surprised he asked. "You mean on the mayor? Not so far. Who do you think did it? You think someone from his staff was involved? Is that why Collins took off?"

"You know I can't talk about—"

"An open investigation. Yeah, yeah. I've heard it all before." Sam drummed his fingers on the bar. "Nathan would say the same thing." Suddenly he was suspicious. "Wait a second. Did Nathan ask you to keep an eye on me?"

Rivera didn't flinch. "Nope."

"But if he had, you wouldn't tell me."

"Probably not. But if he had, I wouldn't be ordering you a drink." Sam looked down at his glass, which was empty, and Rivera motioned for another round.

Panic started to creep into Sam's gut. He had told himself just one, and then had two. And the next would make—four? He didn't want to stop, and he wasn't sure he could. A cold feeling of disgust settled over him, but he fought it and raised the glass to his lips.

He and Rivera continued their conversation as they drank. They talked about sports, and Sam realized Rivera was a pretty funny, self-deprecating guy under his gruff, FBI-agent exterior. Predictably he was a Yankees fan, since he'd gone to NYU and lived in New York ever since. Unlike Yuri he could at least admit the Sox had some good seasons. Sam was tempted to ask him about Donna Howard, but he figured that was too personal.

When he returned from a piss break, Rivera slapped him on the shoulder. Next to his cell phone on the bar, there was another drink. Sam picked it up with a feeling like relief.

"So, you off the wagon for good?" Rivera asked.

"Nope. This is a minor setback. I'd appreciate you not mentioning it to Nathan." His words came out slightly slurred, but he knocked back the liquor anyway.

"Your secret is safe with me." Rivera winked.

"'S not a secret." He'd tell Nathan on his own terms, but he wasn't about to go running to the phone, whining like a needy baby. Nathan would think he couldn't even make it a few days without him. "What about you?"

"Me? My father was a drunk. I figure I'm doing better than he did, so why stop now? What about yours?"

"My father?" Sam thought. He'd often seen his dad with a glass of whiskey in hand, but not out of control. His father had never had a habit. "No."

"Good on you, then." Rivera tipped back the rest of his drink.

Sam hardly realized how much time had passed until the bartender flashed the lights for last call.

"Dammit," Sam said, head swimming as he stood. "I gotta work tomorrow." His stomach lurched in protest. Yuri would be so pissed if Sam called out. They were on a tight schedule to finish for Monday.

"Are you okay to get home?" Rivera asked as they exited the bar to the empty sidewalk. It had started to drizzle, and the oily pavement gleamed under yellow streetlights.

"M'fine," said Sam, though he thought he might be sick. He squinted and tried to remember how many rounds they'd had. Maybe five. Six? Shit. Six was a lot, especially since he hadn't had much for dinner. A trembly panic fluttered inside his chest.

"Good to see you, Sam." Rivera patted Sam's arm. "Take care of yourself."

"Hey," said Sam. "Don't tell Nathan you saw me tonight."

"I told you your secret's safe with me."

Those words dogged Sam's footsteps as he made his way home.

# Chapter 8

SAM STABBED at the radio dial and turned it to another station, where an annoying commercial droned on about some super savings discount at a mattress emporium. He sighed and switched off the damn thing. His head was pounding as he made the drive to Shady Brook to see Tim.

He stopped at a gas station to grab a coffee and fill up, and he chewed a couple of antacid tablets—his old standard breakfast. It wouldn't do to show up with an obvious hangover.

It had been a week since the night at the bar with Rivera. He hadn't gotten drunk again until Nathan called. Their conversation was brief—almost like Nathan wanted to get off the phone. He said he was tired from working long days, but Sam knew he meant long nights. The news wasn't good either. Nathan still didn't know how long it was going to take to wrap up the case, and he couldn't tell Sam any of the details. For all Sam knew, it might be another month. Maybe two.

Sam only remembered the rest of the night in a blur. After hanging up with Nathan, he went to the corner store and bought a fifth of whiskey. He wound up watching sitcom reruns and drinking half the bottle before he even knew what he was doing. He was going to pour out the rest, but he didn't. He would later.

There was a text on his phone when he got out of the truck.

*Talk tonight?*

*Maybe. Might have plans*, he sent back.

He knew it was bitchy, but he was too grumpy to be pleasant. Nathan returned the text almost immediately.

*I know you're angry. I'm sorry I've been busy. Please talk tonight? We can Skype if you want.*

*You're starting to sound like a broken record. There's a reason they don't sell.*

*Maybe I deserve that. But I think you're being a little unfair. You know I hate this as much as you do.*

Sam's irritation grew, and he pocketed his phone without replying. At least he had been keeping himself busy, working at Manella's whenever he got the chance—and writing. Apparently missing Nathan was turning out to be good for his output. He'd already done a couple personal pieces for his blog about the repairs to the Episcopal Church and his own scorched-out building, and he planned to get in touch with some of the families who'd been affected. Maybe it would give him some insight into the White case too.

He was also in the middle of revisiting his old piece on the Streets Clean incentive program for high school students and planned to slam White's administration for hypocrisy. He'd already gotten Damon and the program director on board for an interview.

Still no amount of work could drown out his love for Nathan, or the intensity of his loneliness. Of course he missed the sex. But more than that, he missed the warm, casual touches they shared, the way Nathan laughed at his stupid jokes. He missed the crinkle of skin next to Nathan's eyes when he smiled. He missed the steadiness of his breathing in the night. The way he felt like home.

He grabbed his phone again.

S: *Sorry. Got a lot on my mind. Miss you.*

He thought about the half bottle of whiskey. He knew he was lying to himself about pouring it out. He had every intention of finishing it later.

SAM SET down his glass on the coffee table, and Shadow gave him an irritated look from the floor near his feet and raised her head from where it was pillowed on her paws. The phone rang again. After another moment's hesitation, Sam answered it.

"What's going on with you?" Nathan sounded concerned. Sam had avoided his call the previous night.

"Nothing's going on."

"Yes, there is. You think I don't know you?"

Sam scrubbed a hand over his face. His visit with Tim the day before had been a disaster, and when he got home from Shady Brook, he went straight to the kitchen to polish off the rest of the whiskey. He had promised himself no more, but that only lasted until an eight-o'clock trip to the package store. He was only slightly buzzed, though, so there was no way Nathan could tell he'd been drinking. Sam had enough practice over the years to be able to fool people. "I don't want to be a burden. I know you've been busy with the case."

"Screw the case. Dammit, Sam. I feel like you're hiding something from me. Is this about the mayor's murder? Have you gotten yourself into some trouble?"

"No. It's Tim," he said. "He had a seizure yesterday when I was visiting."

It was horrible. Every time he closed his eyes, he saw his brother's flailing limbs and gasping mouth. Though it seemed to go on forever, in reality it had lasted less than a minute. The doctors stabilized him, but they weren't sure what caused the seizure or what it meant, and they practically kicked Sam out at the end of the day. He went back again that morning and stayed until the early afternoon. To add to his concern, even Lisa looked worried, though she tried to mask it for Sam's sake.

Nathan sucked in a sharp breath. "Is he okay?"

"He is now. But it freaked me out. It could mean he's waking up, or it could be something bad. The doctors don't know. We have to wait and see." *Wait and see.* The most hated words in the English language. They weren't much comfort when you were the one waiting, as they basically meant, "we know fuck all."

"I wish I was there," Nathan said.

"Me too." Sam closed his eyes and rested his head against the couch. He had many questions on the tip of his tongue, but he felt like he couldn't ask any of them. "How's Eric?"

"Oh, he's Eric. He's fine. But I'm... I'm starting to feel it."

Sam knew what he meant. He would probably have the same problem if their situations were reversed, but it stung all the same. He eyed the half-drunk glass of whiskey and grimaced. "Yeah. I guess it's pretty hard not... to participate."

"That's not what I meant. It's the case wearing on me. I only want you. God, when I get home—"

A voice on the other end of the line interrupted Nathan. Sam could tell it was Eric speaking, but he couldn't make out his words, only their emphatic tone.

"Shit," Nathan murmured. Sam heard a few muffled exchanges. From the low growl in his throat, Nathan sounded like he was arguing.

"Let me guess—you have to go," Sam said when Nathan returned to the call.

"Something's come up. I'm sorry."

Sorry was starting to feel like an empty word.

They disconnected, and Sam picked up his glass. The ice tinkled, and he hesitated and considered the amber liquid. A slow-spreading misery took hold of him. He was self-medicating. It wasn't Nathan's fault he had to work. The case took precedence, and Sam hated feeling so needy.

What had Nathan meant—the case was wearing on him? Sam knew Nathan's work sometimes upset him, no matter the calm, rational exterior he presented to the rest of the world. Maybe the case was worse than expected. It was frustrating not to be able to hear the details and maybe offer some comfort. Then again Sam was barely holding it together himself, and the whiskey in his hand was proof.

He thought about reaching out to Alex and Rachel, but he didn't. They were happy, and he didn't want to drag them down. Yuri was busy mooning over his hot, young employee.

What would he do if Tim passed? Was it selfish to want his brother to continue living—if it could be called living—in his current limbo state? What if he was suffering, and Sam didn't know? He'd been so young when his life was stolen. They'd never had the chance to discuss what-if scenarios. There had only been the future, overflowing with promise, but cruelly ephemeral. You should never have to wonder whether your brother would want to die.

"What are you staring at?" Shadow was still giving him a know-it-all look. She could judge away. He was going to finish his drink. And talking to his cat was a pretty sad substitute for human conversation. He was well on his way to becoming a drunk, crazy cat guy, if there was such a thing.

His cell rang again. He answered without bothering to look at the caller ID. "Look, Nathan. Really. It's—"

"Hello? Is this Sam?" The voice was vaguely familiar, and it stopped Sam in his tracks. He set down his whiskey.

"Barney?"

"Yeah."

"Holy shit. I went to your apartment the other day, but the cops said you'd left. Where are you?"

"I can't tell you that, and I can't talk for long. Listen. I don't know who killed the mayor, but I might know *why* they did it."

"Oh yeah?" Sam's pulse started to race. He was on the precipice of something huge—something that might change his career entirely. All of his other worries vanished as Collins continued.

"The mayor was involved with the Voronkovs."

"I knew it." Sam slapped his knee and laughed in triumph. One of his first suspicions had been a mob link. "Is that why you took off?"

"Listen carefully. There's a mailbox on the corner of Regent and South Street, a few blocks from my place. Taped to the underside, you'll find a key to a safe-deposit box at the Union Trust, number 203. Be careful no one follows you."

Sam didn't need to be warned twice. A small, tight scar on the top of his head served as a continual reminder of his encounter with Bernhardt Hoff, one of the Voronkov's henchmen. The injury could have been much worse, but he was lucky. He managed to escape with only a concussion and a few bruises, because Nathan got there in time to save him.

"And you knew about this?" Disappointment quickly replaced excitement. Barney had seemed like an okay guy, but he'd obviously been covering for the mayor. Then it dawned on Sam, and he could have kicked himself for being so stupid. The fancy watch, the nice car, those top-shelf martinis. "You were getting paid off. Weren't you? You son of a bitch."

"I'm not proud, but I did what I did." Collins sounded a little too haughty for Sam's liking.

"Who else?" Sam demanded. "The deputy mayor?"

A pause. "It's all in the files."

"Shit." Sam was up on his feet, pacing around the room. His mind whirled in a thousand different directions, fueled by an adrenaline rush. Not only had White been involved with the mob, his successor was crooked too. "Why are you telling me this now? Why incriminate yourself?"

"I guess you could say I had a crisis of conscience. I'm leaving the country now, and I won't be back. Do whatever you want with the evidence. But I suggest you burn it. It's dangerous. I've got to get going—"

Sam cut him off before he could hang up. "Wait. So you don't have any idea who did it?"

Collins sighed. "It could have been anyone. Rodger was using more heavily after what happened last October. I tried to stop him, but he wouldn't listen. He thought he had everything under control."

"He was getting sloppy?"

Sam spun on his heel and headed to the coffee table to grab his keys. If the mayor had ceased to be useful and become a liability, it made sense that others, who wanted to retain power, might have killed him, especially if the deputy mayor was involved.

"Yes. And I was working my ass off to keep him out of sight. Anyway you seem like a good guy, Sam. Don't… trust anyone. Okay?"

Sam was already heading toward the elevator when Collins hung up. He pocketed his phone and stood facing the doors as they closed and left him in the quiet, enclosed space. He was clearheaded. The minor buzz he had before the phone call was gone.

He wasn't surprised by Barney's revelation. According to a recent report, drug arrests had begun to decline over the past few months. The mayor's office had spun it as a result of the increased effectiveness of the new programs, but Sam had his doubts. It was common knowledge Stonebridge remained a major gateway for trafficking between New York and the rest of the Northeast. Just because there hadn't been any major busts recently didn't mean drugs were no longer coming into the city. In fact it could simply mean the trafficking was continuing unchecked. After all the Voronkovs had many members working throughout the area, like tiny spiders skittering around on one large, complex web. If one thread broke, they would simply build another.

The elevator dinged when he reached the ground floor. Sam gave his surroundings a sweep as he made his way to his parking space and climbed into his truck. There were a few people on the street, but no one paid him any attention as the engine roared to life.

Other questions ran through Sam's mind as he reversed and headed toward the address Collins had relayed. Was he being stupid for trusting his word? What if he was walking into a trap?

He hesitated at a red light with his hands on the wheel.

If Collins was telling the truth, Sam was about to gain possession of information that would make him a target if the wrong people found out he had it. He thought for a second about calling Chief Howard and telling her. But could he trust her? And Nathan was out of reach at the moment.

He made the final turn and curbed his truck a block away from the mailbox. After a cursory rummage in the glove compartment, he found an old blank envelope—his cover in case someone had eyes on the area.

He fingered the folded paper. "Cautious" wasn't an adjective anyone had ever used to describe him, but was he bordering on reckless? Ever since seeing Tim seize up, he'd been thinking about how fleeting life was. With Nathan gone, it felt like he was on hold. But he had always wanted to make a difference, and he wouldn't get there by sitting on his hands.

His blood hummed with excitement as he hopped out of the truck, started to whistle, and made his way toward the dark blue shape of the mailbox. Collins had chosen wisely. The street was quiet. After he slipped the empty envelope into the box, he purposefully dropped his keys, cursed, and kneeled down to find them. Running his fingers gingerly along the underside of the cool metal box, he encountered cobwebs, rusty metal, and then a smooth bump of plastic tape.

The key.

He removed it and gripped it tightly in his palm. As he retraced his steps to his truck, it seemed to get even hotter, until it was searing a brand in his skin. The night stretched long before him. He thought about the bottle of whiskey waiting at home. Tomorrow he'd find out what was inside the safe-deposit box.

Union National Trust was a small brick structure with an even smaller parking lot. When Sam entered with the key in his pocket, there were only a few pensioners in the lobby and a bored teller at the long, faux mahogany desk. A security guard gave him a disinterested glance and then continued pacing the scuffed marble floor. Beyond him a narrow hallway led to what looked like the vault.

Sam had spent the morning wondering if he should go to the bank or wait to talk it over with Nathan. After a few hours of internal debate, his disobedient streak won out. With Nathan out of state, it was easier to ignore his inevitable objection. Still, with every step he took, he could feel Nathan's disapproval. A shrink would probably say he was courting trouble on purpose.

Sam peeked into one of the cubicle offices flanking the wall of the bank. He'd never rented a safe-deposit box, and he wasn't sure how the process worked. Would he need a photo ID or something, even though he had a key? What if they denied him entry?

He didn't have much time to wonder. A woman wearing thick horn-rimmed glasses looked up from her computer. He smiled at her as sweat started to bead on his forehead. He'd worn a blazer to conceal his holster, and the room was warm. Coupled with the state of his nerves, he was sweltering.

"Hi," he said, giving her his most winning smile. "I need to retrieve something from my safe-deposit box." He raised Nathan's black work briefcase, the one he used for his teaching trips. Sam had found it in the closet while rooting around for something professional to wear. It seemed the perfect solution to stow whatever was in Barney's box, assuming it didn't contain something large or cumbersome... like a severed head. That thought had been enough to encourage him to investigate the gun safe. It felt strange to be carrying a concealed weapon, but it was the one concession he made to the list of Nathan's imagined objections. Once he got home, he'd lock up Barney's evidence.

She blinked owlishly. "Key?"

He held it out.

"ID?" She typed something on the computer.

Sam held his breath. *Shit.* The woman slowly blinked again, like his hesitation was paining her. He had to make a decision.

"Sam Flynn." He fished out his license and handed it to her, and his heart hammered as she typed out his name. He should have asked Collins what name the thing was under. He should have—

"Right this way, please," said the woman.

—given the guy a little more credit.

The deposit vault smelled musty, like dust and a thousand old possessions left behind. The woman procured a key from a ring on her belt, slipped it into one of the two keyholes, and motioned for Sam to do the same. She pulled out the small rectangular box and set it on the sole metal table in the center of the room.

"Ring the bell when you're finished."

Once she'd gone, Sam opened up the hinged box and peered inside. There was a manila envelope filled with receipts and tax documents dating back years. A quick flip through them suggested the mayor's accountant had been creative with his returns. The only other object was a small red flash drive. Sam slipped both items into his briefcase and rang the bell.


THE CAR wasn't turning.

Sam glanced in the rearview mirror at the silver sedan that had been following him for the past several minutes. He hadn't noticed it in the bank parking lot, though, and he told himself he was being paranoid. But at the next light, when he turned left and the car continued to trail him, his stomach dropped uncomfortably. He couldn't see the driver through the car's tinted windows. *Shit.*

He'd loaded a few rounds into his gun before he left the apartment. Even so he hadn't honestly considered the possibility of a confrontation. What would Nathan do if he were here? Thinking quickly, Sam slowed to well below the thirty-mile-per-hour speed limit, and instead of passing him, the sedan slowed too. *Double shit.*

He sped up, and the sedan sped up. Whoever was driving didn't appear to be making any attempt to conceal the fact they were following him. His hands slipped against the wheel as he made the first left turn he could. The sedan turned too.

Sam glanced into his rearview as adrenaline revved up his fight-or-flight instinct. Even though the sedan was close behind, he couldn't make out the driver—only a vague shadow of a genderless person who appeared to be wearing sunglasses. The car didn't have a front plate either, so he couldn't tell whether it was from out of state or local. And Sam had made a tactical error. The road he'd chosen was becoming more and more rural by the second. Why had he turned left, away from downtown? Cursing himself for his stupidity, he pressed the gas pedal, and the engine roared. The speedometer read fifty, then fifty-five.

The road was relatively straight, with only an occasional house on either side, and soon Sam realized he was heading toward the old Stonebridge airfield. The corrugated metal roof of the old hangar was barely visible through the thick growth of trees, but he remembered it well. He'd had his first driving lessons there as a teenager. His father took him onto the abandoned tarmac in order to avoid traffic and to give him a chance to make mistakes. His father's stern but patient face flashed before him. *Ease up on the gas, bud. Turn the wheel with both hands. Keep them at ten and two. Remember to use your mirrors to check for traffic.*

But leading the sedan onto the tarmac would only continue the cat and mouse game. To make matters worse, another spring thunderstorm was brewing on the horizon, filling the sky with dark clouds. Sam drove faster. His truck rumbled underneath him, the vibrations reminders that the engine was old and not accustomed to speed, in spite of some recent repairs. He hoped it would hang on a little longer.

The first few fat drops hit his windshield, splattering loudly with the impact and streaking out along the glass as more rain followed. A flash of lightning up ahead lit the nearly black afternoon sky. He was running out of options, and the sedan didn't show any signs of backing off. Even though he had chosen his route, it almost felt like part of a plan—as though the sedan was purposely forcing him into the storm and making him speed up. Almost like it was a trap. What if he couldn't get out of it? He imagined the truck spinning out of control into the thick bank of trees. He would die, and Nathan would be alone again.

*Keep those hands at ten and two.*

His father had always driven so cautiously, and he'd taught Sam to do the same. Why was he speeding on the night of the accident in a snowstorm?

Pushing the random thought out of his mind, Sam focused on the road ahead. His chest ached when he thought of Nathan getting the inevitable phone call. *I'm so sorry to tell you, but....*

Moreover, if Sam died, no one would ever know about the mayor's supposed mob ties. He was likely the only one on the outside who knew the truth—besides Collins—and the evidence would die with him. He doubted Collins would stick his neck out again.

Sam tried to calm his panic and consider his options. On the left a chain-link fence enclosed the abandoned airfield. On the right tall maple trees lined the road, their green leaves frothing in the rising wind of the storm. Rain started falling harder, coating the windshield in sheets. Despite being on the highest setting, Sam's wipers were hardly doing the job. He couldn't see more than a few feet in front of him, and pellets of hail soon joined the rain and clattered loudly on the roof. Behind him the sedan's driver had turned on the car's high beams. It was gaining on him.

A turn curved sharply to the right, and Sam slammed on his brakes to make it without skidding off the road. His hands slipped on the steering wheel as the truck lost all traction, and Sam's stomach lurched. Hydroplaning. His father had warned him about that too. Miraculously the wheels found the ground, and he made the turn without incident. But he wasn't out of the woods. Not a hundred yards ahead of him, there were taillights in the darkness, and beyond them, a line of oncoming headlights on the other side of the road. Even through the rain, he could tell they were slow moving. He was trapped.

*Fuck no.*

Whipping his truck over the barely visible double yellow lines to face the traffic, he passed the car on his right and made it back to the proper lane just in time to hear the blare of a car horn from his left. The line of slow traffic continued to pass, making it impossible for Sam's pursuer to follow him. Sam floored it.

Once he'd made it a safe distance, he took the first turn he could onto a dead-end street with a few rundown houses and flicked off his lights. A minute or so later, the silver sedan sped by on the main road. He squinted to try to make out the plates, but they weren't legible through the rain.

What the hell had just happened?

He sucked in a quick breath and then another. He was light-headed, and his heart was pounding loudly enough in his ears to be audible above the rain and the occasional rumble of thunder. With trembling hands he felt for the gun in his holster, drew it out, and placed it on the passenger seat next to the briefcase. It didn't do much to calm him down. He was having a panic attack.

Forcing himself to breathe deeply, he leaned his head back and took stock of the situation. Whoever had tailed him had seemed willing to run him off the road. Had they followed him to the bank? He thought again of the woman who assisted him. Had she been paid to call someone if he showed up?

Sam ran a hand over his face and through his sweat-damp hair. He was in deep, deep shit.

Then again, what else was new?

ONCE HE made it home, he locked and bolted the apartment door from inside. He grabbed only the essentials—computer and chargers, a few changes of clothes, more ammo, and, of course, Shadow. The cat complained loudly when he stuck her in the carrier, but he appeased her with a few treats and the promise of wet food whenever they arrived at their destination. For her, a local pet hotel.

He was back on the road again in fifteen minutes. He deposited Shadow at the Furry Friends Hotel and Day Care Facility, left his truck in a grocery store parking lot, and called for a ride to take him to a cheap motel across town. There was no sign of the silver sedan or any indication he was being followed. Sam checked in under a false name, paid the front desk attendant with cash, and was sure to lock the door behind him and leave his gun on the side table next to the bed, where he could reach it easily.

The room was a dingy affair with stained yellow wallpaper and an orange shag carpet that was matted and dark in places. He didn't want to know with what. It was the kind of place you rented for sex or cleaning up after a murder. Nathan would have hated it.

"Yeah, yeah. It's not the Ritz," Sam muttered to himself. "Try to stay calm."

He called Nathan, but it went straight to voice mail. Nathan's deep, smooth voice made Sam's chest twinge.

*Hello. You've reached Nathan Walker. Please leave a message, and I'll return your call as soon as possible.*

"It's me," Sam said after the beep. "I need to talk to you. It's an emergency." He threw down the phone and booted up his computer. He had to find out what was on the flash drive so he knew what he was up against.

He clicked open the first file.

There were several photos from what looked like surveillance video of an intimate gathering. A slightly slimmer Mayor White sat at a table with a man wearing a black suit. He had close-cropped white hair. Both of them held cigars, and they were smiling. Sam didn't recognize the white-haired man, but he'd bet money he was a Voronkov. Another man stood behind

85

them, slightly apart and to the left, and Sam would have remembered his face anywhere. He seemed to be watching the proceedings with interest. Sam zoomed in.

It was the guy who killed Emma Walker and almost killed him. Bernhardt Hoff.


By NIGHTTIME Sam had gone through all of the files, and he was livid. While some were more incriminating than others, taken together they were enough to prove, beyond a shadow of a doubt, that Mayor White and the former deputy mayor—now Mayor Rick Morgan—had been taking regular bribes from the Voronkovs over the years. The files revealed a trail of corruption that brought new insight to recent events. The mayor had known about and directly benefitted from the Voronkov's former arrangement with the PD and the Feldman Foundation. While the Voronkovs sent their drugs by land and sea through Stonebridge, to destinations in the north, and laundered their money through the Feldman Foundation, they gave the PD a cut to keep quiet.

The mayor's "tough on crime" reputation was an illusion, based on his strategy of going after small-time dealers and their customers, rather than focusing on the big money. Sam had once considered Chief Sheldon a friend, and he was enraged to discover that he had played right into the mob's hands for financial gain. He was less surprised to find out that White had been involved all along. But how, even with Collins's assistance, had he seemed to keep his hands clean?

Why didn't Sheldon expose the mayor and his cronies during the trial? He and his staff took the entirety of the blame. Bernhardt Hoff was a made man, as well as a torpedo—a hired gun—but he hadn't ratted out his bosses during the trial either—even for a lesser sentence. He probably knew what thanks awaited that sort of betrayal. Maybe Sheldon kept quiet out of fear for his life.

But since the trial and conviction, the city had been lulled into a false sense of complacency, and that naïveté had allowed the same corruption to flourish under a different guise. Mayor White's Streets Clean policy was appeasement at its worst. There was even a recording, secretly obtained by Collins, which consisted of a very stoned mayor boasting about how stupid the people of Stonebridge were to buy into "that load of crap."

If the mayor were still alive, Sam would have kicked his substantial ass.

He flipped his computer shut with disgust. He couldn't look at the mayor's self-satisfied grin anymore. Whatever the case, in the last few months, the tide had turned against Mayor White. Maybe the fallout from the Halloween bombing and arsons had made him a liability, or maybe his increased drug use had signed his death warrant.

It seemed probable at least someone in the PD knew what was going on. Because the mayor had appointed her, Chief Howard was the most likely suspect. And either one of the Voronkovs or someone on White's staff had killed him. Rick Morgan? It made sense. He had the most to gain.

Or maybe not.

One item—an e-mail from the mayor to Collins—pointed the finger in another direction entirely. White suspected his wife was having an affair, but he didn't know with whom. So the entire mob connection *could* be unrelated, and the mayor's death attributed to the cold-hearted calculation of two people who wanted him out of the way for personal reasons.

Sam scratched the rough growth of stubble on his chin. He hated the idea of Chief Howard being involved. In spite of his cynicism, he wanted to believe there were good people in the world, working in public service and politics for the right reasons.

What the hell was he going to do?

He needed a plan—and fast. No doubt the driver of the silver sedan was looking for him. They knew he had the files. The smartest thing he could do was get rid of them. But who could he trust? Antonio Rivera was a possibility, but Sam didn't have his number, and asking anyone but Nathan for it might arouse suspicion.

His phone was still silent. Sam sent another text message.

*Answer your damn phone.*

Then there was the errant thought he had during the car chase, about his parents' deaths. The official report said his father had lost control of the vehicle on an icy patch of road. Sam never doubted that what happened was an accident. He hadn't let himself even consider another cause.

But several months before, when he and Nathan were working to crack the Stonebridge arson case, his father's former colleague, Frank Chancellor, made a troubling throwaway comment about the crash.

"Suspicious, if you ask me...."

Though Frank never elaborated, the statement struck a chord deep in Sam's gut. For so many years, Sam had been angry with himself. And he could finally admit he was angry with his father too. He felt guilty for not being in the car with his family that night—for surviving while his brother wasted away in a coma. And he was furious with his father for being the one behind the wheel and accidentally shattering all of their lives. But what if it wasn't an accident after all?

Nathan still hadn't texted back. It wasn't like him to ignore Sam's messages, especially if they were urgent.

What if something had happened to him?

Sam wished he'd brought his collar along. More than ever he needed tangible evidence of their connection. He touched his neck and imagined it there, but the gesture only served to confirm its absence.

He needed a drink.

TEN MINUTES later Sam found himself across the street at a dirty liquor store, asking the guy behind the plexiglass for a pint. He returned to the hotel room with the paper bag and grabbed one of the disposable coffee cups. Then he thought better of it, unscrewed the bottle, and took a swig. Why bother with the illusion that he wasn't going to drink the whole thing?

The whiskey burned its way down his throat and warmed his empty stomach. He sat on the armchair closest to the parking lot window and peeked through the dusty blinds. With the lights out in the room, he wouldn't be visible to anyone, but he wanted to make sure he hadn't been followed. Going out to get booze was a risky move.

It was worth it. He continued to drink, and the whiskey did its job, dulling his worry over Nathan.

But what if—

Sam bolted upright in the uncomfortable chair. The whiskey swished and spilled as he set it down on the table, right next to his loaded gun. He grabbed his cell phone and scrolled for Nathan's number.

Three rings. Four. *Don't go to voice mail. Don't go to voice mail—*

"Hello?" asked a silky male voice. "Who is Sam, and what does he want with my Nathan?"

"Who's this?" Sam had trouble making the "s" sounds. He tried to wrap his lips around them and failed.

"I asked first." The voice was teasingly seductive and held a hint of a British accent. Sam's flesh crawled as the whiskey in his otherwise-empty stomach threatened to rise.

"Simon, who is it?" It was Nathan.

"Someone called Sam. Who is he, love?"

"Give me the phone."

Sam hung up before Nathan could get on the line. He ignored the phone when it rang again and stared straight ahead at the ugly yellow wallpaper. One portion of it had started peeling off and showed the stained concrete wall behind it.

He felt numb, so he brought the whiskey to his lips again and sipped robotically. The bottle was already half gone, and Sam was drunk. Too drunk. He knew if the person in the silver sedan found him here, he wouldn't be able to defend himself. He could barely focus and he was pretty sure he was going to puke. He couldn't get the man's voice out of his head. Simon. Who was he? Someone Nathan met at the club?

Sam thought back to their abbreviated conversations over the past couple of weeks. Never once had Nathan mentioned a Simon, but it certainly seemed like they were on familiar terms. He'd called Nathan "love." *What the actual fuck?* And where was Eric?

Maybe they were having a threesome. How fun.

Whiskey dripped down his chin, leaving a cool trail, and he wiped it away with the back of his hand. The disgust he felt with himself for turning to his old crutch was less powerful than his desire to get blackout drunk. He didn't want to think anymore, even if it meant he was weak.

He looked out the window again. Except for the three cars that were in the lot when he checked in, it was empty. He was safe for the time being. He closed his eyes, and the world started to spin. It was too quiet.

What if Nathan had lied? What if he was fucking other people? What if he'd made the deal with Sam simply to placate him, but had no intention of keeping his word?

Sam felt the bile rise in his throat. He stood up and set the empty bottle down. Moving as quickly as he could, he staggered to the bathroom and vomited up most of his binge. It was horrible, and the linoleum floor killed his knees. He flushed the toilet and lay down on the cold tile.

What the fuck was he doing? He grabbed his phone.

Nathan had left some text messages, in addition to several voice mails. Sam couldn't focus to read unless he closed one eye and read with the other.

*Dammit Sam answer the phone*

*Won't you at least let me explain?*

*Why don't you trust me?*

The last one got to him—like Nathan probably expected it would. When his phone rang again a few minutes later, he answered, even though he didn't want to hear any canned excuses.

"What?" Sam snapped.

"Before you say anything else, will you please listen to me? Simon is helping us with the case. He's a friend of Eric's."

The familiar sound of Nathan's voice was so welcome, it almost made Sam forget why he was upset. Almost. "He called you love."

"That's just his way. He's a flirt. I promise there's nothing going on."

"Why didn't you tell me, then?"

"I haven't had the chance." Nathan's words echoed over the line. He sounded far away. Farther than New Jersey.

"You been busy, haven't you? So busy you wouldn't even call me back when I needed you. I needed you today." Sam tried not to slur, but it was difficult—even though he felt a little better since he'd been sick. He overcompensated by speaking very slowly.

"I'm sorry I missed your call. We've been tied up, and I just turned my phone back on. Did I wake you up? You sound strange."

A derisive laugh spilled out of Sam's mouth before he could stop it. "Tied up, huh? How's that working out for you?"

"Very funny. Will you please tell me what's going on?"

Sam rubbed his temples. His brain was having a hard time putting his thoughts together. He knew he had to explain, but so much had happened. He didn't know where to start. "I think I might be in trouble."

"What do you mean?" A pause. When Nathan spoke again, his voice was serious. "Have you been drinking?"

Sam stared at the ceiling. There was a stain on the white paint, probably from a roof leak. He teared up. "I didn't mean to. But a sedan chased me today, and I think my parents might have been murdered, and I'm at this shitty motel on Route 33 because I can't go home, and I don't know what to do. I can't trust anyone but you, but you're not here, and I have this evidence they must want. Barney Collins said so, but I still don't know who killed the mayor."

"What are you talking about? Who chased you, and where are you now?"

Sam tried to explain further, but his words came out in even more of a jumbled rush. The alcohol made it hard to maintain control of his emotions too, and his eyes kept welling up. Tears dripped down the sides of his face in warm, wet trails. To his great shame, he let out a sob, and his whole chest quaked with the effort of holding back an even louder one.

Nathan's calm, controlled voice wavered. Sam heard him curse under his breath.

"Sam, listen to me. You're going to be okay. I'm sending someone over to check on you. Don't open the door for anyone until I call you back."

"No." Sam shook his head emphatically, even though there was no one to see. "I don't want the police. Collins said I shouldn't trust anyone. I brought a gun and I'll be fine. I'm sorry I made you worry." He tacked the last couple sentences on as an afterthought, though they didn't sound very convincing.

"Jesus. You're obviously not fine. How much have you had to drink?"

"Uh. Some. Okay. Maybe a lot." This would be it, the final straw. A few more tears slipped out. "Please don't hate me," he whispered.

"I could never hate you. Not ever. In any case this isn't the time for this conversation. Now don't answer the phone or the door until I figure out what to do."

"Okay."

They hung up and Sam closed his eyes and let darkness sweep him under.

# Chapter 9

A POUNDING headache greeted him in the morning, which made sense, since he'd spent the night on the damn bathroom floor. Sam groaned and rolled over on his side, but his whole body hurt. His mouth tasted like ass, and he vaguely remembered waking up to vomit. With some effort he finally managed to right himself and reach for the small green bottle of complimentary mouthwash—a surprising amenity given the rest of the accommodations. He swished it around and considered his reflection with disgust.

Bloodshot hazel eyes stared back at him in the mirror. His hair was a mess, standing up at odd angles, and there were traces of vomit on the front of his blue T-shirt. He needed a shave too, but just as he was about to turn on the shower, he heard the *rat-tat-tat* of someone knocking on the door.

As quietly as he could, Sam emerged from the bathroom. He grabbed his gun, unlocked the safety, and held the cold metal grip tightly in his right palm. The knocking continued.

Maybe Nathan had ignored his wishes and sent someone to check on him. The thought, though unwelcome, was better than the alternative—the occupant of the silver sedan had tracked him down.

The motel was a one-level job that opened directly to the parking lot, used mostly by truck drivers passing through town. It wasn't exactly the most secure location, but Sam hadn't been picky the previous day. Now he regretted his choice. If Silver Sedan was outside, Sam's position would be virtually indefensible. There was no other exit.

He held his breath and peered through the peephole. The sight was so unexpected Sam did a double take. He blinked, stared, and then blinked again.

"Nathan?"

His fingers trembled as he struggled with the chain latch. The door let a warm waft of fresh air into the stale room. Nathan scanned the scene with hawklike precision. His dark hair had grown a bit and was tousled like he'd been raking his hands through it. Sam thought he detected a hint of cigarette smoke too, an old habit Nathan rarely indulged unless he was stressed. As soon as the door shut, Nathan bolted it and turned his focus on Sam.

"Did you drive all night?" Sam asked dumbly. He still couldn't believe Nathan was there.

Nathan's jaw ticked. "Are you okay?"

"Uh. Mostly?"

Nathan's eyes tracked over Sam's body, and Sam saw what Nathan did—the wrinkled, stained shirt, his missing left sock. There was a hole in the toe of the remaining one. Nathan always tried to make Sam throw his old socks away, but Sam figured as long as they were mostly intact, they still served their purpose. He tried to hide it by wrapping his socked foot behind his bare one.

Nathan stepped forward. He paused, eyes searching, and then slowly reached for the gun. Sam had almost forgotten about it. Nathan flicked open the chamber and frowned.

"You shouldn't be drinking with a loaded gun. God, do you know what might have happened?" Nathan's eyes flashed with concern and anger.

Sam winced. "I've been careful."

"I've seen people accidentally shoot themselves while sober. Believe me, you can't be too careful."

"Okay. I get it. I don't need a lecture right now. And you didn't have to come here at all," Sam said. "I'll be—"

Nathan cut him off by pulling him forward into a fierce embrace, and the air left Sam's lungs in a great whoosh. He returned the hug as soon as he got his bearings, wrapping his arms around Nathan's back and holding him close. The tight knot in his chest unraveled as he breathed in Nathan's familiar scent and felt the contours of his body.

For a few minutes, they simply held each other, neither ready to speak. But when Nathan's grip started to relax, Sam sighed and pulled back with reluctance. He didn't know if he was ready for the conversation they were about to have. His head was still pounding.

"I could use some coffee and some aspirin," he admitted. "And a change." He hated to think of how he smelled, and he took another step back. On the foot of the still-made bed, he found his bag. He pulled off his dirty shirt and grabbed a fresh one.

"You had quite a night." Nathan spoke tonelessly.

"I'm not proud."

To his credit Nathan didn't press the matter. "I could use some coffee too." Nathan had dark circles under his eyes. He'd likely driven straight there after they hung up, leaving his case to check on Sam. He obviously hadn't even slept.

"But I don't understand how you *are* here. Aren't you still undercover?" Sam's heart skipped. If Nathan's boss found out he'd gone AWOL, he'd be fired. "You can't put your job at—"

Nathan cut him off and squeezed his shoulders. "It's fine. I took a few days for R & R. Let's get out of this place. Do you have to check out?" His lip curled as he glanced around the room, and Sam wondered if Nathan's revulsion extended to him.

"I already paid in cash."

"Good. Where's Shadow?"

"I brought her to a pet motel. Listen. I need to tell you—here, there's a flash drive and some papers. We need to keep them safe." They were sorted into a messy pile on top of the briefcase. Nathan flipped through a few pages, eyebrows drawing together.

"I'm going to need to hear the whole thing from the beginning, now that you're sober," he said without looking up.

Sam winced again. There was no ignoring the disapproval in Nathan's tone, but how had he expected him to react?

"All right. Well, Collins called me and said he was leaving the country. I found all this stuff in a safe-deposit box, but as soon as I got it out, I was chased by a silver sedan. Couldn't see the license plate—"

"Wait, wait. Let's get out of here first. You can tell me the story over breakfast."

Sam knew resistance would be futile. He closed his eyes and nodded. His stomach grumbled loud enough to reply for him. A greasy breakfast sounded like heaven.

THE CAR in the parking lot was unfamiliar, a perfectly conditioned, rusty-red classic Buick Skylark. Sam glanced around for Nathan's Mercedes even as Nathan walked with purpose to the driver's side.

"Is this a rental?"

Nathan shook his head. "It's Eric's. I figured it would be safer to drive this, considering what I think you told me."

"And he has your car?"

"Don't remind me."

Sam couldn't help smiling. The car exchange must have hurt. The leather interior smelled like fresh pine, and a small black pouch hung suspended from the rearview mirror. Almost unconsciously Sam reached for it and stroked the soft velvet. He thought it might be a gris-gris.

"But Eric flew in. How did he get his car?"

"Simon," said Nathan simply, throwing the Buick into drive. They peeled out of the parking lot and left the dingy motel behind.

THEY CHOSE a small diner in the next town. The coffee was weak but fresh and steaming hot. Sam sipped it and tucked into his breakfast. His stomach gratefully welcomed the food.

As they ate, Sam stole glances across the table at Nathan, who seemed similarly ravenous. The server returned and refilled their coffees. She looked from one to the other, probably wondering why they weren't talking. The silence between them stretched even after they'd eaten away the worst of their hunger. It soon grew into a strained tension.

Sam regarded Nathan over the rim of his mug. He didn't know what to say. He was so relieved that Nathan was there, he couldn't stop staring. He'd never understood the phrase "sight for sore eyes" until then.

When Nathan broke the connection and gazed out the window, Sam's stomach tumbled with disappointment.

"You'd better start at the beginning," Nathan said.

"I guess I wasn't making much sense last night."

"Not really." Nathan didn't smile, and Sam flushed with shame. Admitting what he'd been up to while Nathan was away—that his drinking the night before hadn't been an isolated incident—was going to take the kind of courage he wasn't sure he had. In any case there were more pressing issues to deal with.

"Where should I start?"

"How about when you last heard from Barney Collins."

Sam took another sip of coffee. Luckily the painkillers had started to cut through his headache, dulling it to a throb at his temples. He could hardly believe only a couple of days had passed since then.

He went over the important events in more detail than he'd managed the night before. As he spoke, Nathan paled. He gripped his coffee mug so hard that his knuckles whitened. When Sam got to the part where he was followed by the sedan and nearly run off the road, Nathan's lips thinned into a grimace.

"Dammit. You never should have gone to the bank on your own. Why didn't you tell me what was going on?" He whispered the words harshly.

Sam's defenses rose. "I tried. We haven't exactly been communicating very well the past couple of weeks. And it's not like you could have stopped me anyway. You know that."

"It wasn't a good idea."

"Yeah, Maybe not. But it's done now, and we've got the evidence," Sam whispered back. Even though the diner was almost vacant, he was justifiably paranoid.

Nathan set his mug down and ran both hands through his hair. Then he rubbed his face in a frustrated gesture. "I don't like it. I don't trust Barney Collins. What's in it for him? He's not exactly a Good Samaritan."

"You think he might have set me up? The thought had crossed my mind. I'm not completely stupid."

Nathan fished for his wallet and threw down a few bills to cover the food before Sam could object. "This isn't something we can sit on, twiddling our thumbs. You do realize that?"

"I know. But what if Donna Howard was involved? We can't bring it to the police."

Nathan frowned. "I need to take a look."

"I don't think we should go back to our place." And heading to Rachel or Yuri's would only put their friends at risk.

"Agreed."


NATHAN DROVE them an hour north, closer to the Massachusetts border. Luckily there was no trace of the silver sedan, and nothing out of the ordinary happened on the trip. They registered under false names and settled into a much nicer hotel room. Sam booted up his computer and inserted the flash drive so Nathan could check it out while he showered.

"Everything's on here?" Nathan asked, scanning the file contents.

"Yeah. Except for the tax stuff."

"Got it." Nathan carried the computer to the desk. He was so wrapped up in reading and clicking, he didn't even notice when Sam stripped and headed for the bathroom.

He found a gorgeous blue-and-white marbled wet room with three showerheads, a bench, and a sliding glass door dividing the shower portion from the rest. Fluffy white towels were laid out in a fresh pile on top of a waist-high wooden shelf. Sam ignored his reflection in the mirror, stepped under the tap, and groaned as warm spray began to flow from every direction. He stood there for a long time, letting the water stream over his aching muscles. He was too tired for anything else.

Of course he understood Nathan's desire to see the evidence as soon as they arrived. It was the FBI agent in him, and they were working on borrowed time. But Sam couldn't help feeling something had shifted between them. Aside from the hug when they first saw each other, Nathan hadn't been physically affectionate all morning. He was probably angry about Sam putting himself in danger. But it was more than that. Almost like he couldn't look at Sam for too long. Was it guilt—or disgust? Sam wasn't sure, and neither alternative was appealing.

He could hardly remember their conversation from the night before, save for the fact he'd cried like a goddamn baby. It was the definition of pathetic. Small wonder Nathan wouldn't touch him.

He wasn't going to do it again, but even as the thought entered his mind, he craved a drink to take the edge off his hangover.

*No.*

He grabbed the bodywash and lathered himself up. It smelled like his father's old aftershave, and his throat went hot and itchy as a long-forgotten memory flooded over him. He was thirteen, in the bathroom with his father's razor, sprouting the first few growths of beard on his chin. His father walked in and chuckled, but Sam saw the pride on his face too. He showed Sam the correct way to shave, letting Sam lather his face, even though he didn't need more than a few cursory swipes. When they were finished, his father splashed a cool, burning liquid onto Sam's cheeks and neck. Sam grimaced but didn't complain, and his father rewarded him with a smile and a firm pat on the back. *You're a man now, son.*

97

Once he'd showered and shaved, he returned to the bedroom with one of the fluffy towels wrapped around his waist. Nathan was still at the computer, but he looked up.

"Feel better?"

"A little." Sam came closer. "So, what do you think?"

"I think we need to do some serious strategizing."

"You think the mob killed him?" Sam dropped the towel. He was gratified when Nathan tracked his eyes over his body, but the ogling didn't last long. Even as Sam's cock started to fill hopefully, Nathan looked back at the screen. The rejection sent another wave of disappointment and confusion through him. He reached for his clean boxer briefs and turned away to pull them up.

"Maybe," said Nathan. "But that doesn't explain why you were chased. It seems to me Rick Morgan or someone who had something to lose by the association must be involved."

"What about the mayor's wife or her lover?"

Nathan nodded. "Could be. Whatever the case, my bet is whoever chased you isn't going to give up easily."

"I was afraid you'd say that."

"Come over here." Sam pulled on a T-shirt and approached. He stood about a foot from Nathan, unsure if he should get closer while Nathan maximized a PDF of some of the mayor's e-mails. Sam watched Nathan's long, capable fingers glide over the keyboard. He smelled fresh, like he'd sprayed some cologne while Sam was showering. Sam leaned to see the screen, and his throat tightened with longing. The Nathan he remembered would never be able to resist the proximity. This Nathan didn't seem interested at all.

"What am I looking at?" Sam asked, trying to disguise the misery in his voice.

Sam had read the e-mails over before. They seemed to be in a code based on sports references, but he hadn't made much sense out of them.

"It's meant to sound innocuous." Nathan frowned as he scrolled down. "Take a look at this." He pointed at the screen. The e-mail address was random, consisting only of numbers and letters, and it wasn't signed.

"Someone working for the Voronkovs?" Sam asked.

"I think so." Nathan scrolled back up. "Here's the first one, dated March 4, 2014. Sounds like an introductory e-mail. *'Don't worry about missing out on any games. I'll have the tickets for you when you need them. Let me know how many you want. "'*

"Right around the time of Sheldon and Hoff's trial." It had only been a year and a few months, but so much had happened since then, it seemed like much longer.

"I'm thinking this person could be the connection who took over for Hoff once he and Sheldon were out of the picture," said Nathan.

"And tickets could be code for money or drugs. How quaint."

Nathan sighed and rubbed the bridge of his nose. "All we know so far is that these payoffs were happening. We might have a motivation for murder in these files, but like you said, it could have been personal rather than political. I'd like to look into this supposed affair, see if there's any truth in it. But the first thing we need to do is find the owner of this e-mail address."

"How?"

"I'm going to put in a call to Tony, if it's all right with you. He'll be discreet about getting the ball rolling."

Sam frowned. The last time he saw Rivera, they got drunk together. He hoped the guy would keep his mouth shut and give Sam the chance to tell Nathan on his own. In any case they couldn't even go back to their apartment until the whole thing was sorted. Who knew how long it would take? Or if Nathan would even want him to come back....

"All right," he said with some reluctance. "If you think Rivera will help."

"Of course he will. Oh. And one more thing. This man in the photo, the one with Hoff and White?" Sam looked as Nathan brought up the picture of the mayor and the white-haired man smoking cigars. "That's Victor Voronkov. I honestly can't believe Collins managed to get a picture of him."

"Holy shit. The head of the family?"

"None other."

"But I thought he lived in Moscow?" One of the frustrations of dealing with a crime family like the Voronkovs was that the leaders couldn't be extradited to the States. Their underlings and made men carried out their orders, and when they were jailed or killed, others rose to take their place—like a hydra.

"He does," Nathan agreed. "But this picture dates to 2007."

"The year my parents died."

As Sam absorbed the new information, Nathan busied himself with his call. Silver Sedan was looking for him and knew he had the contents of Barney's safe-deposit box. What if, in trying to get to Sam, they got to his friends, or Tim instead?

Nathan must have noticed his expression. "What's wrong?" he asked, pausing with his phone in hand.

"We need to go to Shady Brook. I need to see Tim."

"I don't think that's a good idea." Nathan's frown deepened. Sam hated seeing him so worried, and he knew he'd fucked up badly. Maybe beyond repair. But his brother might need help.

"What if they know about Tim? Do you think they could try to use him against me?" His words almost caught in his throat.

Nathan seemed surprised by the idea, and then gave a quick nod of assent. "Why don't you call Lisa while I talk to Tony? We can see about getting him transferred to a secure ward and hiring extra security. Cost isn't an issue."

Well, at least Nathan still cared about Tim. Sam tried to answer as many of Lisa's questions as he could without giving away the reality of the situation. Luckily she got the hint pretty quickly. She was familiar with the kinds of cases Sam worked on.

"We got this, kid. He'll be taken care of. We've been working with a great security firm, and I'll make sure there are two guys on duty at all times." After the arson in October, many patients' families had been uneasy with their loved ones returning to the building—even if the perpetrators were in prison. In response the administration had new high-tech cameras installed, and they hired more on-duty guards.

"Thanks. How… how is he?" He hadn't seen his brother since the day after the seizure, and the guilt of it ate at him.

She hesitated for a moment. "I'm sorry, hon, but there's been no change."

"I see." It wasn't like he really expected Tim to wake up. He was used to the disappointment. "Call me if anything happens. Okay?"

"Of course."

Next Sam called both Yuri and Rachel and put them on the alert. Neither was exactly pleased to hear they had to keep their eyes and ears peeled. And unlike Lisa, they didn't accept Sam's vague answers without pushing back.

"Man, what's going on? Did Nathan get you into something crazy?" Yuri sounded wary. Sam couldn't exactly blame him. After being kidnapped and nearly left for dead by his ex's sister and her deranged boyfriend, Yuri had earned the right to be skeptical.

"It has nothing to do with Nathan. But we're taking care of it, and I wanted to let you know in case someone tries to approach you. Just… stay away from people in silver sedans, okay?"

"Riiight. Maybe I'll crash at Nick's to be on the safe side."

"The twink from work? Are you fucking him?" Sam asked the question too loudly. Nathan raised an eyebrow from the other side of the room and then went back to his conversation with Rivera.

"A gentleman never tells." Yuri was so full of shit. His self-satisfied tone made the truth clear enough.

"It's a good thing you're not a gentleman, then. How is it?"

"Best sex of my life." Yuri said the words in a half sigh.

"Hey."

"You wanted to know."

The talk with Rachel went a little easier. "I haven't heard from you in days. You're sure you're okay?" Rachel asked. There was noise in the background. It sounded a little like fighting, but was punctuated by occasional laughter. He was going to ask, but then he remembered Alex's parents were visiting from Colorado.

"I'm fine. Nathan's here now. Anyway how's family time going? Did you tell them about the engagement yet?"

"Tonight's the big night, actually. Wish me luck." She sounded nervous.

"I do, Rach. I wish you all the luck in the world." And with any luck, Silver Sedan would stay far away from Rachel. It helped she had family and friends close by.

Content his friends were as prepared as they could be, given the need for secrecy, Sam hung up and waited for Nathan, who was on the phone with Rivera and typing away on his work computer.

"So Tony's going to run the e-mail address. See what he can find out," Nathan said. "He's getting a team together to look at the material on the drive. I sent it to him. Let's just say city hall's going to be in for a rude awakening very soon. And hopefully there'll be something in the package that leads to the murderer."

"But if the Feds start snooping around, whoever chased me will know I gave up the evidence. Won't they come after me?"

Nathan narrowed his eyes. "It's out of your hands, so it's too late to stop the information from getting out. You should be safer. We'll be okay here for a few days."

Sam hoped Nathan was right. Part of him was irritated the Feds would get the credit for cracking the case. He felt strangely possessive of it. "I want to take another look at the list of suspects."

"Be my guest."

Nathan relinquished his seat and stood behind him. Another pang of longing shot through Sam. To distract himself he pulled up the list of suspects he created when he learned the mayor had been poisoned. He needed to regain the focus he'd lost.

*Who Killed Mayor White?*

*Deputy Mayor?* Asked the first bullet point, which then listed the obvious motivation. Power and authority.

Nathan read over Sam's shoulder. "He still seems to be a top suspect. Let's keep him in play."

*His wife?* She found the mayor's body and had most easy access to his food. While Sam originally thought the motivation might be anger at her husband's drug use, Collins's files suggested she might have had an additional reason.

"I think we can add *or her lover* to that one," said Nathan.

"Agreed." Sam did. "Okay. Next. *His dealer?*"

"Yes. Especially since we know about the mob connection now. On second thought, better make the Voronkovs a separate entry." As Nathan spoke, he rested his hands on the back of the chair, and Sam felt it shift a little with the added weight. He wished Nathan would touch him instead.

The last entry, *someone with a personal vendetta,* was the vaguest and encompassed the largest group of people. Collins's evidence didn't provide much support for the theory, but appearances could be deceiving.

"Let's keep it in mind," said Sam through a yawn. Though it was only afternoon, he was exhausted. "But damn. That's still a lot of suspects."

"And they might even be working together," said Nathan.

Sam read over the list again. He hoped he never lived to amass so many people who wanted to kill him.

"So, now what?" Sam turned around in his chair.

"What do you mean?" Nathan asked. Sam couldn't tell if he was feigning ignorance.

"Don't you have to get back to New Jersey?"

"I'm not leaving you alone."

"But Nathan—"

Nathan cut him off. "I told you. It's taken care of."

"Nice use of the passive voice." Sam stood up. His headache returned, bringing with it an irritability that could only be assuaged by sleep—or more whiskey. He wondered if room service would have a nice, expensive twelve-year.

"Do you want me to leave?" Nathan asked quietly, with his hands in his pockets. They faced one another, and Sam blinked rapidly. He hated the way Nathan was staring at him, like he was a stranger. A stranger he'd come back to help. Not out of love, but out of responsibility. Sam was nothing but a burden.

"I don't need a babysitter."

"No. Of course not." Nathan scoffed, and the sound went right to Sam's heart, piercing it like barbed wire.

He retaliated in kind. "Fine. Then yes. I do want you to leave. I don't want you here. Get out and leave me the fuck alone."

"So you can drink in peace and quiet?" Nathan raised his voice.

"Yeah. Exactly." And with that, Sam reached for the phone with a shaky hand and dialed 0.

"Hi," he said when the front desk answered. "I'd like a bottle of your most expensive scotch. Charge it to the room." He figured if Nathan wanted to pay for everything, he could. Sam would gladly exploit his generosity.

The next few minutes passed in tense silence. When the room service arrived, Sam tipped the guy with a twenty. He set down the bottle on the drink caddy and poured two fingers into the crystal rocks glass.

"Care to join me?" he asked.

"Why are you doing this?"

Sam took a sip to steel his nerves. Then he slowly turned around. "Did you fuck someone else? This Simon guy? Is that why you can barely look at me?"

"Of course not. Sam—"

Nathan started forward, but Sam backed up. He held the glass between them like a shield. "I can't even tell if you're lying."

"And how the hell do you think that makes me feel? What if I doubted your fidelity at every turn? I told you I wouldn't, and I haven't. Why isn't my word enough for you?" Nathan's expression fell, and Sam's belly churned with remorse. He tamped it down by polishing off his drink. It was robust and tasted of smoky peat. It wasn't meant to be gulped, but he didn't so much as wince.

"I take it last night wasn't the first time," Nathan said.

"Nope. And this won't be the last."

"I see." Nathan frowned as Sam poured himself another glass. "Maybe I should go."

"No one's stopping you." He took the small, two-person loveseat and sprawled out. He'd never felt so acutely miserable. "'Poor little codependent Sam.' I know what you're thinking. 'Can't even stay sober for a week without me.' Well maybe it's true, but I don't want you around feeling obligated to protect me and save me from myself. You're free to go at any time."

"I'm sorry I haven't been there for you."

Sam finished his second whiskey and couldn't hold back his grimace. It didn't mix well with breakfast. "You've been busy." He believed Nathan was telling the truth about being faithful, but still he said it. "I always admired you for keeping your priorities straight."

"You want me to quit my job? I will."

"So you can hang that albatross around my neck? No thanks. I won't make you regret me more than you already do." Sam eyed the glass in his hand. He couldn't even look at Nathan.

"Regret you? Are you serious?" Nathan's voice was hard.

He didn't mean it. He didn't think it. But he said it because he was an asshole, and he wanted it to hurt. "I'm the biggest mistake you've ever made. Admit it."

He got up and went for the bottle, but Nathan was already heading for the door.


ONE HOUR.

Two hours.

Three hours, and Nathan still hadn't returned. He'd left his stuff, which suggested he hadn't gone forever. Sam latched on to the hope with one hand and his glass in the other.

He stalled along the way. His drunkenness faded to a slight buzz, and then back to a headache. His anger, on the other hand, had faded instantaneously—as soon as he heard the door click shut behind Nathan.

The glass was pretty. It was real crystal. Sam turned it around and watched the light hit the detailed facets. Then he threw it against the wall. It shattered into a thousand tiny pieces, each of them catching a glint of light on the carpet.

Sam paced, careful to avoid the glass. It was dark, and Nathan had left his cell behind, so calling him to apologize was useless. He'd also taken the Buick, and Sam didn't have any idea where he might have gone. He didn't know the town at all.

He warred between leaving to find Nathan and staying put, and the indecision resulted in a long night of sitting on the bed, flipping through channels until his eyes glazed over. No sitcom could erase the hollow, achy feeling in the center of his chest, or the knowledge that he'd ruined the one good thing in his life. He wanted to rewind time and take back all the awful things he'd said, but he couldn't. They would be there between them forever.

He must have dozed. When he woke, there was a warm body in the bed next to him. His heart leapt. But when he reached out, Nathan stiffened.

"You're back," he said, like a child might. "I was so worried."

"Were you?" Nathan smelled like cigarettes. Sam bit his lower lip hard enough to draw blood.

"I'm so sorry, Sid. I know it doesn't mean anything, but I'm so sorry for what I said. I love you." He moved closer, not daring to touch again, but unable to stay away. "I'm sorry." He kept saying it because he wasn't sure he could say it enough. He wasn't sure what else he could say.

"How could you say you're a mistake? That I'm only here because I feel obligated? I want to make sure you're okay because I love you. I can't control this, and it tears me up." Nathan's voice cracked, and Sam sought him in the darkness. Nathan didn't flinch. They faced each other, side by side. Sam wished he could see Nathan's expression, but he could only make out the curve of his cheek, the dark bristle of beard.

"I know. I didn't mean it. I was lashing out because I was ashamed. I was afraid of you leaving me. I guess my instinct is to drive people away first."

"I know." Another beat. "How did it happen?"

"The drinking? Collins bought me a martini when he was thinking of telling me about the evidence." Sam sighed. "I didn't even want it, but I drank it. I guess I thought I could handle one drink. You know? But moderation has never been my strong suit."

"What do you want to do?" Nathan asked.

"I don't know. I don't… want to be like this."

"Maybe you should talk to someone."

Sam had never been fond of therapy. He prided himself on dealing with his own shit in his own way. But maybe he could find someone he got along with and trusted. "Maybe so," he said. "It's just been a lot of things piling up all at once—this case, you being gone on yours, Tim. I know I can't lean on you for everything. I want to tell you I'll never drink again and I'll be fine…."

Nathan took his hand. "I'm not asking for guarantees. I want to go back to where we were before things went to shit. I want you to let me help you, if I can, and support you if I can't. I want you to believe what I tell you, even though I know it's hard. I want us to trust each other."

Sam swallowed. After a day filled with high-velocity emotion, he was exhausted. "I want that too. I'm sorry." Their mouths found each other, and Sam shuddered and held on. The closeness soaked into his skin like water into a parched field. After a moment, Nathan drew back. For that night, it was enough.

He wanted what Nathan wanted, but he wanted more—so much more. He wanted to be with Nathan forever.

# Chapter 10

THE NEXT morning while Nathan was still asleep, Sam slipped out of the hotel room to call Frank Chancellor. It had been a few months since the last time he spoke to his father's colleague, and he wondered if Frank had been following the Stonebridge news. He also wondered if the old man would remember what he said to Sam about his parent's accident. It was possible it was simply conjecture. Sam knew he might not learn anything. But he still had to try.

Though he'd slept well, the vague recollection of a bad dream about the car chase still hung over him. In the dream he hadn't been able to outmaneuver Silver Sedan. Then the scene changed, morphed into another time and another place. He could still see his father's bloodied head lolling back against the driver's seat.

Frank's nurse answered the phone. "Hello, Chancellor residence."

"This is Sam Flynn. I'd like to speak with Frank, please."

"I'm sorry. He's still sleeping."

Sam frowned. Getting ahold of Frank was like getting the president on the phone sometimes, his nurse was so vigilant about screening calls. Then again it was only eight. "Oh."

"I'll let him know you called—"

He heard Frank's hoarse voice. "Give me the damn phone, woman." A few seconds later, Frank's phlegmy cough echoed on the line, a symptom of his emphysema. "Who's this now?"

"Hello, Frank. It's Sam Flynn."

"Well, how the hell are you, son? And why are you calling me?"

107

Sam chuckled at Frank's gruff, direct manner. "I'm fine, sir. How are you?"

"I know you didn't call to find out how I am. I've been watching the news, even though they try to keep me away from doing anything useful. Crazy business down there. I've never been so glad we moved away when we did."

Frank and his wife Beth had retired to upstate New York more than ten years earlier. They lived there with their three granddaughters, who were orphaned during the arsons. Sam had the good fortune to meet the Chancellors when he and Nathan were on the case, and Frank had provided them with the lead that finally cracked it.

"Actually I've been thinking about what you said about my parents' accident."

"What did I say?" Frank sounded surprised. "You'll forgive me, but my memory isn't what it used to be."

"You said you always thought it was suspicious. Like maybe you thought it was foul play."

Frank tsked. "Ah. I never should have run my mouth. And anyway, Beth will have my head if I start putting ideas in yours."

Sam turned his back as another hotel guest passed by. He spoke quietly, not wanting to be overheard. "Look. I'm not going to tell Beth. Come on, Frank. You know how much this means to me. If there's anything I don't know, you need to tell me. I have a right."

The older man didn't say anything for a moment. "Sometimes it's better to let sleeping dogs lie."

"So I've heard. Unfortunately I've never been very good at that."

Another pause. "All right. All right. So here it is. You know I was a defense lawyer, so when I saw your daddy in court, we were always on opposite sides. But we were friendly. He started as lead prosecutor a few years before I retired. Brought some interesting ideas with him too." Sam nodded as Frank spoke. His father had been politically moderate, but he'd had a more strategic plan for local prosecution. "I got a social call from your daddy's assistant a couple months after the accident. We'd been living up here for some time," Frank continued. "Do you remember her? Janice?"

"Of course." She'd been his father's assistant and paralegal for as long as he could remember, but she left town soon after the accident. They hadn't kept in touch. "What did she say to you?"

"Well, that's the thing. It was more what she didn't say. With a career in defense law as long as I've had, you get to know when people are keeping secrets. When I asked her about the accident and how she was holding up, she got real flustered."

Sam blanched. "You think Janice might have had something to do with the accident?" They were talking about the Janice who always gave him candy when he visited the office—the Janice who doted on his little brother.

"I don't know. But she might know more than she's letting on. There was one last thing she said to make me think so."

Sam braced himself against the door as his heart started to hammer in his chest. "What?"

"She said she was never coming back to Stonebridge so long as she lived, and me and Beth were smart to get out when we did. She also said to lose her number. After that she got off the phone pretty quick. Left me wondering. I tell you. And then I thought about the accident and what they said about it in the news, and I couldn't help thinking maybe there was more to it than we were being led to believe. I'm a cynical man, son. You must excuse me. It comes from years of practice." His voice broke, and Sam knew he must be thinking about the daughter he'd lost to the arsons.

"I'm sorry to bother you with this, sir. I appreciate you talking to me. It makes me think I might not be crazy after all."

Frank cleared his throat. "Oh, you're not crazy. But be careful out there. You hear?"

Sam got off the phone with hollow assurances about safety and a promise to visit soon. He reentered the hotel room quietly, so as not to wake Nathan, but with a single-minded focus to locate Janice's number and call her right away. Instead he found Nathan sitting up in bed. The sheets were tangled around his legs and waist, and he looked like he might want to spring at the door and tackle the intruder to the ground. When he saw Sam, he visibly relaxed.

"Where were you?" The concern in Nathan's voice mingled with accusation. After the rough previous day, he probably figured Sam had run off to get drunk. Or maybe left for good.

"Sorry. I didn't want to wake you while I called Frank."

Sam approached his side of the bed and hesitated. On any other day, he would have leapt on Nathan and straddled him—which would inevitably

109

have led to sex. Even though they shared a tender moment the night before, there was still a residual tension between them. He wasn't sure how he was supposed to act.

"Come here," said Nathan, opening his arms.

Sam went. Nathan was still warm and rumpled from sleep, and Sam breathed in his familiar scent as he situated himself.

"What did you talk to Frank about?" Nathan asked.

Though he still didn't have any proof to back it up, the talk with Frank had strengthened his suspicions and piqued his curiosity.

"So that's what you were talking about the other night when you mentioned your parents," Nathan said, once Sam finished relaying the conversation. "Are you sure you want to pursue this?" There were dark lines between his brows, and his lips were slightly downturned.

Sam couldn't explain the feeling in his gut to Nathan. He could barely explain it to himself, but he knew he couldn't let it go. He thought Nathan, of all people, might understand.

"I know it's bad timing. But yeah." He paused, trying to make sense of Nathan's expression. "You think I'm crazy?"

"Of course not. I'd feel the same way. I *have* felt the same way."

*Emma.* Sam traced Nathan's tightly clenched jaw with his fingers. "I hate feeling like this whole time I've been duped. I need to know what really happened, and maybe Janice can help."

"Okay." Nathan nodded, seemingly resigned to the new development. "Let's see if we can track her down while we wait to hear from Tony."

Nathan made a couple of calls, and Sam tried to find a number or address for Janice. He hadn't spoken to her since his parent's funeral. He was so messed up those days that he hadn't given much thought to her getting another job and leaving town. Still, looking back, it seemed peculiar she hadn't kept in touch. The last he heard, she'd moved to New York, but he couldn't find any listing for Janice Wilkins in the online directory. He found several women with different last names. Out of those, surprisingly few stood out to him in the correct age range. He googled them one by one and had no luck until he reached *Janice W. Davis, age 43*. A quick scan of her resume confirmed he finally had the right woman. She'd been single when he knew her, so it was very possible she'd married since her move.

"Any luck?" Nathan asked once he was off the phone.

Sam gestured to the computer screen. "Looks like she's been living in Westchester these past few years. I've got an address to try, but no phone number. Was that Rivera?"

"Yeah. Seems like the e-mail address leads to a dummy account. He traced the IP to a public computer in DC."

"Well, that's disappointing. You feel like taking a drive?" Sam stretched and yawned, and his shirt rucked up over his belly. He rubbed at it, but Nathan didn't take the bait.

"I can get her number," Nathan suggested.

Sam slumped back in his chair. He was hoping they could make love before they left the hotel, but that didn't seem to be on the agenda. Sex was the one thing he could do without messing up.

"Well?" Nathan's question brought him back to himself.

"Something tells me I should show up in person. I'm afraid if I call, and she doesn't want to talk to me, I'll lose my chance to hear the truth. Better to catch her off guard. See her reaction firsthand."

There would be time later for love, Sam told himself. He just had to get through the day.

SAM FELT positively itchy as they crossed the state border into New York. The I-95 corridor was backed up, so it would take them several hours to get to Janice's house. It was Saturday, so he hoped they'd find her at home, but there was no guarantee. He drummed his fingers on the passenger armrest and earned a look of irritation from Nathan.

"Sorry." He stopped, only to realize his leg was jumping too. With some effort he managed to control his limbs and take a deep, cleansing breath. "Maybe I should take up yoga or something." What he really wanted was a shot of JD, but he tamped down the urge. Nathan was intently focused on the road, though the traffic was bumper to bumper, which hardly merited deep concentration.

"Being on the run isn't as glamorous as it is in the movies," Sam went on. "I mean if this were a Bond flick, we'd be speeding down the highway in an Aston Martin with a couple of hot chicks in the backseat. Not a Buick." Still nothing. "Or maybe a chick for you and a hot dude for me." Nada. Nathan was obviously brooding. Sam was tempted to react in kind, but he knew it wouldn't get them anywhere. He'd done enough damage the day before.

"We're not okay yet. Are we?" Sam asked.

Nathan glanced at him out of the corner of his eye. He seemed to be weighing his response. "We're getting there. But I can't pretend yesterday didn't happen."

It hurt to be reminded when he couldn't stop reminding himself, but Sam understood. "That's fair."

"And when we visit Janice, I hope you won't be disappointed if she doesn't have any info. And if she does, well…." Sam could hear the end of the sentence.

"You think I'll do something stupid? You think I'll go on a bender?" Of course, with his recent behavior, he couldn't exactly blame Nathan for the thought. He winced internally at the realization he'd harmed Nathan's perception of him—maybe forever.

Nathan gripped the wheel with both hands. "That's not what I was going to say. I know you want closure. I want it for you. But if there's one thing I've learned over the past couple of years, it's that closure comes from inside. I hope, whatever happens, you get what you need."

A stadium rock anthem came on the radio, and Sam leaned forward and switched the channel to something lighter. Nathan brought new perspective. Sam had learned to live with his parents' deaths and Tim's condition, but he never experienced the kind of closure Nathan described. And what if whatever he learned in his search made it worse? What if he learned nothing?

He'd have to let go. What if he couldn't?

There was obviously something else on Nathan's mind. He kept sneaking looks across the seat. "I also wanted to tell you…." Sam steeled himself for the worst. He had no idea what to expect from the length of the pause. Nathan let out a long exhale. "I really am sorry about how distant I've been. We've had a little trouble with the case, and I've been questioning whether I want to continue doing this kind of work."

"What do you mean? What happened?" When Nathan said he would quit his job, Sam hadn't taken him seriously. Maybe he had been.

"To be frank I'm not sure anything illegal is going on in Jersey, aside from some recreational drug use. I've spent some time with the local cops. Some good people, but the chief down there is a real homophobe, and so are some of the detectives. They're not exactly respectful of the subculture either. You should have seen them look down their noses at Eric. And one of the guys we met at the club is an outspoken critic of the cops down there. He's got a following too. It reeks of entrapment to me."

"Shit," said Sam. "So you think they're looking for any reason to arrest this guy?"

Nathan nodded. "Could be. As far as I can tell, there aren't any mob ties either. I feel like this whole thing has been a waste of time and resources. I guess you could say I'm disillusioned, and maybe I've been avoiding telling you. It makes what I put you through.... Well, let's just say these haven't been the best weeks of my life. I feel like a fool."

"I'm so sorry. I had no idea." Sam rubbed Nathan's knee. He hated the despondent look on Nathan's face. He was so honest. He believed in the law and he needed to know he was working for the greater good. Sam hated to think all his hard work—all this distance between them—was for nothing. "And you're not a fool. Don't ever say that. It's not your fault you were misled. So, what can you do?"

"We're putting together an advisory report for the agency, recommending a cease of the investigation," Nathan said tightly.

"So it's over?"

"Just about."

A car honked at them as they switched lanes, and Sam flipped him the bird. He was getting sick and tired of being in the car, and he wanted to give Nathan a hug.

"Nathan?"

"Yeah."

"You're not serious. Are you? About quitting?"

"I don't know. I... it's more than this case, but maybe it took this case to make me see it clearly. I lost Emma because of my work, and I almost lost you. Nothing is worth that price. You're the best thing that ever happened to me." Nathan was quiet for a minute, and a slow song started on the radio. It was a song Sam's mother had loved—a seventies ballad crooned by a woman with a beautiful voice.

"Me too, Sid," Sam said. Nathan gave him a grateful smile, and the knot in Sam's gut began to unravel. Things weren't back to normal yet, but they were close.

"What would you do if you quit the FBI?"

"I don't know. And I guess that's what scares me. But whatever happens, I want you to be there."

Sam squeezed Nathan's thigh. Nathan was always so sure of himself. It was no wonder he'd kept his troubled thoughts secret. It made Sam feel horrible for his suspicions and his selfish needs.

He would make it up to Nathan—somehow.

"I will be," he promised.

IN SPITE of Sam's former eagerness to speak with Janice, his feet were leaden as he followed Nathan to the door of the quaint blue house. Unlike many of the other homes on the street, the yard of 325 Elm was unkempt, and the weeds growing from between the flagstones of the front walk were evidence it hadn't been tended in some time. Sam might have worried the inhabitants had moved, if not for the car in the driveway. The June sun beat down on Sam's neck from behind. He rubbed at it and shuffled his feet while Nathan knocked. The bell didn't seem to be in working order either.

A few seconds later, a woman answered the door, her look of confusion plain when she encountered Nathan. When she saw Sam, however, she visibly tensed. A thin smile formed on her lips, but it didn't meet her eyes. She was still pretty, but she'd lost the bloom of youth, and her wariness put Sam on alert. He came forward and held out his hand.

"Hello, Janice. It's been a long time."

"I can't believe it," she said. Her face paled considerably. "Sam Flynn. How many years has it been?"

Her palm was clammy in his hand. "Too many. Can we come in?"

With obvious reluctance Janice opened the door wider, allowing both Nathan and Sam to pass through. The interior of the house was messy, and though the furnishings were of high quality, they were dusty. On the living room mantle, there were several framed photographs of Janice with a man in a wheelchair.

"You must excuse the state of the place," she said, as though reading Sam's mind. "My husband passed recently, and with work, I've had a hard time keeping up."

"I'm sorry to hear about your loss," said Nathan. "I'm Nathan Walker, by the way. Sam's partner." As they shook hands, her eyes widened.

"His.... Oh. Oh. How nice." She tried and failed to disguise her surprise.

Sam took a seat on the couch next to Nathan, and Janice sat across the coffee table in a large, overstuffed armchair, her thin frame dwarfed by its size. It was hard to know where to start. Launching directly into "Hey. Do you by any chance know if my parents were murdered?" seemed a little insensitive, especially given the fact she'd recently lost her husband.

"I didn't know you'd gotten married," he said, perhaps equally tactlessly.

"About five years ago. Steve had ALS, and we knew we didn't have much time. It doesn't make it any easier, though."

"Of course not." Sam nodded. "I'm so sorry."

"How's your brother?" she asked, obviously eager to change the subject.

Sam met her eyes. "He's the same."

"I always hoped he'd wake up."

"Yeah," Sam said. "I still do." A moment of uncomfortable silence passed as they looked at each other, and Sam realized they needed to cut to the chase. "You're probably wondering why I'm here."

"I have a feeling I know why." She sighed. "To be honest I've wanted to reach out to you for a while. But in the end, I thought it best to let the matter drop. I wondered if you'd ever contact me."

"You do know something about the accident. Don't you?" Instinctively he reached for Nathan's hand and laced their fingers together. "Please tell me."

She sat back in her chair and stared up at the ceiling, her sloping shoulders relaxed. Then she took a deep breath and steeled her face into a determined expression, more like the Janice he recognized from his childhood. "Your father and I were having an affair."

"What?" Sam felt the blood drain out of his face.

"I'm sorry to blurt it out, but it's the truth. I didn't know how else to say it."

"For... you and my father?" Sam was stunned. She had to be lying.

"I know this is difficult to hear. I'll spare you the details, but I want you to know I loved him very much. I think he loved me too, but of course he loved your mother more. He never would have left his family for me. I knew that going into it."

"My mother. Did she know?"

Janice smiled sadly. "I don't know. And believe me, I would rather not have told you, Sam. I don't want you to think any less of your father for this. He was a good man."

"Then why are you telling me?" he nearly croaked.

"Because it explains what happened about a week before your father's death. He seemed out of sorts. Sometimes he got a little moody, so I didn't think much of it. But one night I forgot my house keys at the office and I went back to get them. Your father was still there. He was sitting at his desk, having a drink."

She trailed off, as though lost in the memory, and Sam squeezed Nathan's hand harder. He couldn't imagine what she would say next. "What happened?"

"I remember it so clearly. Like it was yesterday. I asked him if everything was okay, but he just laughed. It scared me, frankly. And then... he kissed me and he told me it was over. He told me I should leave. Not only that night. But for good. He said he'd give me a good reference for a firm in Boston or New York."

Sam held his breath. Nathan sat equally tense at his side.

"I was heartbroken of course. He apologized—profusely. He asked me to forgive him. I understood why he needed to break off the affair, but when he kept insisting I leave town as well, I got angry. I accused him of being heartless. I suppose I could have sued him, but I would never have told our secret to anyone." She smiled mirthlessly. "I haven't... until today."

The information sunk in slowly, and Sam nodded at her to go on. Janice wasn't lying.

She leaned forward. "I told him I refused to leave. I knew there was something else. He wasn't himself. It wasn't just the drinking. He was drinking a lot more in those days."

Sam's gut lurched. His palm was sweaty against Nathan's, but he didn't let go.

"Finally a lightbulb went off in my head. You see, about a month before all of this happened, we'd started a folder on a man named Victor Voronkov. I assume you know the name?"

Nathan cleared his throat. "Of course." He exchanged a glance with Sam, which Sam read as "keep your mouth shut." According to the picture in the files, Victor Voronkov had met with Mayor White that year, but it would be huge if Janice could independently confirm the connection.

"I knew he was a mob boss, but I didn't know why we were working on him. He wasn't in our jurisdiction. In those days he lived in New York. So I asked your father, point-blank, if he'd been threatened. He broke down and told me yes."

"Shit. By Voronkov himself?" Sam couldn't stop himself from interjecting.

"No. No. That was the worst part. He told me an old friend was involved. The friend had approached him with a payoff, but he hadn't accepted it."

"Did he tell you who the friend was?" Sam asked. It had to be Dan Sheldon. It had to be.

Janice frowned. "No. He was very drunk by then and kept calling him 'The Tiger.' Later I knew it must have been Dan, but at the time, I had no idea who he was talking about. I wouldn't have guessed Dan was involved with the mob—not in my wildest dreams. The two of them had always been such good friends, and Dan was absolutely devastated when the accident happened."

Sam let go of Nathan's hand and scrubbed both of his over his face. "And you never told anyone."

"I was scared for my life. And I had no idea who was involved. Anyway that was it. He made me pack my things, and I left the office. I went home. A week later he was dead."

Sam swallowed and stared at Janice when she stopped speaking. He always wondered if his father knew anything about the corruption in Stonebridge, but he never had any proof. If what Janice said was true, it seemed probable his father had discovered the connection between his good friend the police chief and the Russian mob—just like Emma had. That discovery led to her death at the hands of Sheldon's crooked cops and Bernhardt Hoff, their mob connection. Of course Sheldon didn't carry out the dirty work, but he orchestrated it. He allowed a woman he supposedly cared for like a daughter to be murdered in cold blood and had nearly destroyed Nathan in the process.

Had Sheldon coordinated the car accident that snowy night? Or had he gotten someone else to do his dirty work then too? A hot, slow-spreading rage started to burn its way through Sam's chest. Even to the end, Sheldon had maintained his allegiance to Sam's father's memory and acted like he was trying to protect Sam for his father's sake. It had been his only redeeming feature—the one aspect of his character not blackened by lying. But it had been a deception. Sam felt his gorge rise. He'd been so blindly naïve.

"Son of a bitch," he whispered. "That no good, murdering son of a bitch." He could have punched something—or worse. If Dan Sheldon had been present, Sam would have killed him.

"After the accident, I convinced myself it was a coincidence." Janice's voice held a trace of shame. "Your mother and your brother were in the car. Why target them if it was your father they were after? But eventually, when I heard about what Dan was involved with, the conversation came back to me. And I knew… I knew your father had been speaking about him."

She paused, and Sam took the opportunity to launch his attack. "But you left town like my father told you to. If you really believed it was an accident, you wouldn't have done that." If what Janice was saying was true, she might have reopened his parents' case as homicide, but she chose to stay quiet.

"You're right and you have every reason to be upset. I did have my doubts and I took precautions. Sometimes… we have to tell ourselves stories to be able to go on with our lives, even if those stories aren't completely true. So I rewrote that night in my mind as your father being drunk and confused. I tried to forget about it. I moved, I met Stephen, and we married. I was happy."

Sam winced visibly, and Janice gave him a sad smile.

"Of course you can only lie to yourself for so long," she continued. "But by the time I realized I should have come forward, Steven was dying. And I had other things on my mind. I figured Dan was going to be put away for life anyway. I didn't want to waste the last few days of my husband's life by dragging us into the case. And in the end, justice was served. Wasn't it?"

Sam sat back like he'd been pushed. City hall was still benefitting from the drug money that had likely cost Sam's parents their lives. Of course Janice wouldn't know. She probably believed the corruption in Stonebridge had been eliminated. She didn't know about Mayor White's mob ties— yet. "But not for my family," he said. "No justice for my brother. He was innocent."

Janice's expression remained stoic and a little sad, and Sam glared at her. A more rational thought flickered through his anger. The loss of her husband, which was much more immediate than the long-ago accident—murder. She didn't have anything left to give, and he couldn't expect any more.

"All I can say is I'm sorry. It's been good to see you, Sam. You don't know this, but I've been following your blog. You're an excellent writer. I think your father would be very proud of you."

Sam couldn't respond.

"Thank you for telling us the truth," said Nathan. "I know it wasn't easy." As Nathan and Janice spoke, an object on the coffee table drew Sam's eye. The brass elephant paperweight was familiar. It took a moment to place it, but when he did, he sucked in a breath.

"This was my father's," he said, turning the heavy, dusty thing in his hands. It had been a graduation gift from a favorite law school professor, and Sam remembered seeing it on many occasions on the bookshelf in his dad's office.

"Yes," said Janice, with a trace more emotion. "I took it when I left, to have something to remember him by. You can keep it if you like."

Sam set the weight back down. "Thanks. You keep it."

"An elephant never forgets," she whispered. There was a faraway look in her eyes, but it was gone in an instant. She stood. "I'm sorry you had to come all this way to hear such bad news. What will you do now?"

Sam balled his hands into fists. He knew exactly where they were going, and he knew exactly what he'd do when he got there.

# Chapter 11

SAM WALKED numbly to the Buick. Janice's words swirled around his mind, making it hard to focus on any one thing. The late-afternoon sun burned his eyes, and he blinked back the threatening tears.

Nathan turned to him from the driver's seat. "Are you okay?"

"I want to see Sheldon." Sam tugged the seat belt over his lap with a bit more violence than necessary.

"I told Tony we'd head over to the New York office."

"No. I need to see that son of a bitch, Dan Sheldon, with my own eyes and ask him if he killed my father. I want to see his face when he admits my mother's death was his fault."

Nathan frowned. "I don't think it's a good idea."

Sam clenched his jaw. "If you don't take me, I'll go alone." He started to open the door. He'd walk to the damn place if he had to.

"Sam—"

"What are you going to do, tie me up? I have to do this. You heard what she said. My parents died for the same reason Emma did, because my father found out something he wasn't supposed to know about Sheldon. Doesn't that make you angry?"

It was Nathan's turn to raise his voice. "Of course. You know how much I hate Sheldon for what he did to Emma. But listen. I know you don't want to hear this, but even with what Janice told us, we don't know the whole story. It might not have been Sheldon your father was talking about. Janice simply inferred it later on. And then of course there's the possibility it's a coincidence, and even if he did find out about Sheldon, it was still an accident."

Sam shook his head vehemently. "Bullshit. You heard how upset my dad was about this 'friend.' Sheldon must have approached him to keep quiet about Voronkov." He didn't even want to think about the affair. He resented Janice for telling him, even though he'd asked.

Nathan exhaled loudly. "I think we should head to another hotel for now. Think about it overnight. Okay? The prison's a few hours drive, and visiting hours would be over by the time we got there. There's also the possibility he'll refuse to talk to you."

Though Nathan's reasoning irritated him, Sam didn't protest as they drove away from Janice's sad house. His mind was a swirling mess, and he wanted to make it stop. He wanted to lash out, and he wanted to hurt. He needed *something* to keep him from imagining his father alone at his desk, slowly drinking while he tried to think of a way to keep his family safe. Why hadn't he left town immediately? Why hadn't he acted sooner?

*He was drinking a lot more in those days.* Sam hadn't known. Had anyone?

By the time they checked into another bland-but-nice hotel off the highway, he could hardly stand to be in his own skin. They passed the hotel bar on the way to the elevator, and he stared longingly at the laughing bartender, who was talking to a couple of travelers who seemed to have hit it off. It all seemed so easy. But waking up with a hangover wouldn't do anything for his mood, and it wouldn't bring his parents back. *He was very drunk at that point.*

He looked away too late. Nathan had already seen him watching. The concern and love on his face made Sam's gut twist with guilt. He scowled, hoisted his bag up on his shoulder, stepped inside the claustrophobic space, and felt his stomach lurch as they began the ascent. Being treated like a kicked puppy was starting to wear on his nerves.

Like the place they'd left that morning, the room was overly lavish, but they weren't exactly on vacation. A huge, comfortable-looking white bed served as the centerpiece, and there was a flat screen on the wall adjacent. Sam wasn't interested in napping or watching TV. He threw his bag on the bed and unzipped it, then rustled through the front pocket for supplies. He could hear Nathan pacing behind him, scoping out the place for bugs—and not the creepy-crawly kind. Sam might have called him paranoid another day, but given the current circumstances, he almost expected Nathan to find something.

"What are you looking for?" Nathan asked.

Finally Sam encountered plastic. He grabbed the small bottle of lube and held it up with what he hoped was a sexy, rather than manic, grin over his shoulder. "Always come prepared."

He wriggled his ass and then stood to face Nathan, discarded his jeans and shirt, and pulled down his boxer briefs. His erection sprung free and poked straight at Nathan like a divining rod.

Nathan crossed his arms and kept his eyes focused on Sam's face. "It's not a good idea. I think you should put your clothes back on."

That was it. The last straw.

"I knew it. You don't want me anymore." Sam turned away as tears started to well in his eyes. He couldn't hold them back. It was all too much—the car chase, the cravings, the revelation of Janice's affair with his father, and this rejection. He thought he'd hit his lowest point when he learned his parents' deaths might have been murder, but he was wrong.

"Sam, look at me. Of course I want you."

Sam responded to the commanding tone almost against his will. He saw love and compassion in Nathan's eyes. He saw trust. His world righted itself as warmth spread through his stomach. He could trust Nathan. He loved Nathan.

"I don't think now is a good time—"

"Shut up." Sam stalked across the room—trying to muster as much dignity as he could with his swaying hard-on—and planted himself in front of Nathan, who stood his ground, staring down at Sam with a defiant expression on his handsome face. The difference in their heights made it difficult to appear intimidating, so, in an effort to turn the tables, Sam laced his hands behind Nathan's head and pulled him down into a bruising, closemouthed kiss. Sam's teeth pressed punishingly into his lips, and the shock of pain made his cock twitch in response. After a moment of resistance, Nathan kissed Sam back and wrapped his arms tightly around him as their bodies fit together. Their mouths opened and the kiss softened as the hardness in Nathan's jeans gave him away. Sam reached down, felt for the zipper, and rubbed Nathan's trapped erection for good measure.

"I think you should stop treating me like a damn five-year-old," he whispered against Nathan's lips.

"Well, *I* think we should talk about what just happened." Nathan grabbed Sam's wrist to stop the unzipping process, and Sam grunted in disapproval and tried to yank his hand away.

Sam felt his face heat—with anger, not with shame. "I'm sick of talking. I don't need you to be my therapist. I need you to give me what I need."

"And what exactly is that?" Nathan's voice held a hint of the dark promise that always made Sam's toes curl.

"You know what. I want you to blindfold me and tie me up so I can't move. I want you to spank me and bite my neck as you fuck me. I want you to use me. I want to forget my own name." He panted at the last words, already floating as adrenaline and endorphins fired his blood. He rubbed his needy cock against Nathan and whimpered as the rough material of Nathan's jeans scraped against his excited flesh.

It seemed like Nathan might give in. His eyes kindled, their pupils blown wide, and he relaxed his grip on Sam's wrist. Sam took advantage of the moment to free himself and continue his pursuit of Nathan's cock, which was still rock hard. If he could just get it in his hand, Nathan wouldn't be able to resist.

Nathan stepped out of the embrace, backed away, adjusted himself, and refastened his fly.

"I'm not sceneing with you like this. And I'm definitely not tying you up or hurting you in any way. I don't think it would end well, and I think you know that too. It's okay if you don't want to talk, but I can't do it. Don't ask me to."

Standing naked and vulnerable in the center of the room, Sam instinctively covered his softening cock with both of his hands. His eyes felt hot again, and he turned away to find his clothes. Maybe he'd leave, go down to the bar and drink like he wanted to in the first place.

His lips were numb as he pulled up his jeans and buttoned them. It was almost the way he felt while being chased by Silver Sedan. Intellectually, he knew he was in a mild state of shock. He stared down at his discarded T-shirt. If he bent to get it, he'd keel over.

"Come here," Nathan said. "Sam?" His voice seemed far away.

"I'm sorry," Sam whispered. He saw his mother in the hospital with blood matted in her reddish blonde hair. He scrubbed his hands over his face to erase the picture, but it wouldn't disappear. An affair. How could his father do it? He pressed the pads of his fingers against his closed eyelids, which were hot and scratchy. His heart felt like it might tear out of his chest, it was beating so hard.

Nathan wrapped strong arms around him from behind. "I've got you," he said.

Sam turned around and ducked his head, mildly worried he was getting Nathan's shirt wet. "Sorry," he said, not recognizing his own voice.

"It's okay. I've got you."


SAM WOKE the next morning feeling drained but oddly calm. It took him a minute to place where he was, since he only vaguely remembered the previous night. He didn't want to think too hard about it. It was tempting to close his eyes again and drift back to sleep, but the bed shifted, and he rolled over to find Nathan sitting up with his computer in his lap, his hair disheveled. He had circles under his eyes, like he'd been up all night.

"You're still here."

Nathan raised an eyebrow. "Of course I am. How're you feeling?"

"Better." Sam struggled to sit up under the thick down comforter. He couldn't meet Nathan's eyes. "Sorry for the, uh, breakdown last night." He winced as the memories started to return. Yeah. There had been deeply unsexy crying.

"You don't have anything to be sorry about. I'm glad you're feeling better."

"Thanks, by the way." Sam bit his lower lip. "You were right about… you know."

"It's not about being right. It's about looking out for each other. You'd do the same for me. And in fact you have. So don't be embarrassed."

Sam raised his eyes to meet Nathan's. "Okay."

"Okay." Nathan smiled, and it was enough for Sam to smile back and let the previous night go.

He shifted closer. "What are you working on?"

"Oh, nothing that can't wait." Nathan flipped his laptop closed and set it on the bedside table. He was naked, and desire curled in Sam's belly as Nathan stretched and flexed his sleek muscles. Then Sam pulled him close, urging him up and over so that Nathan was on top of him. He could feel Nathan's cock nudge his belly. He was already mostly erect. But Nathan's eyes were even more captivating. They were filled with hope and sleepy arousal. On a whim Sam rubbed the tip of his nose against Nathan's. Nathan chuckled.

They were both fully hard, but there was no urgency. Sam figured they could take things slowly. He would happily stay like that for the rest of the day. "Is there any way we can rewind a week or so?"

"I have a better idea. Let's let it go and move forward from here." Nathan ran his fingers through Sam's hair, scratching lightly against his scalp.

"Sounds like a plan."

They kissed, tongues meeting and twining together. Nathan swiveled his hips in a slow, tantalizing motion. His smell and taste filled Sam's senses until his entire body was alive with desire. It had been weeks since they'd been so close, and Sam didn't ever want to wait so long again. He grabbed on to Nathan's back and reveled in the warm skin, the hard plane of muscle.

"I'm so glad you're mine," he said, because it was true.

"Always."

Sam's throat constricted with emotion. Never again would he let his feelings of inadequacy cause him to doubt Nathan's affections. Never again would he self-sabotage the good things in his life. Those reactions had never brought him anything but pain.

He would trust, as he wanted to be trusted, and Nathan would learn to trust him back the same way.

He must have said something out loud, though it didn't sound as fancy as it had in his head. Nathan grinned at him—a glorious sight—and then rolled them over so Sam was on top.

Sam looked down. He loved every one of the fine lines around Nathan's eyes, the occasional gray hairs within the blackness of his beard, and his expressive mouth.

"I need you to move. Please," Nathan said thickly. Sam didn't need to be asked twice, but Nathan wasn't inclined to be passive either. He gripped Sam's ass with his strong hands, urging him to strike a steady rhythm. Maybe Nathan was his magnetic north, the one person he couldn't turn away from and who wouldn't turn away from him. Maybe love could last, could grow strong roots and break through even the toughest rocky earth. He kissed Nathan and reached between their bodies to stroke them together.

"Here," Nathan said. "Let me." He covered Sam's hand with his own. Everything fit together—their hands, their leaking cocks. They belonged like this—not apart, but side by side. They would be all right. Sam could feel it in his bones.

Sam cried out as he tumbled into release, his cock pulsing against Nathan's belly and hand. Nathan came seconds later with a muffled grunt and caught Sam's lips in a kiss. It was over far too quickly, but as Sam lay in Nathan's arms, their skin sticky and wet, he realized he'd never been happier.

"I'm not going to drink anymore," he said as his heart rate started to slow.

Nathan leaned over him. Sam expected to see skepticism, but Nathan only nodded. "Okay."

AFTERWARD THEY talked and filled in the more benign details of what they'd both missed over the last couple of weeks. It was almost better than sex, but of course there was more of that too. Soon it was late morning, and Sam disentangled himself from Nathan and headed to the shower. In spite of the news from the previous day, he felt good. Unfortunately he was out of clean clothes, and Nathan was running low too. They needed to stop at a store or a Laundromat in the next day—or go home.

Home would be nice.

Sam showered and shaved. He reentered the bedroom to find Nathan at his computer again. His expression was grim.

"Oh great. What happened now?"

"Tony sent an e-mail. Looks like he wants us to come in to HQ today. They—they found Collins."

"Shit. Really? Where was he?" Sam approached the desk when Nathan beckoned and scanned the brief e-mail from Rivera. As he read, Nathan wrapped an arm around his waist.

*Dangerous to be on your own… our guys in Florida found his body… bullet wound to the head. Report to the New York office immediately.*

"Collins is dead?" Sam said blankly. He reread the e-mail again and again, but he couldn't make sense of it. It couldn't be right. Collins had been heading out of the country when they spoke. Hadn't he? "I don't understand."

"It looks like a hit. I'm sorry, Sam."

Sam thought about the guy's thinning hair, his fragile features. He hadn't been a good guy, but he hadn't been evil either, and it sounded like he met a brutal end. Poor bastard.

"Yeah. Me too. So what do you think we should do?" Rivera's e-mail was pretty cut and dry.

"It's up to you."

"What do you mean?" Sam frowned, and Nathan's arm tightened around him. "You mean you'll go with me to see Sheldon?" He never thought Nathan would agree—not in a million years—and especially not given Sam's reaction the night before.

"Do you still want to talk to him?"

Sam didn't have to think twice. "Yeah. I do."

"He might not want to see you."

"I know. But I have to try, at the very least."

"Tony's not going to be happy," Nathan murmured. He typed back a quick message. "But this is more important. And he knows I have another case."

"Are you telling him where we're headed?" Sam read over his shoulder, indulging his curiosity.

"No need to rock the boat. We'll be fine." Nathan snapped his laptop shut.

"How are we going to get in? Don't we need to be on a list or something?"

Nathan smirked. He reached for his badge. "That's where this comes in."

"Oh." Sometimes being in love with an FBI agent had its perks.

THE FEDERAL prison where Sheldon was incarcerated was several hours from their hotel. Sam had tried to visit his father's old friend once during his trial and had been turned away. At the time, he saw it as a cowardly refusal on the part of the ex-chief of police, but he hadn't suspected then that the guy was hiding something about his parents.

He knew Sheldon had coordinated the whole thing. He was positive—as sure as he'd ever been about anything. He clenched his jaw and stared at the summer scenery through the open Buick window. The gris-gris swayed in the wind. Sam wondered about it. He wasn't a superstitious person, but he hoped it would bring them good luck. They could use a dose.

They crossed the border to Pennsylvania at around noon. The land was flat and green, punctuated here and there by a farm in the distance, though the road was mostly lined with trees. Half the time, Sam expected Silver Sedan to pull up alongside them and try to run them off the road. But aside from a necessary pit stop halfway through the drive, nothing eventful happened.

It seemed almost too easy.

Nathan didn't say much, though he did have to take a call from Eric. From what Sam could tell, he was wondering when Nathan was coming back to Jersey with his car. The brief vacation would have to end soon. Nathan needed to head back to wrap up his case, and Sam would be who knew where—maybe in a federal safe house, if Rivera had his way.

Sam had received a couple of texts too. Rachel had apparently won over Alex's parents, and Yuri was gloating over his new boy toy. But he was equally concerned over Sam's whereabouts.

Eventually Nathan made the turn off the highway to Lafayette Prison. A network of concrete buildings, bundled together by twenty-foot-high chain-link fences, appeared in the otherwise-pristine valley. There were towers along the perimeter manned by guards holding sniper rifles. Sam's blood chilled. He'd never been to a federal prison before, and he was glad he was visiting on the right side of the law.

The narrow road finally diverged in front of the foremost building, and they followed the signs to the visitor's lot. It was half-empty. Unfortunately they'd arrived at the tail end of visiting hours. Sam hoped he'd still have enough time to do what he needed to do.

They parked the Buick and then crunched over the gravel lot toward the visitor's entrance. Sam trailed Nathan, relieved he wasn't alone. The first guard they encountered was a short, muscular man who looked like he might have done some time too. He stared at them from behind yellowed plexiglass.

"We're here to see Daniel Sheldon," Nathan said. He pulled out his badge and held it up for the guard to see. The guy raised his eyebrows. He had small, beady eyes and nose hair for miles.

"He hasn't had many visitors," said the guard, who was already flipping through a list attached to a clipboard.

"Will that be a problem?" Nathan asked. He had a connection at the prison if they ran into any trouble. Sam held his breath. He was so close to answers that he didn't think he could bear a setback.

"Shouldn't be. Your name?" The guard nodded at Sam.

Sam slid over his ID, and the guy squinted at it, and then at a page on his clipboard. "All right. You two are good to go. But just so you know, visiting hours are over in twenty minutes."

Sam turned to Nathan with a grateful smile. "Looks like we're in."

They emptied their pockets, made it through the gauntlet of security measures, and were met by a guard at a far door. Sam was about to step through, but he noticed Nathan's hesitation.

"What's up?"

"Sheldon isn't going to talk to you if I'm there, not after what happened with Emma. But he might if you go alone." Nathan's voice was gruff, and he kept it low so the waiting guard couldn't overhear. Sam could feel the tension radiating from him. He wanted to take Nathan's hand, but he wasn't sure it was a good idea, given their surroundings.

"So you're not coming?"

Nathan shook his head tersely. He must have noticed an expression on Sam's face. "Are you sure you want to do this?" he asked. For a moment they were in the bedroom, and Nathan's question held a whole other meaning.

Sam swallowed and met Nathan's gaze levelly. "Yeah. I'll be okay."

"I'll be here."

Nathan squeezed his arm, and then the guard buzzed Sam through the door to the interior of the prison. Everything was an institutional, dingy taupe, from the walls to the uniforms the guards wore. Sam followed a female guard down a hallway, and then through a sally port out into the sunlight. The visitor's room was in another building. They passed a fenced-off area with a basketball court, where a few prisoners were shooting hoops. One guy with a resentful, predatory look on his face, stood off to the side, smoking and watching Sam pass.

They reached a second building. The guard unlocked the thick metal door, led Sam through an additional metal detector, and then down a short hall to finally knock twice on yet another door. A guard opened it and ushered Sam inside. He could hear the huge bolt slide shut behind him.

The visitor's room was large and consisted of about twenty metal tables with chairs on either side. Inmates and their guests occupied half of them. The rest sat empty, the same dull color as the rest of the place.

Sam nodded as the female guard gestured to one of the tables toward the front of the room. His palms felt clammy as he sat as instructed and stared down at the table. He finally realized why guys in old gangster movies referred to prison as the can. Maybe the monotone color scheme was intended to make prisoners feel hopeless, or maybe the state simply didn't have the budget to care for appearances. Whatever the case Sam was pretty sure he'd go insane if he were an inmate. Not that it made him feel any sympathy for Sheldon.

A door opening on the left interrupted his thoughts. Another guard—this one burly and about seven feet tall—led an elderly man wearing a blue prison jumpsuit through the entrance and toward Sam's table. For a split second, Sam didn't recognize him. But there was no mistaking those huge, bushy gray eyebrows.

Prison hadn't been kind to Sheldon. He walked with a slight stoop, and his face, which had always been grandfatherly, seemed flabby and jaundiced. The guard handled him firmly but without force.

Sam found himself with nothing to say as Sheldon took the seat across from him. His hands were cuffed, and he set them on the table.

"You have fifteen minutes," said the guard, who then stepped back to become part of the scenery.

"Hello, Sam." Sheldon's mouth was set in a grim line. "How have you been?"

The usual niceties seemed impossible. How could Sam reply with a "Great. Thanks. How are you?" A juvenile impulse rushed up in him—the urge to rub his and Nathan's relationship in the man's face. *You lied to me about him. You tried to frame him for his wife's death. You're a fucking murderer.*

He stared for another moment and then replied. "You look like shit."

Sheldon chuckled. His blue eyes still held a trace of their old vitality. "Prison will do that to you. But so will cancer."

"You've got cancer."

"Pancreatic. Docs say, with treatment, I might live another year. But I'm too old to drag this out. Never did like hospitals. They're worse than prison."

It was a sentiment Sam might have agreed with, were Sheldon any other person. "How long?"

Sheldon shrugged as though they were talking about the weather. "A month, maybe two."

"Do you expect me to feel sorry for you?"

"No."

How had they lapsed into conversation? Sam balled his hands into fists on his lap. This was the man who'd killed his parents. This was the man who made his life a living hell, the man who put Tim into a coma. He didn't deserve normal conversation. Still, Sam found himself surprised at the emotion mingling with his anger and hatred—pity.

"I hoped you'd come," Sheldon continued. "I thought about writing, but I've never really been good at that kind of thing. And I wanted it to be your choice."

"How noble of you." Sam was surprised by the nastiness in his own voice.

"I know I don't deserve your forgiveness, but I wanted to say I'm sorry."

The words hit Sam like a slap across the face. He reeled back in his chair and might have toppled over if the thing hadn't been bolted to the floor.

"How dare you. How dare you apologize to me after what you did to my parents." He left the statement hanging in the air while he gauged Sheldon's reaction. The old man seemed bothered. Sam leaned forward and nearly snarled. "Did you think you could keep me in the dark forever? An accident, you told me. All these years I believed the lie, when it was you all along. And I was your dupe because I wanted to believe in you." He hated the way his voice quavered at the end. He hated how Sheldon could still get to him.

"I don't know what you're talking about."

"Don't you fucking lie to me." Sheldon had manipulated him before, and it wasn't going to happen again.

Sheldon drew his caterpillar brows together in a frown. "You think *I* killed your parents?" he said, almost to himself.

"Yes. I think my father found out what you were up to with the Voronkovs. I think he confronted you, just the way Emma confronted you, and you had him killed." He was confused by Sheldon's refusal to take ownership of what he'd done, though he didn't know why he should be. "I'm right. Aren't I? Tell me the truth for once in your life."

"Your father was my friend."

"Like how Emma was your friend. And Mark Feldman. I bet he was your friend too, until you decided he was no longer useful." Sam spat out the words. He wished they were as poisonous as he felt inside.

"I'm not saying I'm a good man. I've done terrible things. But I didn't have anything to do with what happened to your folks."

"You lie."

Maggie Kavanagh

Sheldon took a deep breath and looked Sam right in the eye. "I know you don't believe me. I don't blame you, after the lies I've told. But I didn't get involved with the mob until about a year after the accident. Maybe if your dad had lived, I'd have made a different choice. But when the money started coming in…. Eventually I forgot what it was like to be on the right side."

"Don't you dare blame my father for your crimes." Sam could hardly believe what he was hearing. Sheldon's corruption was staggering. Even now he denied responsibility, when the truth was so obvious. "He knew what you were up to, and you murdered him. You murdered my mother. You took away my brother's childhood. You ruined my life."

"You're saying you think they were murdered? Well, now. I guess that makes sense." Sheldon paled. He already looked dead.

"You're expecting me to believe you thought it was an accident this whole time? You're telling me you weren't involved. You never approached my dad to pay him to look the other way so the Voronkovs could move in?"

"Who told you this?"

Sam shook his head. He wouldn't give up Janice's name—not for anything. "What does 'the tiger' mean to you?"

Sheldon's expression remained blank. "Nothing. Never heard it before."

"You're a fucking liar." Sam's whole body vibrated with rage, made worse by a creeping doubt. What if Sheldon was telling the truth? If it hadn't been Sheldon, who?

Sheldon raised his hands, and Sam wanted to wipe the sympathetic expression off his face. "Okay. If you need to blame me…. Well, all right. I understand."

Unbelievable. Now he was making himself into some kind of twisted martyr. Sam was disgusted with himself for thinking he would ever get closure from Sheldon. "You don't understand anything."

"I do. More than you know. It's good to see you, Sam. You always were like a son to me, in a way. I did want to see you one last time."

"I hope you burn in hell."

Sheldon's shoulders seemed to slump further, and the sign of physical weakness made Sam irrationally angry. How dare the man be sick? How dare he not fight back? He looked so much smaller than the Sheldon in Sam's memory.

"Did you get Hoff to do it?" Sam asked, crossing his arms over his chest. He needed to regain the equilibrium he'd lost. He couldn't let himself be taken in by lies. "Did he do your dirty work for you?" At his trial Sheldon had pled the fifth when asked how he met Bernhardt Hoff and the Voronkovs. Sam figured the omission was intended to cover up the link to the accident.

The guard approached the table. "Time's up."

Sheldon looked like he might want to protest, but then he simply nodded and stood. He looked at Sam, but if he was waiting for exoneration, he wasn't going to get it.

"You're a traitor," Sam said, standing to face him. "I hope you know that."

"Good-bye, son," Sheldon replied, and Sam knew it was forever.


BACK IN the waiting room, Nathan was pacing. When he saw Sam reenter, he closed the distance between them in two long strides.

"Are you okay?" Nathan asked. He looked like he might be bracing himself for another nervous breakdown.

Sam mustered a weak smile. "Yeah. I'm all right."

"What'd he say?"

"He said he didn't have anything to do with the accident. He insisted." Sam glanced over his shoulder at a curious guard who was pretending not to listen, and then turned back to Nathan. "I'll tell you about it on the way to… wherever we're going. Let's get out of here."

They exited the prison and stepped into the sun. The warm June day was welcome after the cool dampness of the prison. Their feet crunched on the gravel in the otherwise-silent parking lot. Nathan slipped his arm around Sam's waist for a brief squeeze.

"Well, I have good news. Tony called while you were with Sheldon. They arrested two guys at the border for Collins's murder. Looks like they might know something about the mayor too. Both Voronkovs."

"Wow. That was fast." The development should have come as a relief, but Sam was out of emotion. "So can we go home?" He slid into the hot interior of the Buick and rolled down the manual window.

Nathan threw the gear into reverse and backed out of his spot. "I think you should come with me to Jersey."

Sam perked up. "You mean on your case?"

"I need to head back, and I'd feel better if I knew where you were. We still don't know who was in that sedan, and until then I'm not letting you out of my sight. Plus there are still some arrests to be made down at city hall. These guys were probably working with Rick Morgan to get rid of Mayor White all along."

Sam considered that. They had no idea whether the guys the Feds had arrested for killing Collins were the ones who chased him. And there was the added temptation of seeing Nathan at work. "Isn't it against the rules to bring your boyfriend along on a case? I thought you guys were sharing a room."

"We moved to a bigger suite when Simon arrived. I don't think Eric would mind if you suddenly showed up." Nathan kept his eyes focused on the road. "So, are you going to tell me what Sheldon said?"

"Nice change of topic," Sam said wryly.

He spent the next few minutes relating what had happened in the visitor's room. Nathan listened intently, wearing the expression he reserved for very serious matters. Once Sam finished, Nathan glanced over with a raised eyebrow. "So you don't think he was telling the truth?"

"He couldn't have been. The worst part was I got the feeling he believed it himself. Almost like he'd spent so much time rehearsing it in his mind, he doesn't even remember what happened." Sam laughed with incredulity. He shook his head and waited for Nathan to chime in his agreement. But he was silent. "Don't tell me you believe him."

"I don't know" was all Nathan said. They drove past a massive cornfield, the foot-tall stalks bright green in the sun. The ambivalence of Nathan's answer began to infect Sam, and the doubts he'd had back at the prison started to attack the weak points of his conviction. He beat them back. He wasn't about to let himself be duped by Sheldon's lies again.

"There is something still bothering me. I asked him if he knew anything about 'the tiger,' and he said no." It was the one thing Janice had told him that didn't quite make sense. Then again, his father had been drinking at the time. It could mean nothing at all.

"I've been wondering too."

"Do you think there's anything to it?" It probably didn't matter that Sheldon's reaction had seemed genuine. Or did it?

"Hard to say."

Sam closed his eyes and leaned his head back. He hated not knowing what was real, but there was no escaping the fact he'd never heard his father or anyone else refer to Sheldon as a fucking tiger. "What would you have said to him, if you'd gone in with me?" He felt sorry Nathan had given up his chance to give Sheldon a piece of his mind. If anyone deserved to, Nathan did.

"I guess I would have asked him why… how. How he could have done it. She trusted him." Nathan blinked rapidly. It was still difficult for him to talk about Emma's murder, and probably always would be. Sam extended a comforting hand to his shoulder.

"He's got terminal cancer. Pancreatic."

"It couldn't have happened to a more deserving guy." Nathan's frown deepened. "He say that to try to get sympathy from you?"

Sam shrugged. "Maybe. He looked like hell." No matter how he felt about Sheldon, it wasn't going to be a pretty end.

And if he was dying… why would he lie?

# Chapter 12

"The prodigal Dom returns." A man unfolded himself from the couch of the outer room of the hotel suite. He wore a pair of tight black jeans and an equally tight T-shirt. The combination emphasized his petite physique.

"Hello, Simon," said Nathan, setting down his bag on the floor. Sam swung his off his shoulder and did the same. Beyond the living room space, Sam could see two darkened doorways. If one of the bedrooms was Eric's and one was Nathan's, he wondered where this guy was sleeping.

"Oh, and isn't this fun. You brought a new toy." Simon smiled and cocked his head at Sam. His British accent was even softer and silkier than it had been on the phone.

"Uh. Hi," said Sam. "I'm Sam, and you can call me Sam."

Simon clapped his hands. "Excellent. Duke said you were quite the smartarse. Turn around, would you?"

"Very funny," Nathan said. "Don't listen to him."

"You're no fun at all." He crossed his arms over his chest and flopped back on the couch, like the effort of standing was too much. Simon was small but lithe. He had reddish brown hair and a wash of light freckles across his cheeks and the bridge of his nose. He didn't look older than twenty-five.

"So, what's been going on around here?" Nathan injected business into his tone.

"Oh nothing. It's been horribly boring, but Duke insists we can't leave."

As though summoned, Eric appeared in the doorway with a yawn. He scratched his crotch, not bothering to hide the massive erection tenting his pajama bottoms, and looked from Simon to Sam and Nathan. "What are you all yammering about in here? Can't a man get some shut-eye?"

"Late night?" Sam chuckled. Even though he didn't know Eric well, it was good to see him, even if he was getting more of an eyeful than he bargained for.

"Mmm-hmm." Eric yawned again and padded into the room. "Heya, Nate. Hey, kid. How are you doing?" He directed the question at Sam.

"Fine. Thanks." Sam flushed, wondering how much Eric knew. "I'm... better."

"Nate was pretty worried about you. You sure do keep him on his toes."

"Something like that," said Nathan under his breath. Sam gave him a dirty look.

"You bring my baby back in one piece?" As Eric passed the couch on the way toward the kitchenette beyond the living room, he reached out to give Simon's shoulder a brief squeeze, and Simon responded with a surprised, slightly nervous smile. Though the moment was fleeting, it made Sam curious. He filed it away.

Nathan let out an exasperated sigh. "Yes. Of course. And if you put one scratch on my car—"

"I don't understand how you can drive that thing," Eric said. He reappeared with a bottle of water in one hand, and a bottle of aspirin in the other. "It's got no character. Not like old Bess."

"How dare you," Simon interjected. "I think it's divine, Nathan dear." He arched an eyebrow at Eric from the couch. "Much better than that rusty old heap you made me drive across this vulgar nation."

"Rusty old heap?" Eric nearly snarled.

"Our room's this one," said Nathan, nudging Sam. They escaped from the escalating bickering into the relative quiet of the room. Like the rest of the suite, it was clean and modern, but not too fancy. The bureau didn't spring for five stars. Nathan shut the door behind them.

"So that's Simon," said Sam.

"That's Simon."

The two of them looked at each other. Sam wished they were alone. He wanted to have the kind of sex that would rattle walls.

"So what now?" Sam sat down on the edge of the bed.

"Now I catch up with Eric and see where we stand on this case. Then touch base with HQ. Once that's settled, we'll figure out what to do about the rest." He stepped forward between Sam's spread legs, and Sam leaned his forehead against Nathan's belly. He inhaled deeply, bracing himself to say what he'd been thinking.

"I want to see about getting the accident investigation reopened."

Sam looked up, and Nathan brushed a hand across his cheek. "I thought you might."

"What do you think?"

"I think we should wait until the dust settles first."

Sam was quiet for a moment. He wasn't ready to confess his doubts about Sheldon's involvement. The certainty he'd experienced after the visit with Janice had been comforting in a strange way. With Sheldon the responsible party, a known, hated entity already under lock and key, Sam could rest. But if the killer was an anonymous threat and still at large, that was a different story. Unless they opened the accident investigation again, they might never know the truth.

He wanted it to be Sheldon, which was the biggest warning sign of all. He was allowing his emotions to mislead him, and he needed to think with a clear, dispassionate mind.

"All right," he said. In any case, Nathan was right about timing. He couldn't imagine the uproar in Stonebridge once residents found out what had gone down with the mayor over the years—and the fact his death was likely due to his mob connection. Of course the new mayor and several of his staff would be arrested.

It made Sam wonder about Donna Howard again, and whether she was as crooked as the rest of them. Even though she always seemed on the up-and-up, her previous mayoral appointment made Sam seriously question his trust in her. Either way they'd find out soon enough.

He only hoped the people of Stonebridge could weather the coming storm.

THEY ORDERED in for dinner, and while Eric and Nathan sat in the small dining room beyond the dividing wall to catch up on the case, Sam found himself watching some British fashion show with Simon.

"So how did you start working with the FBI?" Sam asked, bored out of his mind and only half tasting the Thai food on his plate. He wished he were in the other room, taking part in the conversation there. It was hard not to feel like he and Simon were being relegated to the sidelines while the real men took care of business, though he knew the thought was uncharitable.

Simon laughed. It sounded forced. "Oh, I'm not with the agency. I'm a rent boy. A high-end rent boy, of course. I've known Eric for ages." He drew out the last word, injecting it with a bit of meaning Sam easily deciphered. "I help him out on occasion, when the matter in question is related to my subject of... expertise."

"Ah." Sam stabbed a piece of shrimp with his fork and waited for him to go on. But Simon didn't seem inclined to elaborate on the intimate details. He set down his half-eaten plate of food and stood up.

"Let's have a drink. Shall we?" He swayed his thin hips as he made his way to the liquor cabinet Sam had been trying to ignore. Sticking his ass out, he bent over and picked up a bottle of expensive vodka. "I can make a passable martini," he said, turning around. "Or perhaps you'd prefer a whiskey? The selection's not very good, I'm afraid. Nothing that isn't American." He wrinkled his pert nose.

"Uh. I'm good. Thanks."

"Suit yourself."

Sam forced down a bite of food as Simon grabbed the cocktail shaker. He'd meant what he said to Nathan about not drinking anymore, but desire smacked him in the face with tinkling ice, crystal, and the pungent scent of olives.

"So what do you do, Sam, other than our dear Nathan? What a darling he is. I am so sorry about the misunderstanding the other night. He was quite cross with me."

"It's fine," Sam said. "I overreacted."

"You mustn't mind me," Simon continued as he mixed his drink, "I have a shameful lack of concern for anyone but myself. Just ask Eric." There was a bite to the last statement not meant for Sam. He walked back to the couch, sipping carefully. "So?" Simon said once he sat down. "What do you do?"

Sam shifted away from the smell. He focused on the TV show, where three judges were frowning at an atrocious-looking ensemble created by one of the contestants. "I guess you could say I'm trying to be a journalist."

"Trying to be?" Simon fished one of the several olives out of his glass and held it to pursed lips.

"Well, I've had a measure of success, but I've been a little distracted lately." He wasn't about to spill his guts to a stranger.

"Hmm. Writing seems so difficult. I abhor hard work. You can ask Eric that too. He knows I can't be bothered to lift a finger." He raised his voice again, and this time Sam heard a muttered curse from the other room. Simon stretched out his legs and propped them up on the coffee table, seemingly satisfied. Sam couldn't help feeling like he was putting on an act.

"Why do I not believe that for a second?"

Simon gave him a hard-edged smile, and his rent boy persona wavered like a mirage.

"Believe what?" Nathan stood in the doorway looking edible in a Henley and jeans. Sam was getting used to the sexy casual clothes. He moved over on the couch to make room.

"Oh nothing. Your boy and I were having a little chat," said Simon, waving his glass casually.

While Sam didn't mind thinking of himself as Nathan's boy, hearing it from the mouth of a kid who was probably no older than Tim made him bristle.

Simon smiled sweetly. "Oh, you don't like me calling you that. But why? I should think anyone would be proud to be Nathan's boy."

"You making trouble in here, Si?" Another voice joined the conversation. Eric swung his massive arms as he stalked across the room toward the liquor cabinet. Contrasted with Simon to Sam's right, he was mountainous.

"As always, darling." There was no emotion in the drawled endearment, and Eric responded with a vinegary frown as he made his drink. The air in the room felt like it had chilled thirty degrees—obviously something had changed in the last few hours. Sam remembered the tattooed initials he'd seen on Eric's arm and the conversation they had back in Stonebridge about love, though it seemed an eternity had passed since then. Whatever the relationship between the two men, it was complicated.

Nathan seemed as eager to escape the tension as Sam. "Well, I think we're headed to bed," he said, putting his hand on Sam's thigh. "Eric, let's talk again in the morning and finish the report. Hopefully we'll be out of here in a couple days."

Eric grunted his assent and raised his glass of whiskey, which he downed in one large gulp. His usual good humor was gone. "Night."

Simon didn't seem to notice them leave. He was too busy staring at Eric.


"SO WHAT did you and Eric decide to do?" Sam asked later, his voice husky from the blowjob he'd given Nathan. He was sleepy and boneless from the reciprocal attention, but still curious about the case and the men in the other room. At the moment Eric and Simon were having either an argument or very angry sex. It was hard to tell which.

"He agrees with me the case is going nowhere. He and Simon have gone back several times and there's no sign of illegal activity, not even solicitation. They can still be shut down for operating without a permit, but the cops don't need us for that."

"So you're out?"

"We're out." Nathan pulled the blanket over them and then turned out the light. From beyond the far wall, Sam heard a moan that was definitely sexual. It probably would have gotten him going again, if not for the whole being-exhausted thing.

"What about Simon?" Sam asked as another, louder groan punctuated the air.

"What about him?"

"Does he solicit?"

"No. Of course not." Nathan sighed and flung an arm around Sam.

Sam turned toward the embrace. "He made it sound like he did. Called himself a rent boy."

"Oh. He was, years back, until he was arrested."

"Who arrested him?" Sam had a sneaking suspicion he knew how Nathan would answer.

"Eric."

"Hmm." Sam yawned and snuggled closer. He was going to sleep like the dead. "So are they in love or what?"

"I don't think they know."

Sam closed his eyes. No matter the uncertainties in his life, at least there was one person he could count on.


SAM'S RINGING cell phone dragged him from sleep early the next morning. He grabbed for it as Nathan grunted his protest.

"Hello. This is Sam," he whispered, pushing back the covers and exiting the bedroom with haste. He'd recognized the ring. Shady Brook.

"Sam?" said a familiar voice on the other end of the line. "It's Lisa."

"What's going on? How is Tim?" His stomach clenched. If something happened while he was away, he'd never forgive himself.

"There's been some movement. And some vocalization."

"What do you mean? Another seizure?"

"No, no. Nothing like that. The doctors.... I don't want to get your hopes up, and that's why I didn't call right away... but they think he might be responding to stimuli."

Sam froze in the doorway. He'd heard the words clearly enough, but his brain refused to absorb them. The early light had started to filter in, and the sound of commuters on the street below combined with the pounding of blood in his ears. He almost thought he was dreaming.

"Are you serious?" he whispered.

"I am." There was a smile in her voice, but it faded quickly. "But listen. We need to talk about expectations. I know you know this, but even if he does wake up—and it's still not a guarantee—there's a long road ahead. We don't know the extent of the damage. And of course the effects of being unconscious so long...." In the silence Sam heard the litany of warnings she'd stopped herself from elaborating—the possibility he might never walk, or speak... the possibility he might not know Sam. But none of that mattered.

"I'm just trying to prepare you for any eventuality. Okay?" she continued. "I want you to keep your expectations realistic." It was too late. He was already flying. The hope he'd come to dread, long repressed and withered, seared his chest with joy.

"We think it's a good idea for you to come down. Having someone familiar nearby.... Family is really important."

"I'm already on my way. Thanks, Lisa. Thanks so much."

"I'm hoping for the best for both of you." The smile in her voice was back, and Sam found himself foolishly grinning at the air. He nearly tripped over his own feet in his haste and ran smack into Nathan's bare chest as he emerged from the bedroom.

"Whoa. What's the hurry?" Nathan asked, steadying him with hands on both shoulders. "I heard you talking out here. Is everything okay?"

"It was Lisa. The doctors think Tim's waking up. I need to go home."

Sam braced himself for the inevitable objection, preparing for battle. Nathan wouldn't want him heading back alone under the circumstances, but nothing could hold him here, not when his brother needed him.

Instead Nathan smiled as the words sank in, and Sam's gut clenched in an entirely different way. Nathan always looked younger when he smiled. His face was open and unguarded. It reminded Sam of the hundred times he'd seen that expression before they were together, when that smile and the man behind it were nothing more than a dream. The reality was so much better than anything he could have imagined.

Sam leaned up on his toes and dragged Nathan's head down. Their mouths met in a smiling, laughing kiss that stole Sam's breath and made his heart pound.

"I want this more than anything for you," Nathan said, murmuring the words against Sam's cheek as they broke apart.

Sam hugged him tighter. "Thank you. I know it might not happen, or that he might be…. But I don't care. I need to get to Shady Brook."

"Of course. Let's get you a rental. I'll catch up with you later this afternoon," Nathan said, releasing Sam from the embrace.

"Really?" Sam raised an eyebrow. "No warnings about being safe? No dire predictions about a certain sedan?"

"Well… I do think you should go directly to Shady Brook and stay until I get there."

Sam was confused for a second before he remembered. "Oh right. The security detail." They'd made sure to give Tim's room extra cover, and surely the guard would still be there. He wasn't going to object to the precaution. Getting killed was not on the agenda for the day.

His brother was depending on him.

# Chapter 13

RACHEL, ALEX, and Yuri met him in the care facility's waiting room, adjacent to the lobby. All three of them looked up anxiously when he entered. Sam stopped in his tracks, surprised to see them.

"Did Nathan call you guys?" It was the only explanation. Sam had spoken with his grandparents in Florida on the drive over, but he almost got pulled over by a cop, so he hadn't chanced any more calls.

"Yeah. He thought you might need some friends," said Rachel. She smiled and pulled him into a hug, and Sam hugged her back gratefully. Alex smiled as she watched, twirling a strand of her bleached-blonde hair around her finger.

"Thanks. Have you seen Tim yet?"

"No. They wouldn't let us into his room without you," said Yuri as they all started to walk down the hall. "What's with the security? Does it have to do with your secret trip out of town?"

"I'll tell you about it later."

"You're so damn enigmatic these days."

"Believe me, I don't want to be. So how goes the parent visit?" he asked Rachel and Alex, buzzing with nerves. He was both excited to see Tim and afraid there hadn't been any change after all. What if Lisa was wrong?

"My 'rents left this morning," said Alex. "It's great to have the place to ourselves again."

"Mmm-hmm," Rachel agreed, giving Alex a knowing smile. Sam rolled his eyes.

The guard stationed outside Tim's door—a burly guy who could have played Zangief in a *Street Fighter* movie—asked for ID and eyed all of them, including Sam, until Lisa came by and gave them the go-ahead. She was wearing scrubs covered with cats and mice playing poker.

"It's great you got here so fast," she said, squeezing Sam's arm. "I think it'll help."

"I hope so." Sam sidled by the guard and entered the familiar white room behind his friends. The television hanging from the ceiling was on and tuned to a sitcom with a laugh track. Lisa switched it off.

"You might not notice any change right away. He's been vocalizing a little more each day, but it's sporadic. Be patient."

"Okay."

Sam stared at the figure in the bed. The white hospital sheets were fitted snugly around Tim's thin body. His brother's eyes were closed, and his mouth was slightly open, as though he'd been caught midsentence.

"Hey, buddy." Sam moved closer and carefully sat down on the edge of the bed. He could hear his friends settling in the furniture behind him, whispering quietly together, almost like they were in a museum.

He took Tim's warm hand. It was a man's hand, not a child's anymore, though unblemished and pale. If Tim woke up, would he understand how much time had passed? Sam couldn't imagine the shock of realizing years had vanished without you knowing, but Tim was still young. He had a full life ahead of him.

Sam squeezed his brother's hand. "I hear you've been making a racket. I really want you to wake up, Timbo. I hope you can hear me. I love you." He felt self-conscious talking with his friends in the room but was glad for their support all the same.

Yuri approached and stood next to the bed. "Hi, Tim," he said.

Sam squeezed Tim's hand again, hoping for a response or a reciprocal movement, but there was nothing. He tried to tamp down the disappointment, remembering Lisa's injunction to be patient.

"Does he look any different to you?" Yuri asked.

Sam squinted. Instead of the usual pale, bloodless color, his brother's cheeks were slightly rosy. He looked like he was sleeping and could wake any moment. It was enough to give him hope and brush aside some of the initial disappointment. "I think so."

"Does this mean you're back in town, in spite of all your weird warnings?" Yuri asked.

"For the time being."

145

Yuri smiled, and his cheeks dimpled. "Good. Because I've got a big job coming up."

Sam laughed and punched Yuri's arm. "So that's what you're after. You got it."

He turned back to Rachel and Alex, who were sitting side by side on two matching hospital chairs. "You guys wanna come say hi?"

Of all his friends, Rachel was the only one who'd known Tim before the accident. She stood on the other side of the bed and brushed Tim's hair away from his forehead.

"We're all waiting," she said. "Whenever you decide the time is right. Your brother needs you."

Sam swallowed down the raw emotion and stared. He could have sworn he saw Tim move.

NATHAN ARRIVED shortly before visiting hours ended. Sam could feel the concern radiating from him when they embraced.

"How is he? Any change?" Nathan asked.

Sam couldn't hold back his grin. "He moved his foot. I've never seen him do that before." It happened a little after three o'clock, when Yuri, Rachel, and Alex had left for the day. Sam was reading a book, and he looked up to see his brother's toes slowly flexing under the blanket. It might not have been a conscious movement, but it was still something. Tim's body seemed eager to wake up, even if his mind wasn't quite ready.

Afterward one of the doctors had come in to speak with Sam about Tim's prognosis. She seemed cautiously optimistic, though she also made it clear they wouldn't be able to determine the extent of the brain damage or the effect of the long-term coma until Tim was fully conscious. Sam couldn't wrap his mind around the prospect that it might finally happen.

"I want to go look through his stuff, see if there's anything in storage worth bringing over here so he won't feel so weird when he wakes up. Mentally he'll still be fifteen. The doctors think it might help." Sam hadn't visited the storage unit in years. He packed the thing with some help from Rachel, but he hardly remembered what was in it.

"That's a great idea." Nathan's smile was strained as he looked from Sam to Tim on the bed. Sam realized his mouth had been running a mile a minute.

"Is something wrong? Did you finish up the report?"

"Yes. And my supervisor isn't exactly happy about it. I think the PD down there will be getting a piece of his mind."

Sam nodded. "Good." He was glad Nathan wouldn't have to keep working on a dead-end case, but he still wondered what Nathan would decide. He hoped he wouldn't quit his job rashly and regret it. Then again, Nathan didn't do much without thinking it through.

"What about Eric and Simon?"

"Headed back to Texas. At least Eric is."

Sam was almost disappointed. He liked the guy, but he supposed they all had to get on with their lives.

"And we're headed home."

"Home?" Sam asked.

"Yes. They solved the mystery of the silver sedan. It was Judy White trailing you."

"The mayor's wife?" Sam couldn't believe it.

"Yep. Looks like she's been sleeping with the city comptroller. The two of them figured out Collins had some dirt on them, and that he'd given it to you before he split."

Sam frowned. "But there was hardly anything incriminating in those files. White only suspected his wife was having an affair."

"But she didn't know that. Tony says she was worried they'd suspect her or her lover in the mayor's murder if the cops found out about the affair. They were both at the gala."

"So she decided to run me off the road?" Sam wrinkled his forehead. It seemed a little extreme.

Nathan shrugged. "Love makes people do strange things."

"More like people will do anything to save their own skin." Sam was pretty sure love had nothing to do with it.

"Touché."


SAM FLEXED his muscles, but his arms and legs were tied to the bed, so he could do little more than writhe. On his chest, Nathan had applied two small nipple clamps—stolen from Eric's bounty—which were tightened to the point of pain. Nathan kissed one, and then the other, and Sam's cock twitched.

They were both naked, but with the blindfold over his eyes, Sam could only guess where Nathan would touch him next. The sensory deprivation heightened every sensation, and Sam shivered as Nathan flicked his tongue out and teased his sore nipples. A firm hand slipped down between his legs, avoiding his cock, and Sam whined as two slick fingers breached him.

He'd never felt so helpless, and the primitive urge to fight rose up in him. He tested his bonds again, but they were strong. Nathan had used a set of four leather cuffs that linked together via nylon rope under the mattress—a contraption they purchased online but hadn't yet used.

A surge of adrenaline pulsed through Sam's body.

"Shh," Nathan whispered close to his face. "Are you okay?"

The voice was familiar. Loved. Sam knew Nathan would let him go if he used their safeword. He started to relax as the fight dissipated. The cuffs weren't there to hold him back, but to make him feel secure. They were an extension of Nathan, like his hands, or his arms. He nodded.

"Good."

Nathan angled his fingers to rub Sam's prostate, and his erection started leaking on his belly. He wanted something—anything—to touch it, but he knew Nathan wouldn't give in easily. They had waited too long for it to be a quick session.

"Mew." Shadow jumped onto the bed. Sam laughed as her cold nose tickled his side. He'd missed the little beast.

Nathan tutted. "Okay. I'm sorry, cat, but you need to go."

Sam's world only existed through sound and sensation—the bed bouncing as Nathan moved to exile the cat, the sound of running water in the bathroom. Then all was silent.

Sam's eyelashes fluttered against the blindfold, but he couldn't see more than a thin strip of light near his nose. His nipples ached. He closed his eyes and let the comforting darkness surround him.

As he listened to his own breathing—in and out, in and out—warmth spread over him. The adrenaline surge ebbed, leaving him fuzzy-headed and content, and he melted into the mattress. His cock was still hard, but it didn't seem to matter anymore.

He waited what felt like hours, floating on the edge between wakefulness and sleep. When the mattress dipped, Sam opened his eyes to darkness. Nathan's warm hands spread out over his chest and then pulled the clamps on his nipples. The sting traveled straight to his groin, and his cock leapt on his belly, slapped it and then rose again. It didn't get any satisfaction. Nathan continued to ignore it and moved between Sam's legs. Something pressed into him. Slick plastic, not quite as wide as a cock. It fit easily into his relaxed body. Nathan said something Sam couldn't quite make out, but the tone of his voice was pleased. It made Sam proud he was doing a good job. He waited.

The plastic buzzed to life, and Sam shuddered as the unexpected sensation rocked through him. His toes curled and his adrenal glands fired. This time, Nathan fucked in and out with the vibrator as his other hand worked Sam's cock. It was leaking profusely by then, and Nathan blew on the cool wetness, sending a shiver up Sam's spine. The vibrator sounded loud in the quiet of the room, and Sam realized there was another noise—his own moaning. It felt so good he could hardly stand it. And then Nathan took the head of his cock into his mouth and sucked.

It was too much sensation too quickly. Sam could barely give a garbled warning before his balls contracted and he came.

He waited for the reprimand, but instead Nathan rewarded him with a long, openmouthed kiss. Their tongues slid together, tasting of come, and Sam lifted his head to get closer. His orgasm had left him weak and too sensitive. He wanted Nathan to untie him and hold him, but Nathan didn't seem to have any intention of releasing him yet.

"That was good," said Nathan between sweet kisses. "But don't come again until I say. Tell me if you're close."

Sam didn't think that would be a problem. He almost laughed but he didn't dare. "Yes, sir."

The vibrator was still inside him, angled just so, and Sam whimpered as Nathan continued to jack his softening cock, using his ejaculate as slick. Waves of pain mingled with pleasure, but Nathan was relentless, in spite of Sam's halfhearted protests. He could safeword at any time, and Nathan would stop. But Sam wanted to keep going. He wanted to see how far they could go.

After a few minutes of steady attention, Sam's dick started to stiffen again. His arousal was less potent than before, but grew steadily more urgent with every pull and twist of Nathan's expert hand. Soon he was hard and throbbing, breathing in time to each slow stroke.

His mind started to wander. He imagined he could look down from the ceiling and see them both on the bed. He knew exactly what Nathan would look like, how proud, determined, and single-minded in his focus on Sam. How had he ever believed Nathan wasn't entirely devoted to him? He felt so good. He reveled in the attention his cock was getting, especially when Nathan's wet tongue flicked over the crown in a tease. Again Nathan's hot mouth engulfed him, taking him to the root. Sam couldn't thrust, and he held off. He floated on the precipice of another climax, but he wouldn't let himself fall over.

When Nathan stopped sucking him, Sam arched off the bed, his body reacting automatically. Nathan quickly removed the vibrator, and Sam shuddered as the phantom sensation continued to echo inside him. Then Nathan was at his ankles, untying the cuffs. He pushed Sam's legs back and slid something—a pillow—under his ass, angling him upward.

Sam's first instinct was to hold his legs to his chest to give Nathan better access, but his arms were still bound. His heart pounded in his throat as he imagined how he looked. Earlier Nathan had instructed him to clean himself, and he'd done a thorough job. His hole was gaping, hungry for Nathan's cock, but Nathan seemed intent on edging him into oblivion. Sam willed himself to relax.

Nathan ran his hands over the globes of Sam's ass and spread him wide. Then he teased a finger between his cheeks and down his crack. He pushed in a little, and Sam felt himself welcome the intrusion. He wondered with breathless anticipation what would happen next.

"You look so good." Nathan removed his hand, and Sam let out a whimper. Then, before he could adjust to the loss of sensation, he heard movement, like Nathan was repositioning himself on the bed.

Then Sam felt the wet, hot sensation of Nathan's mouth on his hole.

"Shit," he panted. Nathan nuzzled deeper, licking around his entrance and then kissing him above and below. He swirled his tongue and pressed it against the ring of muscle. Sam almost came as Nathan's tongue opened him up. His cock started to drip onto his belly, and he made a nervous sound in the back of his throat. He didn't want to come until he was told.

"Please, please." His stomach quivered with the effort of being folded nearly in half, and his nipples ached. He sounded broken, desperate.

Nathan simply hummed against him, but he didn't let up. He lapped and sucked, flicked his tongue, and tapped it against Sam's balls.

"Is this heaven?" Sam groaned.

"Your ass was made for kissing," Nathan said thickly. He teased a finger around Sam's rim as he spoke. "Why haven't I done this before?"

Sam had often wondered the same thing, but he hadn't wanted to press the issue. Even though he enjoyed eating ass, it wasn't for everyone. But Nathan wasn't hesitant at all. He was going at it like he loved it, like he couldn't get enough—and it was driving Sam out of his mind.

Nathan's beard scratched against Sam's sensitive skin, providing a delicious contrast to the wet heat of his mouth. When Nathan wrapped a hand around Sam's dripping cock, Sam thought he might die. He let out a shout of warning. "No. Please."

"Good boy." Nathan released him. "That's my good boy. You were close?"

"So close. I—ah."

Nathan laughed. He sounded like his mouth was full and went back to slowly jacking Sam's dick while he licked and sucked. It seemed to go on like that forever, the orgasm building and then receding in waves until Sam was delirious and utterly under Nathan's control.

He almost wasn't expecting the words "I'm going to fuck you now."

Nathan bent his legs back even further, and Sam cried out at the first thrust.

"Put your heels over my shoulders," Nathan commanded as he started to move. Sam did. His arms stretched and strained with every slam of Nathan's hips. Soon Sam was lost in the give and take of the rhythm.

"You feel perfect," Nathan whispered hoarsely.

Sam could only moan and clench around the cock inside him. He was beyond language.

"I need you so much." Nathan's voice was close, intimate. He nosed Sam's cheek and then sucked an earlobe into his hot mouth. "I thought of you all the time when I was away. There was a swing. Wanted to see you on it, full of my cock. People wanting you, watching me fuck you, but knowing they can't. Knowing you're mine."

Sam whimpered as he imagined it too. His ass burned with the stretch of the pounding.

Nathan reared up and pumped more erratically. Even though Sam couldn't see him, he knew Nathan was getting close. "I'll be dammed if I ever have to miss you like that again."

Sam's balls contracted. He was going to come soon, with or without Nathan's permission. Every slide of Nathan's cock edged him closer.

"I own you. I fucking own this ass."

"Yes. Yes," Sam nearly sobbed.

"Tell me how much you love it."

"I love it. I love it so much." In his delirium, Sam thought with shame of his drinking. All he'd really needed was to be completely taken over by Nathan's thick cock.

"What if I fucked you like this all day?" Nathan was panting, punctuating each guttural word with a grind of his hips. "I want to feel you come. Can you do that for me?" He stopped moving, and Sam almost cried. Then he felt Nathan's hands on his chest. Each nipple was sore, but it was nothing compared to the rush of sensation that came flooding back when Nathan released the clamps. The throbbing pain traveled straight to Sam's cock. Sam exploded with a cry as the orgasm rocked him from head to foot.

"Oh damn," Nathan groaned. "Damn." He kissed Sam without finesse as he went deep and stayed there, trembling with the effort. Even after Sam thought it was over, Nathan moved slowly, fucking his come into Sam with a few final, luxurious strokes. Sam wanted to hold Nathan to him and keep him inside, but the restraints on his arms were unyielding. He moaned softly and gripped with his legs instead, wanting to feel every last pulse of the cock emptying into him. *His.*

When he was finally untied, Sam could hardly lift his arms, mostly because the second orgasm had turned his body to jelly. He blinked slowly against the light when Nathan removed the blindfold.

"Hi," Nathan said, his smile fond. He rubbed Sam's arms to bring back circulation.

"Holy shit." Sam's voice was hoarse. He struggled to sit up against the pillows, but his body wasn't obeying mental commands. He fell back and stared up at the ceiling, utterly wrecked.

"I hope that's a good 'holy shit'?"

"It's a fantastic 'holy shit.' I need… I need to take a piss, but I don't think I can stand up."

"Here, let me—" Nathan hooked one arm under Sam's bent knees and fit the other one behind his back.

Sam glared. "If you carry me, I'll be angry."

"How angry?" Nathan grinned as he started to move.

Sam grumbled out a protest against heteronormative bullshit, but Nathan was impossible to argue with. He carried Sam to the bathroom, careful not to hit his head on the doorframe.

"You're an asshole," Sam said as he was restored to dignity on legs that were a lot more stable than he expected. He aimed at the toilet, aware Nathan was scrutinizing him for any signs of injury.

"So you've said before."

"I was right before."

Nathan laughed. He looked gorgeous—carefree.

Sam finished, shook off, and turned around. His belly twisted with a different kind of need. He didn't protest when Nathan turned on the shower and led them both under the spray to wash. He didn't complain either when Nathan rubbed him down afterward, or when they lay together under the covers in the middle of the day, listening to the early summer thunderstorm through an open window. He fingered the collar around his neck as a flash of lightning lit up the cloudy sky. Thunder clapped loudly overhead, sending a tremor through the entire building. And Shadow—returned from exile—meowed and burrowed between them.

Nathan rested his head on Sam's shoulder, and Sam tightened his arms. After all they'd been through in the past couple months, he knew Nathan needed the closeness as much as he did. Maybe even more.

Maybe it didn't make them weak at all.

# Chapter 14

WHEN RICK Morgan was arrested, the town erupted into pandemonium. Stonebridge was without a mayor for the first time in its history, since Morgan's designated appointee from the city council had been arrested as well. A street protest against the corruption in city hall began as soon as the news broke, and it swelled over the next day until the governor declared a curfew. Now the streets were quiet at night, but Sam's keyboard was on fire. The media was full of conjecture about which of the remaining council members would take the temporary office, and Sam wasn't going to be left in the dust.

Chief Donna Howard and her police were under renewed suspicion, and the Feds had launched an internal investigation, led by none other than Antonio Rivera. It was almost like they'd gone back in time two years, but the people wanted answers. They weren't going to settle for anything less than the truth.

Still it was good to be home again.

Sam lay with his feet in Nathan's lap and Shadow tucked close against his left side. The newspaper headlines were even crazier than they'd been during the Sheldon-Hoff trial.

*Feds Bust Former Deputy Mayor And Staff On Conspiracy to Commit Murder, Bribery Charges*, the lead to the *Gazette* article read. Sam continued out loud. "*Barney Collins, White's former assistant and whistleblower, provided the FBI with information linking his employer to the Voronkov crime family before he was found murdered in southern Florida.* I guess it's fitting Collins gets credit in the end."

They decided it was safer to keep Sam's name out of the papers, since it wasn't clear if there would be further retribution from the Voronkovs. The men they arrested in Florida weren't taking credit for the mayor's murder. Still it was a relief to know who'd chased him and nearly run him off the road. A crime of passion was less frightening than a potential mob hit.

Nathan rubbed his feet as Sam scrolled to the bottom of the article. *"Police Chief Donna Howard is working with local prosecutors to pursue further leads, in spite of increased suspicion on her office. Mayor Morgan denies all involvement in White's poisoning last month."*

"So the guy says he's innocent." Sam snapped his laptop shut, set it on the coffee table, and stretched. He unsettled Shadow, who gave a meow of protest and jumped off the couch. "I guess I don't blame him." He thought again of the prison where he visited Sheldon—those oppressive drab walls and unfriendly guards. And of course Sheldon's claim of innocence regarding his parent's accident. It made him wonder about Donna Howard. "So, do you think Chief Howard's involved?"

Nathan wrinkled his forehead. "Not sure. There was nothing in the Collins files linking her to the case. But I think it's safe to say Morgan would throw her under the bus if he had any dirt on her, especially given the aggressive way she's pursing the case. I'd say she's likely clean. Speaking of… Rivera wants to know if you'd like to press charges against Judy White. They've got her in custody."

Sam considered his move. Even though nothing had happened in the end, the car chase had been one of the most terrifying moments of his life. Still it gave him an idea. There was a slight possibility that Judy White had useful information. "I'd like to go see if I can talk to her, first. You wanna come with?" He swung his legs off Nathan's lap.

"Somebody's got to keep you out of trouble." He sounded stern, but Nathan's eyes were twinkling.

THE STAIRS at the police station swarmed with a sea of reporters and photographers, but guards kept most of them back and out of the way. Nathan towed Sam after him as he waved his badge and cut through the throng easily. A few cameras flashed in their faces, eager to capture something—anything—that might be useful on a front page or a website, though Sam knew the assholes didn't have a clue who they were.

Antonio Rivera greeted them at the front desk, looking haggard. Sam realized he hadn't seen him since the night they'd gotten drunk together. It seemed like years had passed since then. Nathan slapped Rivera on the arm, and the two of them shared a greeting.

"Didn't expect to see you back in town so soon, Tony," Nathan said. "How's it going?"

"Controlled chaos, as you see. Barely controlled." Rivera smiled tightly, and Sam's eyes were drawn again to the scar running the length of his face. He'd never asked how Rivera got it. "Feels more than a little like déjà vu. So what can I do for you?"

Rivera looked from Nathan to Sam, and the expression on his face shifted to not particularly pleased when Sam made his request to see Judy. "I'm afraid I can't allow it," he said, shaking his head. "No visitors."

"Come on, Rivera," said Sam. "Consider it a favor?"

"Sorry, but the answer is final. I can't let you through, not during the questioning phase. She's with her lawyer now."

Sam cursed internally as he felt his chance slipping away. "But I need to talk to her."

"About what?" Now Rivera seemed curious.

"Listen. I'm pretty sure my parents were murdered, and there's a possibility Dan Sheldon was involved," Sam said. "Maybe Judy White knows something about it. If White and Sheldon were working together, she must have—"

"Whoa, whoa, whoa. Dan Sheldon?" Rivera's voice rose and he lifted his hands, like Sam was a horse that needed slowing down. "Whatever gave you that idea?"

Nathan sighed, and Sam felt firm pressure on his elbow. "Sam—"

He brushed Nathan off and turned back to Rivera. "I went and had a little chat with Sheldon. He says he wasn't involved, but I've got a source who says an old friend betrayed my father before he died. Now I don't know what to believe and I want to get the accident case reopened. If you let me talk—"

"Sam Flynn and Nathan Walker. Where the hell have you two been?" Donna Howard's voice interrupted him. Sam turned. He had no idea how long she'd been standing there. "What's this about Dan Sheldon?"

Sam flushed. He probably should have brought the matter up in a more private setting, without the whole station listening in.

"Hi, Chief," he said. "Uh."

"Sam's been under a lot of stress lately," Nathan explained. His hand was back on Sam's elbow, and this time Sam couldn't shake him off without making a scene. He glared, not appreciating being manhandled in front of an audience. "And we've already taken up too much of your time, Tony. Donna." Nathan gave her a grim smile, and she looked like she might say something, but her eyes were latched on Sam. Sam stared back.

"I want to take a look at my parent's accident report again. What happened that night was murder, and I'm not going to rest until I find out who did it."

BY THE time they made it outside the precinct, Sam was furious. Nathan had nearly dragged him out the door and down the steps through the crowd of reporters without speaking.

He was surprised to find Nathan just as angry, his lips a thin, tense line. "What the hell were you doing back there?"

"What are you talking about? We were supposed to talk to Judy. I thought you were with me on this." But he hadn't counted on Rivera's resistance. And he'd run his mouth impulsively, even though they had decided they were going to make polite inquiries only.

Instead of waiting for Nathan's reply, Sam turned on his heel and stalked down the sidewalk, thrusting his hands in his pockets as he went. He had no idea where he was going. He heard footfalls on the pavement behind him but didn't turn around.

In few strides Nathan caught up. Sam cursed his long legs. He kept his gaze low, avoiding Nathan's—the sole defense of the vertically challenged.

"Will you hold up a second?" Nathan asked, his voice calm.

Sam scowled. "No. I won't. I have shit to do." For one he'd promised Tim he'd be back to visit that afternoon. For another he needed to go on a run.

"Sam, come on. Don't be like this."

"If you tell me to be reasonable, I'll punch you in the face."

At the next intersection, Sam was forced to stop and wait for the pedestrian walk signal. He thought again about his conversation with Dan Sheldon. Over the last couple of days, he'd wracked his mind for other people who could have been involved. His father had a lot of friends, but not many close ones. Sam discounted the list of names he came up with one by one. It kept coming back to Sheldon, but that solution didn't ring true anymore. It was frustrating as hell.

"I know you want answers," Nathan said, his voice filled with understanding. "I do too. But going down to the station with guns blazing isn't going to help. For one thing the place is in an uproar, and as much as I hate to say this, an accident from almost eight years ago isn't first priority right now. And we need to be cautious. If the mob was involved, do you really want to drag Janice into it? I thought we agreed to wait until things died down."

The pedestrian signal started beeping. Sam was still angry about being patronized in public, but Nathan had a point.

"I guess I didn't think everything through," he admitted once they'd crossed the street.

"You never do." The words were quiet but cut to the bone.

"Oh, don't be shy. Tell me how you really feel," Sam said. "Impulsive Sam, never doing what I'm supposed to do. Good thing I have you to save the day. What about you? You arrogant bastard. Can't you even admit you were wrong to drag me out of there? I'm not your slave."

Sam realized he was panting out the words. They stopped in front of their building, and Nathan watched him, eyes blown wide with pupil. His mouth curled into a smirk. "Oh. I think we both know that's not true."

Sam's cock started to harden in spite of his anger. "Apologize to me."

Nathan came closer. He cupped the back of Sam's neck with one hand, and he used the other to caress Sam's cheek. "I'm sorry. I admit I was out of line. Forgive me?" His voice was quiet, commanding. There was a glint of humor in his eyes. A guy walking his dog passed by and gave them a wide berth.

Sam knew he was a fool, but he couldn't do anything but nod. Nathan's sincerity was impossible to resist. "Fine. But just so you know, I'm not your slave… 24-7, at least." He grumbled the last few words, and Nathan smiled.

"I wouldn't have it any other way. Now get inside and I'll make it up to you."

Sam didn't have to be told twice.

# Chapter 15

THE STORAGE center was a huge compound of temporary and long-term units connected by a maze of muddy dirt and grass roads. Sam pulled his truck into the external lot, not surprised to find it vacant. On the few occasions he'd visited, he often wondered if he was the only one renting there. It was the cheapest place he could find after the accident, when he was broke and struggling with the idea of getting rid of all his family's stuff, even after he unloaded the house.

He hadn't been there in a long time, but he still remembered exactly where unit 438 was located—near the back and to the left. As he slowed to a crawl and steered down the narrow dirt track, his heart started to pick up speed. He could handle it. He'd handle it for Timmy, and then he'd head home.

A brown rabbit scurried across the road, stopped dead in the center, and eyed the oncoming truck with terror. Sam braked and waited for her to continue on her way, flashing his lights a few times to encourage her. The dusk was quickly approaching, and Sam wanted to get home before Nathan did, though he figured he had some time because Nathan had been in New York all day. Sam had told him he wanted to go on his own, but he knew how Nathan worried.

After a few more seconds, the rabbit took off at full speed, and Sam chuckled and pressed the gas gingerly, in case another critter decided to chance its luck.

The storage unit looked lonely when he pulled up in front of it, but he put the thought out of his mind, hopped out of the cab, and slapped a mosquito that landed on his bare arm almost immediately. With all the rain they'd had, the tiny bloodsuckers were out in full force. He swatted at the couple buzzing around his head and fished out the key from his pocket. Then he thought better of it and went back to his truck to douse himself with the last of an ancient bottle of bug spray.

The padlock to his unit had rusted, but it unlocked easily enough. Sam swung up the overhead retracting door. The dull evening light washed over the contents inside. Plastic boxes, chosen to keep out the vermin, were set on slats and stacked into piles without labels. He'd packed them with little thought about organization, and now he regretted it. It might take hours to sort through all the stuff, and the cicadas in the field outside had already started to sing. Tonight he'd find a few things for Tim. He'd do the rest with Nathan another day.

Luckily Sam had a heavy-duty flashlight among his tools. He grabbed it and then returned to tackle the first box.

He sucked in a deep breath. The box held some of his mother's belongings. Old jewelry that wasn't worth anything but what it had meant to her. A few scarves she used to wear tied around her neck, or in her hair. Sam held a purple-and-gold one up to the fading light, and he remembered her washing dishes in the kitchen sink while he snacked at the table after school. *You better eat your dinner!* Even when she scolded him, she always had a smile in her voice.

On a whim, he brought it to his nose and inhaled. But any trace of his mother was gone, replaced by the musty smell of storage.

Had she been happy? His father's long-standing affair with Janice suggested there'd been trouble in the marriage, but his parents had done a damn good job of hiding it from their kids. And then there was the secretive drinking. It sounded to Sam like his father might have had a problem—just as he did—but at least Sam was facing his demons head-on. The previous day he'd gotten a therapist referral from his doctor.

The rest of the box was filled with trinkets from her dressing table. There was a little bottle of perfume, evaporated, and a tiny dog made out of soap and still encased in plastic wrap. It was probably a gift from either him or his brother, though he didn't remember. Sam's throat closed around a swallow. He didn't know why he'd saved those things.

He discovered a box of general household items he had wanted to keep but hadn't been able to fit into his apartment. Another held a treasure trove of books Sam had forgotten existed. He sandwiched his flashlight between chin and shoulder and leafed through a few pages of an old copy of *Robinson Crusoe*. It had been his father's, then his, and then Tim's. He was setting it aside in the take-with pile when it hit him. How would he tell Timmy about the accident? How would he tell him their parents were dead?

*Shit.*

He made his way quickly through the rest of the boxes, occasionally finding something he thought Tim might like. At some point he heard the rumble of another car engine within the compound. It was comforting to know someone else was around.

The photos made him linger. His mother had loved her camera, and there were many framed pictures of him and his brother together as kids—baby Tim perched on Sam's lap as Sam stared down at him, a picture of Tim on his third birthday, covered in chocolate cake. His parents' wedding day album was at the bottom of the box. He set it aside.

He'd lived so long with the idealized versions of his parents that the reality they might have kept secrets from each other—lied and cheated—was hard to face. He'd been blind, but even though it hurt, maybe finding out the truth was for the best. Nathan had said something along those lines the other night. Everyone had struggles. It was a part of life, and it was comforting to know he wasn't the only one with problems.

At the end of the search, he came across a box filled with his father's stuff. He stared down at the New York University Class of 1978 yearbook, and a chill ran through him. There was something he wasn't remembering—something important. Something about NYU. He chased the thought, and his mind scrambled back through the recent past. So much of it was a jumble because of his drinking.

Drinking with Rivera. Hadn't he mentioned attending NYU that night at the bar? Sam could hardly remember the conversation, and he cursed himself for being such a damned fool. Rivera was a Yankees fan, just like Yuri. He was in his fifties, just like Sam's father would have been if he lived.

He held the flashlight with his chin and opened the book. Surely his suspicion was unfounded. Rivera wasn't crooked. He was Nathan's friend.

His father had been on the law review staff in college, and Sam found a picture of the group in the clubs and activities section of the yearbook.

His father was front and center. In spite of the queasy feeling in his gut, Sam chuckled at his heavy-framed glasses and mustache. The rest of the club—all men—stood around him with goofy smiles. One of them looked horribly familiar.

Sam's blood chilled as he read the names under the picture.

*Timothy Barnes '79, Rupert Natick '78.... Antonio Rivera '78.*

Sam's head ached as he tried to remember the night with Rivera. They'd talked briefly about their fathers, but Rivera hadn't mentioned knowing Sam's dad or going to school with him—least of all being in the same damn class and club.

Maybe he'd forgotten? Or maybe he didn't realize he was dealing with the son of the same Flynn?

It seemed impossible. Being in Stonebridge for so long after the Sheldon case, he would definitely have made the connection. And if he followed his alma mater's alumni news at all or talked to other classmates, he would have heard about the accident.

Why wouldn't Rivera mention he knew Sam's father unless he had something to hide? Could that night at the bar have been a stealthy attempt to find out if Sam was onto him?

Sam flipped to the section with individual pictures. When he got to the *R*s, he aimed the flashlight with a trembling hand.

Antonio Rivera '78. Even without the scar, there was no doubting his identity. But it was the nickname underneath the photo that made Sam's stomach lurch. A cold frisson of fear shot through him.

*Tony the Tiger.* Holy Shit. Was he the tiger Sam's father had referred to in his drunken state? It seemed like the only viable explanation.

Sam yanked out his phone to check the time. It was going on nine, and Nathan still hadn't called or texted. Since they'd been home, they made a point to message each other at least a couple times a day. Maybe he thought he was giving Sam the space he needed to do what he had to do. But he couldn't wait. If Rivera was responsible, he knew exactly what Sam was looking for, and he would be dangerous. Dammit. Nathan had been right the other day at the station. Sam should never have blurted out his plans like a complete idiot.

He had to get out of there.

*Think Rivera's our guy. On my way home.* He pressed send and quickly looked around. The take-with pile was too large for one trip, so he grabbed as much as he could and made sure to tuck the yearbook under his arm. Then he aimed the flashlight at the door and shone it directly into the face of Antonio Rivera.

He was holding a gun in one hand, and a cell phone in the other.

"*Think Rivera's our guy,*" Rivera read out loud from the screen. "*On my way home.* I don't think that was very smart of you, Sam."

"Why do you have Nathan's phone?" Sam asked stupidly.

"He's in the car." Rivera gestured over his shoulder with his gun hand, like he was mentioning the weather. "Believe me when I tell you I didn't want it to be this way."

Rage bubbled up in Sam's chest, but it was blotted out by a paralyzing sense of dread. "Is he alive?"

"He's unconscious. But yes, he's alive. And he'll stay alive if you come quietly."

"Do I have a choice?" Sam fought to keep his voice steady.

"It doesn't look like it."

"Did you murder my parents?"

Rivera cocked his head and pocketed Nathan's phone. His gun hand was steady. "Murder is such a loaded term. Don't you think? I certainly didn't mean to hurt your brother and your mother, and I'm sorry about that. It's unfortunate, but it's business. Now put that stuff down and come on out of there. This place gives me the creeps."

"You son of a bitch. Why?"

Rivera scowled. "Spare me the drama. We could have avoided this if you and Nate had come to the New York office like I asked. But no. You had to go snooping around. You never follow the rules. Do you, Sam?"

"Fuck you."

"Why make this harder than it has to be? Get out here. Now."

With the gun pointed directly at his chest and Nathan's life at stake, Sam could do little but obey. He set down the things he'd intended to bring to Tim on the lid of one of the closed boxes.

Who knew if his brother would ever get them? Who would take care of Tim?

"The old college yearbook," Rivera said, a tinge of surprise in his voice. "Better bring that along. But leave the flashlight and toss me your phone and your keys."

Sam was strangely calm as he followed Rivera's instructions. Rivera even had the audacity to help him down off the riser. Sam held his father's yearbook as Rivera locked up the storage unit.

"Let's go."

# Chapter 16

SAM STARTED walking, and Rivera followed behind as they made their way through the muddy grass and then toward the right, where Rivera's unmarked car was parked. All seemed quiet inside as they approached, and Sam's heart leapt with hope. Maybe Rivera was lying about Nathan being inside.

But when Rivera opened the rear door, Sam saw a familiar figure slumped on the backseat.

"Nathan," he called out. Then he felt a hand over his mouth, muffling his speech. "Gef offa me sonfabitch," Sam mumbled. The chilling feel of the gun barrel against his spine stopped his struggle.

"Are you going to be quiet, or am I going to have to gag you and stick you in the trunk? Come on, Sam. Make the right choice."

Sam went limp. He didn't want to do anything to jeopardize Nathan's safety, and he certainly wouldn't be able to help him from inside a locked trunk. If he was hurt....

"Attaboy," Rivera said. "Now get in before I change my mind."

Sam didn't need to be told twice. When Rivera released him, he lunged for the backseat. The door slammed behind him, but he didn't care. Even though it was dark, he could tell Nathan was pale. With trembling hands, he felt Nathan's still body for injuries. He pressed the pads of his fingers to Nathan's throat. His pulse was steady and strong. Sam leaned down and pressed a kiss to his forehead. *Thank God.*

Several minutes later Rivera climbed into the front seat. There was a bulletproof divider between it and the back, broken only by a couple small holes to allow sound to pass through. Sam didn't need to try the door to know it was safety locked. He and Nathan wouldn't be getting out of the car unless someone opened the door from the outside.

"What did you do to him?" Sam asked, resting Nathan's head in his lap. It didn't look like Nathan and Rivera had fought. Aside from his unconscious state, Nathan seemed intact.

Rivera didn't answer right away. He was busy texting someone. "Dose of Rohypnol at dinner," he said absently. "He'll be fine."

"You date-rape drugged him?"

Rivera shrugged as he kicked the car into drive. "It works. He won't even remember this."

"Won't remember he was eating a burger with you and then passed out, only to wake up and hear I'm, what? Dead? Missing? They'll find my truck, you know." Sam wrapped both arms around Nathan to hold him still as the car jostled over the rough track toward the main road.

"It's being taken care of."

That's probably what the texting was for. *Great.* "Where are we going?"

"Oh, out for a little drive. You've been more trouble than you're worth, I'm afraid. Now I think we might be able to work out an arrangement for Nate… if you cooperate. He's a good friend of mine."

Rivera took a left, which led away from Stonebridge. Sam's gut clenched with panic and a strange sort of longing. In all the dangerous situations he'd been in over the past couple years, he hadn't ever really expected to die—not when he was held at gunpoint by Bernhardt Hoff and Rich Petersen, not when he was trapped underground by Randall Palmer. Even in those moments, he never believed it was the end. But Rivera was so cold… so calm. He was a professional. Sam would never again see the home he shared with Nathan.

"Some friend." Sam brushed the hair back from Nathan's forehead. While part of him wanted Nathan to wake up and get them out of there, Sam knew it was for the best that he stay unconscious. Rivera had played his cards well. Sam would do anything he needed to do to keep Nathan alive.

"I'm a better friend than you know. I let you live this long. And if you hadn't meddled in this case, you wouldn't be in trouble now. You're a hard man to help, Sam."

"Help me? You bastard. You killed my family."

"It was business."

"Because my father found out you were a double agent, working for the Voronkovs. That's what happened. Wasn't it?"

"Your father was too self-righteous for his own good. It's a quality you share, unfortunately."

Sam's stomach churned. "How did you do it? Why would you?"

"So many questions. Do you really want to know?"

"I have a right."

Rivera made another turn onto a narrow road. Sam immediately recognized the place, though it was unmarked. They were heading toward one of the more concealed banks of the Connecticut River. As a teenager, he'd swum in it with his friends, though their parents warned them to beware of floating debris. There were urban legends about a girl who was knocked unconscious by a tree branch and swept out to sea. Her body was never recovered.

The small parking lot near the riverbank was dark and silent. Trees folded around them, blotting out the light from the moon and the city beyond.

Rivera seemed to consider whether to answer Sam's question. He killed the engine and lights and turned around so Sam could see his face—and his lack of remorse. "I approached your father. He was an old friend and a state's attorney. A good man to have in our corner. We figured it would be easier to move in with him on our side."

Sam could feel the thump of Nathan's heart under his shirt. He drew strength from its simple, steady beat. "But you killed him when he said no." Sam could hardly take comfort in knowing his father had refused.

"He knew his options, and he made his choice. I would never have rigged the car, but I got word he was planning to run after the party. I had to stop him."

"What?" Sam tried to remember anything out of the ordinary during those last few weeks, but he couldn't. He'd been away at school. If his father feared for his life and the lives of his family, of course he never would have told Sam. He wouldn't have wanted to drag him into it.

Rivera tsked. "He should have made a different choice."

Sam closed his eyes. So his family had been fleeing, all together, and not driving home as he always thought. But where were they heading? Had Tim known? Had his mother? Had they realized what was happening when the car wouldn't stop? Were their final moments filled with terror?

All was silent. Sam wondered how high a dose of roofies Rivera had given Nathan. When he woke up in the morning, would he suspect he'd been drugged or be convinced by whatever lies Rivera would spin?

"But Dan Sheldon…. He didn't know you. He said he worked with Hoff." Sam was still trying to wrap his mind around how Rivera had insinuated himself into Stonebridge society. "Or was that a lie?"

"I left town after the accident and returned to Columbia. I was down there for a couple of years on a joint CIA venture. Made some good connections for Victor. Got this lovely memento, as well." He gestured with his thumb and forefinger, spanning the width of the fierce scar on his face. "Hoff took over up here and made further arrangements."

"Columbia. So that's where the Voronkovs get their supply," Sam muttered, more to himself than Rivera.

"Good story, huh? It's a damn shame you won't be able to write about it."

The reality of the situation returned with crushing force. Sam didn't want to die. He couldn't imagine making Nathan mourn for another lover. And Tim. Sam didn't doubt Nathan and his friends would care for him, but Sam wasn't about to leave his brother behind.

How the fuck could he escape? Rivera had his cell phone and a gun. And of course there was the most obvious issue. Sam was locked in the car. If he waited to make a run for it when Rivera opened the back door, he would kill Nathan. Whatever Rivera said about friendship, there was no doubt in Sam's mind that Nathan was a bargaining chip. The only thing he could buy was time.

"But I don't understand," Sam said as he hoped for a miracle. "You helped Nathan clear his name after Hoff killed Emma. You helped put him and Sheldon behind bars. Why would you do that if you were all working for the same organization?"

"Same reason I got rid of White," said Rivera. "Hoff fucked up. He started acting like a big shot, like he was invincible. And if there's one thing you learn in this business—you're not. Once you get cocky and start making mistakes, well… you get the picture. The boss wanted them all out of there, and they didn't know me. Safer that way." He flashed a predatory smile, and Sam cringed. How could he ever have considered Rivera handsome? And then Sam realized what he'd heard, and his heart skipped a beat.

"Wait a second. *You* killed the mayor?"

Sam had barely asked the question when a flash of headlights through the trees startled him. His body surged with adrenaline as a familiar vehicle pulled up beside them. It was his truck.

A small-statured man he didn't recognize climbed out. Without another sound Rivera exited the car and slammed the door behind him. Sam's truck was still running, and the two men met in the headlights. Rivera reached out a gloved hand.

A muffled shot rang out, and the smaller man crumpled to the ground, disappearing below Sam's line of sight.

Sam's gut heaved, and he broke out in a cold sweat as he watched Rivera turn off his truck and kill the lights. He knew he had to hold it together. He needed time to *think*, but he had none. In a flash Rivera was at the back door, swinging it open. His gun was a cold, metallic certainty aimed right at Sam's temple.

"Can't take any chances. It's so hard to find trustworthy help these days," said Rivera. "Get out."

Sam looked from the gun down to Nathan, who didn't show any signs of waking. He rested a trembling hand against Nathan's forehead and felt the warm skin he had loved so many times. He had to believe Rivera was serious about sparing him. He slid Nathan's head from his lap. He couldn't say "I love you" out loud—not with his soon-to-be killer as audience—but he needed Nathan to know all the same. In a carefully disguised move, he slipped his birthday keychain and the tiny collar key he always carried into Nathan's shirt pocket. Hopefully when Nathan woke up to find the engraved S+N nestled there, he would understand that it meant "Be happy."

"Hurry up," said Rivera.

Of course it was a lie. Sam knew as sure as he knew the pressure against his spine was a gun that Nathan would be devastated. But Nathan was resilient. He would heal.

What would death feel like?

Sam dragged his feet as Rivera urged him toward the gruesome scene in front of his truck. The dead man was young—probably not more than twenty-one—and he was wearing a skullcap and a black leather jacket. His eyes were open with surprise. Sam had the urge to reach down and close them, but he didn't want to touch the body. There was a dark liquid seeping onto the ground near his shoes. He avoided it narrowly.

"Pick him up," said Rivera. "Let's get this done."

Sam seriously doubted he could lift the dead weight of a man nearly his size. He had half a mind to tell Rivera to go fuck himself. Still, with Nathan alive and helpless in the car, Sam couldn't take any chances. He bent down and managed to get a grip under the man's arms. The head lolled backward at a painful angle. The body was warm, but it was obvious in an instinctual way that it was dead.

Would this be what he looked like when it was over? Sam recoiled at the thought, and from the smell coming from the body. The man had soiled himself in his last moments. He turned his head and breathed through his mouth.

"A little help would be nice," said Sam as he started to drag Rivera's latest victim toward the river. The incline was gradual, and the area was covered with a thick layer of grass. The summer night was windy and fresh, and the sounds of the cresting river reminded Sam of those long-ago swims. It would have been a pleasant scene… if not for all the murder.

Rivera pursued the spectacle with measured steps, still holding his gun. "I prefer not to get my DNA on the body."

"What about my DNA?"

"That hardly matters. Does it?"

Despair ran through him in a cold shock, even though he knew he shouldn't be surprised. After he deposited the body in the river, he'd be next. There was no guarantee anyone would even find him. With all the rain they'd had recently, the river had flooded beyond its banks. Worse still, another thunderstorm seemed to be brewing, one of the nightly downpours that made summer mornings at Manella's so painfully humid. If it rained hard, all the evidence of Rivera's kill would be washed away. The bastard would walk free and clear again.

"Nathan will want answers. He'll want justice."

"And he'll get it. Either they find you and determine cause of death a mob hit, or they don't. And with your truck parked here, and how depressed and erratic you've been lately…. Well, maybe Nate will decide you'd finally had too much."

"A suicide?" Sam trembled. No. Nathan would never believe Sam had killed himself. He knew Sam would never abandon Tim. The previous day Tim had murmured something unintelligible yet purposeful. Like he knew Sam was there. But of course Rivera couldn't know that. Yes. Let him think Nathan would buy his story. Let his ignorance keep Nathan alive.

Sam swallowed as he finally encountered the muddy water overflowing the river's normal banks. The ground squelched and squished, and he lost his footing and went knees down, dropping his cargo as he did. He could feel the pull of the river current as the water soaked his jeans up to his waist.

"Stand up," demanded Rivera, standing only a yard in front of Sam with his gun aimed and ready.

"Not so fast. Sam, don't move."

Looking shocked, Rivera turned his head toward the new voice, still aiming at Sam. Sam, on his knees next to the dead guy, was equally surprised. Though he could hardly see for the darkness, there was no mistaking the accent.

"Chief?" he whispered.

Chief Donna Howard stepped out of the shadows. She had her gun aimed at Rivera.

"What the hell are you doing here?" Rivera demanded.

"Drop the gun, Tony. I've got backup on the way. I've been trailing you all night. Drop the gun now and put your hands up, or I'll shoot. Sam. Stay calm."

"Uh, yeah. Calm. Easy peasy."

"Donna, listen to me—" Rivera said.

"No. You shut the hell up and listen to *me*. You thought you were so clever. Didn't you? Thought you could pull the wool over my eyes with a few lousy fucks. Thought I was easy to manipulate. A lady cop. You had as much access to the mayor as anyone else did, and you were pretty quick to hightail it out of town after months of hanging around up my department's ass. So yeah. I started taking notice. I pulled the file on Sam's parents yesterday, and you know what I found? It didn't exist. It was gone, vanished, caput. No pictures. Nothing. Yet I know it was there when I was appointed, 'cause we did an audit after Sheldon went to jail. So I got to thinking. Who could have done such a thing? And why?

"So I broke into your room. I found the files and so much more, you double-crossing son of a bitch."

As she spoke she moved slowly but steadily toward Rivera. He was no longer paying attention to Sam, though he kept his gun aimed in Sam's direction. Sam sort of wished she would stop talking.

"Don't come any closer," Rivera told her. Still, he was giving up ground as she advanced. Water lapped at his feet. He was close now, almost an arm's distance away—and so was the gun.

171

Sam weighed his options. If Chief Howard pulled the trigger, there was a good chance he would go down as friendly fire. Even if Rivera was hit, he would likely retaliate and shoot Sam too. It was a case of mutually assured destruction. And who knew when the hell backup would arrive?

But there was one wild card. Sam himself. Rivera thought he was weak, a coward. He thought Sam would go down without a fight. That he'd consent to be written off a suicide.

Rivera was dead wrong.

Without pausing to think himself out of it, Sam lunged and grabbed for Rivera's gun arm. He managed to catch Rivera by the elbow and held on with both hands, wrenching the man around to knee his groin. Rivera cursed in surprise but didn't drop the gun. He punched Sam square in the jaw with his free hand, and Sam's whole body juddered with the impact, but he didn't let go. He knew what would happen if he did.

They struggled as the muddy earth slipped beneath their feet. Sam had his eyes locked on the gun. It waved wildly in the air as they both fought for dominance. Since Rivera had a free arm, he had the advantage, but Sam managed to dodge a few additional punches with his adrenaline-sharp reflexes. He snapped Rivera's arm back with all the force he could muster, and the man howled in pain. His eyes were murderous, fixed on Sam's face. Chief Howard was shouting at him, but Sam couldn't make out what she was saying over the roar of the river. Maybe going for the gun hadn't been the best idea, but it was too late.

They were deeper now, and Sam felt the current tug at his waist. He was certainly at a disadvantage given Rivera's greater height, and he was going to fall.

"I should have killed you a long time ago," Rivera said. His words were staccato, punctuated by grunts and heaving breaths, and his spittle rained down on Sam's face.

Sam's flagging strength returned and increased tenfold. Now he had murder in his blood too. "Yeah? Just try, fucker."

"Sam, stand aside. I don't want to shoot you," Chief Howard shouted from the bank. She was panicked, but the words sounded fuzzy in Sam's brain.

This man killed his parents, had drugged Nathan—and Sam was going to kill him. Sam held his breath, and with a mighty shove, he threw his entire weight against Rivera. He fell, flailing into the water, and Sam went after him. In the ensuing tangle of limbs, Sam lost his grip on the gun arm. He grappled with Rivera's shoulders and held him down under the water, but just as he thought he felt Rivera's strength slacken, a new surge of force pushed him off and over, flipping him onto his back. Sam sputtered a few feet away, scrambling to regain his footing in waist-deep water. He needed to get hold of that gun before....

A shot rang out. Rivera cursed. He was soaked with water and something darker, but he still managed to stand. He raised the gun and pointed it right at Sam.

"Sam," Chief Howard yelled. "Get down. Get down, now."

Suddenly Sam heard sirens in the distance, growing louder and louder with every passing second. A swell of triumph rose in Sam's chest, and along with it, the searing pain of a bullet piercing his flesh.

The agony was explosive and seemed to spread through his whole body. Sam gasped for breath as he fell back into the water. Another volley of shots went off, but Sam was staring up at the dark sky. Cold, muddy water splashed over his face and into his mouth and nose, and he choked and tried to right himself. There was nothing under his feet. He couldn't move his left arm, and when he tried, a burst of agony radiated from neck to bicep. He clutched for the bank with his right, but the pain made movement difficult, and blackness teased the edges of his vision. Lights flashed on the land beyond, and Sam called out, but his voice was garbled with water. *Shit.* He was going to die anyway.

Wasn't that just his luck?

# Chapter 17

SOMEONE WAS saying his name. Sam tried to answer, but he couldn't move his mouth. His tongue was sore, and it hurt to breathe. Maybe he'd just go back to sleeping.

"Sam? Sam, can you hear me?"

He blinked open and a blurry figure came into focus. A tall man who resembled Shaquille O'Neal was holding a clipboard and standing over him.

"Where am I?" Sam asked. "Where's... where's Nathan?" He started to struggle to sit up, but a sharp pain in his left arm made him gasp, and he couldn't move it. It was tied to his body by some sort of... sling. His arm was in a sling, and there was a thick, white bandage on his shoulder. He must be in the hospital. It came back to him in a rush—Rivera, the struggle, water filling his mouth and his throat. Nathan unresponsive in the backseat of Rivera's car.

"Good to see you again, Sam, though I wish it were in another context. You're going to be fine," Shaq said. No. A doctor. The same doctor who attended him on his last visit. He had a deep, comforting voice. "You were shot in the shoulder, and we had to perform surgery to remove the bullet. It was a clean wound, and it went very well. After a few weeks, you should be good as new." He shone a light into Sam's eyes, and then jotted down a couple of notes and smiled again. "You'll be sore for a while, and you might have some discomfort in your throat and lungs due to the water inhalation, but I'll prescribe you something for the pain. You should be released tomorrow."

Sam had no idea what time it was or what day it was. He nodded dumbly. The doctor still hadn't answered his question.

"Nathan. Is he… is he all right?"

The doc proceeded to inject a needle full of something into the IV tube running into Sam's right arm. "He's out in the hall. I'll send him in, and I'll be back to check on you in a few hours. Try to get some sleep, if you can. This will help."

The doctor's shoes squeaked on the linoleum as he left. Sam's bandaged arm ached, but the drugs were quick acting. He was already pleasantly fuzzy when Nathan entered the room, still wearing the same clothes from the night before. With his messy hair, his beard, and the dirt smudges on his shirt and jeans, he looked wild. Sam had never seen a more perfect sight.

"Sam," he said, his face lighting up with worry and relief. And then he was there in Sam's arms—well, arm.

"You're all right?" Sam whispered hoarsely against his rough cheek. "I was so worried he'd given you something else… something bad." At the back of his mind, he'd worried it had been poison, but he hadn't let himself go there.

"I'm fine. A little tired, but I'm fine. What about you? They told me you fought him. You brave idiot."

"He killed my parents," said Sam. "And he hurt you."

Nathan's eyes were wide with pain and something else—pride. Sam started laughing.

"What's so funny?" Nathan asked, slightly alarmed.

"*The Princess Bride*. I… this is just like *The Princess Bride*. Well almost."

Nathan looked at him like he was crazy, and he put a hand to Sam's forehead. "How do you feel?"

Sam's laughter started to give way to a coughing fit, and his lungs ached. Maybe he was slightly mad. "Like I was just shot, then dredged from the bottom of a river. I thought for sure I was a goner. Who saved me?"

"Officer Jain. Remember him?"

Sam smoothed back Nathan's hair with his good hand. "I've run into him a time or two. Looks like I have a thank-you card to write." If he hadn't arrived when he did, Sam would be fish food.

"He's been working closely with Donna. She's all right, by the way. I imagine she'll want to talk to you soon, but I've convinced her a day of rest won't hurt." Nathan kissed Sam's eyelids and his forehead. His touch was gentle, seeking out tender places. Sam could hardly feel the pain in his arm anymore. Whatever meds the doc had given him were good. But he couldn't sleep yet.

Sam forced his eyes open. "And Rivera?"

"Dead. Donna shot him."

"I'm sorry." The man had killed his parents, but he had been a mentor to Nathan and a friend. At least that was what Nathan had always believed.

"So am I." Sam saw the raw pain in Nathan's eyes. He knew what that betrayal meant. Nathan would need support over the next few weeks, and Sam would be there to give it to him. They would be there for each other. But they didn't need to talk about it yet. Sam stroked Nathan's shoulder. "It's good to see you."

Nathan framed Sam's face with both hands. "When I woke up and they told me you were in surgery, I thought the worst."

Sam knew the feeling. "When I saw you in the back of the car, unresponsive... yeah. I thought the worst too. It made everything we've been fighting over seem so insignificant."

"Perspective's always helpful, but I prefer to get it in other ways."

"Me too. How come I'm the one who always winds up in the hospital?" Sam stifled a yawn. His body felt heavy, like he could sleep for a week. His face was tender where Rivera had landed a particularly nasty punch.

"I'd take your place in a second."

"No. I don't want that either." His eyes drifted shut again. It was nice having Nathan so close, and it would be even nicer if they were in bed together. He wanted to stay awake to enjoy the hands petting his hair. "I don't want you to feel guilty over this. It wasn't your fault."

Nathan sighed. Sam knew he was probably fighting a losing battle, but he had to say it anyway.

"Oh, by the way, I found this in my pocket." Nathan held out the silver keychain. Its tiny key dangled like a promise. "You put it there, didn't you?"

Sam nodded. "Yes. In the car... before he... I wanted you to know... he wanted...." He blinked back the tears that were suddenly threatening.

Nathan leaned down and softly kissed his mouth. "Shh. We can talk about it later. Here." He made a move to put the key back in Sam's hand.

"You keep it." Sam shook his head. It felt like it weighed twenty pounds. "I'm sleepy."

"I know. It's okay." Nathan pressed his warm lips against Sam's forehead. "Get some rest. You don't have to worry about anything anymore."

"But Tim. Is he okay? I didn't get to take… the stuff is there in a pile. I wanted him to have it."

"Of course. I'll call Lisa and make sure we get it sorted out."

"Don't want you to leave."

"I'm not going anywhere. I'll be right here when you wake up." Sam's grip went slack. He was already tumbling into a dream. In it Nathan said, "I'll never leave you so long as I live."

SHADOW WAS a small white blob of fur at his side, purring loudly. They were both curled up on the couch a few days after the shooting, and Sam was frustrated. What good was a fancy new computer if he couldn't type?

"Give it some time. The doctors say you should rest your arm." Nathan appeared in the doorway with a kitchen towel draped lazily over his shoulder. An unpleasant smell wafted from behind him. Something was burning, but Nathan assured him it was fine.

"I don't have a few days," Sam groused. "The news is happening now." He'd even tried typing with his right hand only—an exercise in futility. He'd never be able to finish his article. When the *Times* called him, he thought it was a prank. But it wasn't, and not finishing by his deadline would be career suicide.

"All right. What if I got you some voice-recognition software?"

Sam brightened. "Could you?"

"I have to go out later. I'll see what they have at the store."

"I can't believe I didn't think of that."

Nathan shrugged. "I'm smarter than you."

The doorbell rang, and Nathan went to answer it. Sam smiled at the group of familiar voices mingling in greeting. He missed his friends. They briefly visited the hospital but hadn't been permitted to stay long. Alex and Rachel were both carrying presents, and Yuri, bless him, had two extralarge pepperoni pizzas.

"When you told me Nathan was cooking, I knew I had to intervene."

"You've done the Lord's work," Sam agreed.

"Ha-ha. Very funny." Nathan snapped the kitchen towel at him, and Sam swatted it away with his good arm. He set down his laptop and made room for his friends, much to Shadow's chagrin. She eyed the newcomers with disdain from the floor.

Everyone settled for lunch. Nathan sat to Sam's left and Rachel to his right. Alex and Yuri surrounded the coffee table, sitting on pillows on the floor.

"So how is the patient recovering?" Rachel asked. "Are you behaving yourself?"

"What do you think?" Nathan asked.

"Never do that again, by the way." Yuri glared at him.

Sam returned the look. "What? Get shot? I'll try to remember." He wasn't eager to repeat the experience.

"I meant tackle a mobster with a gun."

"It's all part of the job," said Sam, with just a touch of pride.

All joking aside, there were some things he'd never forget—like Rivera's last victim, the young man he had to carry. Sam could still feel the warmth leeching out of those dead limbs. Antonio Rivera was one of the coldest, most calculating men he had ever met, and Sam was glad he got the punishment he deserved, even if he wasn't the one who dealt the final blow.

It was hard to say if knowing the truth made it easier to take. He still hadn't quite wrapped his mind around what happened, and he was pretty sure Nathan had instructed everyone not to bring it up.

"Are you cold?" Rachel reached for the extra blanket on the back of the couch and draped it over his lap.

"I'm fine. Seriously."

"You always say that. Shut up and let us pamper you."

Sam let his friends fill him in on the more innocuous goings-on in Stonebridge. Rachel and Alex had good news. They were planning a Christmas wedding. Nothing too fancy, just friends and family at the courthouse and a huge party at the Lucky Star. And then the kicker.

"You're buying the bar?" Sam's mouth dropped open.

Rachel made a high-pitched noise and stamped her feet on the floor. "Yes. The owner wanted to sell, and I've been saving, and well, I figured it was time I went for it. We're going to redecorate and reopen in time for the wedding."

"Sacrilege," Sam said. "You better not fire the cook." He loved those burgers.

Alex beamed at her. "Look at my fiancée, would you? A business owner. I'm so proud."

A round of congratulations filled the room, and they all raised their soda glasses to toast. Sam had meant what he said about not drinking. He had too much to lose. In moments when he was happy, he didn't miss it. It was the dark times he had to worry about. Still, he knew he needed some help. He'd scheduled his first session for the following week.

"What about you? How's the boy toy?" Sam smirked at Yuri, who stuck his tongue out.

"He has a name, you know."

"Ohhh," said Alex. "Then it's serious."

Yuri gave Sam a pointed look. "If you can have a sugar daddy, I can have a boy toy."

"I thought you said he had a name," Sam said, throwing a couch pillow at Yuri.

Nathan scowled. "Can you all please stop calling me that? Sam contributes plenty to this relationship."

"I'll bet he does." Rachel waggled her eyebrows and made a blowjob gesture.

Laughter punctuated the rest of the exchange, and Sam settled back while the others fought over what movie to watch. He didn't care, as long as they were all together.

"*Star Wars* it is," Nathan finally said, flicking on the TV. Sam leaned against him, resting his bad arm on Nathan's lap. Alex situated herself between Rachel's legs, Yuri sprawled on the floor, and they all settled into an epic movie. Sam had to write, but the article wasn't due for another couple days. He supposed he could take a little R & R. Doctor's orders, after all.

"Sam, what are you wearing around your neck?" Rachel asked as the music began and the words started to scroll across the screen. Sam's fingers automatically flew to his throat. He flushed and leaned closer to Nathan, who said nothing.

"Uh. I'm going goth?"

"Hmm." Her eyes flicked from Sam to Nathan.

No one else paid it much attention, and Sam thought she might have forgotten about it. But Rachel never forgot anything. About halfway through the movie, when Nathan got up to use the bathroom, she leaned close and whispered into his ear.

"You can't fool me, Sam Flynn. I'm your best friend, and I know sure as I know my own name you're not going goth. I've had my suspicions."

A swell of protectiveness rose up in his chest. "I know. But Rach, you don't under—"

"I don't need to know the details. But tell me… is it what you want?"

He fingered the warm leather and metal. It seemed so natural to wear. He'd forgotten he had it on when their guests arrived. And he wasn't ashamed. "Yeah. It's what I want."

"And he treats you well?"

"He's the best person I've ever met," Sam said.

"Well." She patted his knee. "That's good enough for me. I'm not even gonna get jealous."

"Shut up," Yuri complained from the floor. "We're trying to watch the damn movie."

Sam kicked at him. "Like you haven't seen it a thousand times."

JUNE TURNED into July, and the real heat and humidity kicked in, drenching everything in sticky moisture. The morning of the fourth, Nathan emerged from the bathroom freshly shaven, and Sam blinked, hardly recognizing him. He'd liked the beard, but without it, Nathan was truly breathtaking. From her position curled up next to Sam on the bed, Shadow looked up and blinked sleepy blue eyes.

"Wow."

"You like?" Nathan rubbed at his jaw. His arm flexed with the movement and drew Sam's attention to the black orchid tattoo. Nathan had been talking about getting more ink, and Sam thought they might do it together.

"I love. Does it feel better?"

"So much better. I can always grow it again in the winter." Nathan removed his towel and shimmied it up and down his back. His thick cock swayed between his legs. Even when it was flaccid, it was a sight to behold. He turned around and gave Sam a show from behind, running the towel down his sides and over his shapely ass.

Sam's pulse picked up, but they didn't have time to mess around. They were due to report to the station at nine. The Fourth of July parade would start at ten. To kick it off, the acting mayor was going to award Sam's father posthumous recognition for years of service rendered. Sam would receive the honor in his name.

"Are you nervous?" Nathan asked.

"A little." His stomach swam at the thought of appearing in front of all those people. After the publication of his *Times* piece on Antonio Rivera a couple weeks before, he'd become something of a minor celebrity to those in the know. Even the *Gazette*, the paper that had strung him along on piecemeal assignments for years, had called to offer him a full staff position with benefits. Sam wasn't sure he should take it.

Nathan started to dress, covering up his glorious skin with a white, V-neck tee, and then pulling on a button-down shirt. His movements were graceful and efficient, and Sam figured he might as well enjoy the show. "How about your shoulder?"

"A little sore." Sam touched it gingerly. The external wound had scabbed over, but the muscles had yet to fully knit.

"I'll get you some aspirin," Nathan said in a tone that brooked no objection. Sam had stopped the harder drugs as quickly as he could withstand the pain. He wasn't about to trade one addiction for another.

Sam swung his legs over the side of the bed. "Okay. Thanks. I guess I should shower too."

"I'll make coffee."

They caught each other's lips in a quick kiss as Sam crossed the room. He traveled a few more feet and then turned.

"Nathan?"

"Yeah?"

"I was thinking… after the parade. Would you mind going with me to the cemetery?"

Nathan's expression softened. "Of course."


THE SKY was a clear, brilliant blue, and the grass of the Willow Run Cemetery was green as an emerald. Sam carried the medal in his right pocket. He led Nathan through the main entrance and down the dirt path that led to his family plot. Maybe someday he would wind up buried there. It was a strange, unwelcome thought, and one he pushed quickly out of mind. He had many reasons to live, and one of the most important was walking by his side.

"I haven't been here in years," he admitted.

"I know."

"It's over here." Sam gestured with his good arm.

The grave was well tended, in spite of his absence, and the pink marble stone was in pristine condition. Sam was relieved. He paid a monthly upkeep, but part of him worried his parents were being neglected even so… or maybe it was his own neglect he worried about. He'd talked it over with his therapist the day before, and she was the one who suggested the visit. She was a pretty smart lady. Being in the cemetery felt like the right thing to do.

Seamus Flynn, *March 30, 1957–December 23, 2007*

Laura Flynn, *June 8, 1959–December 27, 2007*

An unknown well-wisher had left a pot of fresh daisies on the ground. It warmed Sam from the inside, knowing someone else cared about his parents. Remembered them. He clasped Nathan's hand, squeezed, and then released it.

"I'll give you a moment alone," Nathan said.

"Thanks."

Nathan retreated to one of the nearby benches, and Sam turned back to the stone.

"Hi, Mom. Hi, Dad. I guess… it's been a while. I'm sorry."

The warm breeze ruffled his hair, almost like a caress. Somewhere in the distance, a dog barked.

Sam kneeled down, not caring if he was dirtying his nice pants. He drew the medal out of his pocket. It was bronze and shimmered in the sunlight. Sam set it down next to the daisies. "This is for you, Dad. I know… we know what happened." His voice cracked, and he blinked back the tears. The ground underneath his knees was warm, and a bee buzzed over his head. He put his hands on the smooth stone. "I love you. I want you to know that. And Tim… I have good news. He's getting better. I promise I'll take care of him."

The truth was, Tim might never fully recover. Sam knew the reality. But every day he seemed to be further emerging from his long sleep.

"And… well. There's one more thing." He glanced over his shoulder and beckoned. Nathan was pretending to look at his phone, but he immediately stood and joined Sam at the grave. He held out his hand, and Sam took it with his good arm.

"I wanted you to meet my parents," he said hoarsely. He didn't bother to wipe the tear tracks off his face. Nathan's eyes shimmered too.

Sam looked back at the stone. "This is Nathan. My partner."

"Hello," said Nathan. "I love your son very much."

They stood for a few more moments with their arms around each other's waists. Sam breathed in the fresh scent of cut grass and closed his eyes. It was a peaceful place. He was glad he picked it.

"Are you ready to go?" Nathan pressed a kiss to his temple.

"Yeah. I think I'm ready to go."

# Epilogue

*Five months later*

"SHIT, SHIT, shit. We're going to be late."

"Where're my cufflinks? Sam, did you 'borrow' them again?"

Sam looked up from buckling his belt, sure guilt was written all over his face. "I needed to wear them for the meeting with the publisher. They're not in the box?"

"No. You little brat. What am I supposed to do now?" Nathan stared forlornly at his gaping cuffs.

"Shit. I'm sorry. Maybe we can use paperclips?"

Nathan glared. "I'm not wearing paperclips to a wedding."

"It's Alex and Rachel. They won't care."

"That's not the point—"

A ring from the other room stopped the conversation. Sam squeezed Nathan's arm. "I've got this."

Sam finished tucking his shirt and hurried into the spare room, where he found his brother sitting on the edge of the bed, his handsome face twisted with frustration. He was wearing a white button-down shirt and black trousers, just as he'd been when Sam left him. When he saw Sam, he opened his mouth, and a garbled sound came out.

"What's up, bud?" Sam waited.

Tim sighed. Sam knew how frustrated he felt. The last four months hadn't been easy, but Tim's progress had defied all expectations and predictions. After a couple months of intensive physical therapy at Shady Brook, they decided to bring him home. His muscular fitness had improved, but he had difficulty with fine motor control. He gestured to his untied shoes, and Sam understood.

"You need a little help?"

Tim crossed his arms.

"Tell me what's wrong, Timbo."

Tim opened his mouth again. While he comprehended everything fully, spoken language was slower to return—and the doctors weren't sure it ever would. To compensate all three of them were learning sign language. Tim and Nathan were better at it than Sam.

*I don't want to go.*

"Why not?"

A few more signs. They were familiar.

*Don't want people to stare at me.*

"They won't."

Tim grunted. "Will."

Sam kneeled down and tied both shoes. "I know Rachel and Alex want you to be there. We don't have to stay long at the party." He looked up. Tim's face cleared slightly.

*Fine.*

Sam nodded. "It's a deal. I know it's hard for you, buddy." Sam ruffled Tim's blond hair, and Tim batted him away.

*Not a kid anymore. Jesus.*

"Sorry."

It was still an adjustment, learning to think of his brother as twenty-three instead of fifteen. Even more shocking—Tim said he'd been aware of his surroundings most of the time, and he'd heard all the things Sam had said to him. He liked being read to.

It had pretty much made Sam's life.

He also knew their parents were dead, but telling him about the murder had been another thing altogether.

It hadn't been a good week.

"How's everything going in here?" Nathan asked from the door. Tim smiled at him. While Sam received the brunt of Tim's frustration, his brother liked Nathan. He hadn't even batted an eye when Sam had told him he was gay. He just shrugged and signed, *Duh. Tell me something I don't know.*

"Yeah," said Sam. "I think we're about ready to go."

"Great. Tim, do you want the chair or are you going to walk?" Nathan asked. Nathan was matter of fact about things, where Sam made a mess of it most of the time, not wanting to cause offense.

*Walk.*

"Sounds good."

Nathan went to get the walker, and Sam let Tim use his arm to steady himself as he stood. The doctors said, in another year, he'd have barely a limp. As of now he still got winded easily and had to take frequent breaks. But seeing the pride in Tim's eyes was totally worth the slow progress.

"You look great, Tim."

And he did. His brother was handsome—classically so, with fine features that bordered on delicate.

Tim flushed and worked his mouth. "Thanks," he managed.

They made it downstairs and to the Mercedes with a few minutes to spare. Tim smiled when he saw the car. He loved it and he kept asking about learning to drive.

Other things needed sorting first. Like where they were going to live.

While having Tim at home was wonderful, it put a substantial damper on their sex life. It was exciting at first—stealing an hour or two at a hotel while Tim napped or watched TV—but the shine wore off quickly. They needed a bigger place, where they could have more privacy, and so could Tim.

Nathan had ideas. One of them was California. A month before, they received some bad news. Nathan's mother had been diagnosed with stage 2 breast cancer. He wanted to be closer to her.

Sam put his hand on Nathan's thigh and squeezed. It had been almost a week since they scened, and he needed it. Nathan gave him a dark glance as they turned onto the main road. *Later.*

There were the practicalities to consider. California would be expensive, though Nathan said they could afford it. There were also more personal concerns. Sam had never lived outside Connecticut, save for college. And of course he'd miss his friends.

But maybe it was time to start fresh. Things were looking up for them all. Nathan had taken a leave of absence from his job and was enjoying the time off. And recent talks with a certain notable publisher gave Sam hope the book project he'd been considering might actually happen, which would mean a substantial advance. Meanwhile he'd been writing so much for various online news outlets that he'd had to cut out his hours at Manella's completely. And Nathan needed to move. Family was important.

Sam's heart swelled when he thought about how brave Tim was, how strong. He belonged with them, wherever they wound up.

THE CEREMONY was short, simple, and sweet. Sam stood at Rachel's side as her best man and watched as she and Alex exchanged their vows. Both of them were beautiful, wearing matching white suits. He couldn't help glancing at Nathan and wondering if they would ever end up at the altar.

Nathan caught his eye and smiled.

BACK AT the Lucky Star after the ceremony, even Tim started to enjoy himself. He found himself in the company of a pretty girl, one of Alex's cousins. In spite of being initially shy, he soon warmed up to her, and Sam took the opportunity to pull Nathan into a dance.

The Lucky Star was freshly painted, and with the new wood floor and furniture, it had a certain class it previously lacked. Rachel was a classy lady.

"Are you having a good time?" Sam asked as they swayed together.

"Mmm-hmm. You?" Nathan wrapped his arms around Sam's back and squeezed.

"Yeah. I've been thinking."

"Oh no." Nathan nosed the side of his face.

Sam nuzzled back. "Ha. No. Seriously. It's about California."

"Oh, about that. I had an—"

"No. Hear me out. I think it might be good for us to make a change."

"Really?" Nathan grinned at him. "Are you sure?"

"Yeah. I'm sure. I guess it's starting to feel like there's not much left for us here. And it's important for you to be with your mom. And… well, I could deal without another long winter. What were you going to say?"

"I have a proposition for you. A business proposition."

"I'm all ears." Nathan spun them around in the gradually thickening crowd. Friends and family had come from all over the country to celebrate. The song changed to a slow jam.

"I was thinking about opening up my own firm."

"Firm?"

"Yes. A PI firm." Nathan tightened his arms. He seemed nervous as he waited to see how Sam would react. It was adorable.

"Shut up. Wow."

"It's only an idea. I haven't worked out the details yet, and I know you're busy with your own work. But I was hoping… well, maybe you would help out once in a while on a case."

"Like partners?" Sam could hardly believe it. Nathan was proposing they work on cases together. He once fantasized about that, but he never thought it would actually happen.

"Like partners."

"And you'd trust me?" Sam bit his bottom lip. He knew that, at one time, he wouldn't have been the most reliable partner. But he'd improved. The therapy was helping, and he was proud of the strides he'd made in his recovery. The writing helped too. It didn't mean he'd never have a setback, but he was healing, taking it one day at a time.

"With my life."

Sam threw his head back and laughed. They had come a long way. "You're not messing with me?"

"You have a lot to offer, Sam. You're smart. You're persistent. We'll have to work on your penchant for plunging into danger without a second thought, but I think it could work. What do you say?"

"Uh, I say yes. Of course. Yes."

Nathan kissed him, and Sam held on for dear life as his legs turned to jelly. Someone hooted at them from the other side of the room. Tim.

"Well, fuck me," said Sam once they finally separated. If they hadn't been in public, he probably would have dropped to his knees.

Nathan leaned down and whispered, "I intend to. For the rest of my life, if you'll have me." He grinned mischievously when Sam opened his eyes.

"What was that?" The song changed again to a louder beat, and Sam wasn't sure he'd heard correctly.

"I'm saying you're it, for me. I love you and I love your brother. I want us to be a family. I want to do this—this whole wedding thing—with you. If you want." He tacked on the last statement with a breathy laugh. "I mean, not tomorrow. But someday."

Sam glanced around to take in the scene. He was in a crowded room, dancing with Nathan and a hundred other wedding guests. A group of lesbians had begun a conga line and were weaving their way through the throng, gaining aunts, uncles, and cousins as they went. Rachel and Alex were ignoring everyone while they dirty danced to a 50 Cent throwback and, a few feet away, someone's grandmother was groping Yuri.

Sam had a pretty fucked-up subconscious, but he'd never in a million years have a dream that weird. It must be real life. He laughed and dragged Nathan's smiling mouth down to meet his own.

"Now that sounds like a partnership I can get behind."

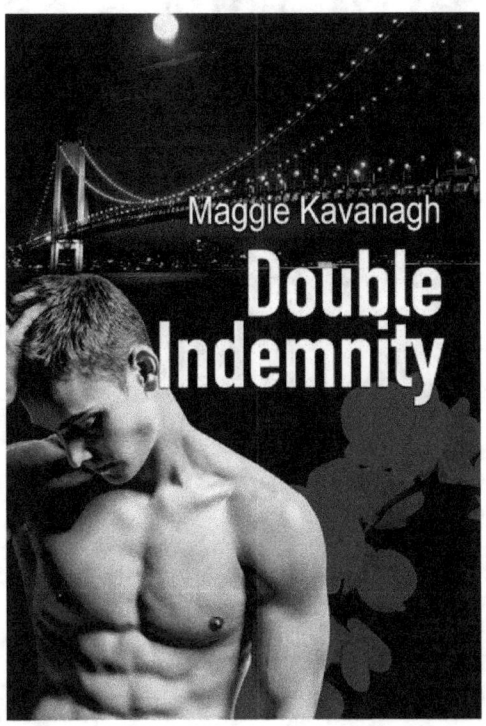

The Stonebridge Mysteries: Book One

Sam Flynn dreamed of being a journalist, until a car accident killed his parents and put his brother into a long-term coma. Now Sam spends his days as a landscaper, toiling in the New England sun, and his nights drunk in bed with the closest warm body. In his limited spare time, he writes about Stonebridge's local crime and politics on his blog "Under the Bridge."

Then Sam's favorite client is found dead in her home—shortly after telling him someone has betrayed her trust. Sam can't believe her grief-stricken husband, Nathan, would be a suspect, but the investigation focuses on him. Sam has always admired handsome Nathan from afar, but now he puts his libidinous feelings aside to help clear his name. But the closer he gets to Nathan, the more he's told to keep away from him and the investigation—by the fatherly police chief, by an officer on the case who's hated him since school, and by Nathan himself.

Sam is determined to expose the real reason his friend died and to clear Nathan's name—even if it's the last thing he does. Which, considering how fast the death toll is rising in Stonebridge… it might be.

www.dreamspinnerpress.com

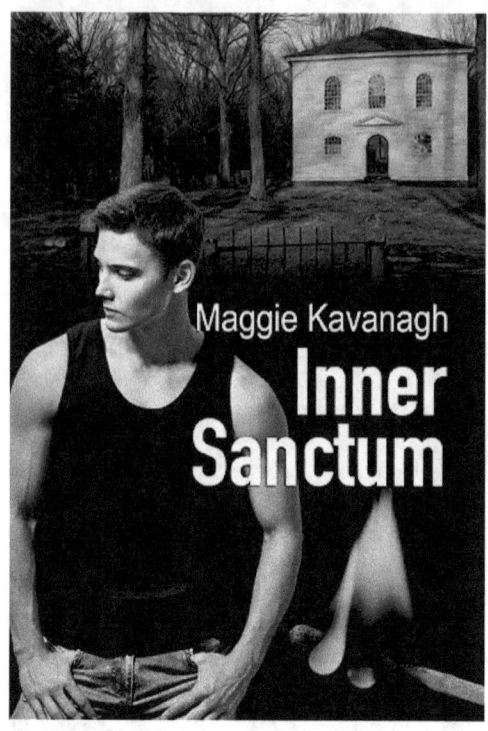

Maggie Kavanagh

# Inner Sanctum

Sequel to *Double Indemnity*
The Stonebridge Mysteries: Book Two

Six months into a relationship, things have heated up between political blogger Sam Flynn and FBI Special Agent Nathan Walker. Though Sam is happy with Nathan and proud of his own sobriety, he's anxious about what their future holds. Things are heating up in Stonebridge, Connecticut, as a series of deadly fires puts the community on edge and eventually threatens Sam's comatose brother. As Halloween approaches, fears rise that the arsonist will strike again.

When Sam encounters the main suspect, seventeen-year-old orphan Damon Blake, he's not sure what to do. Obstruction might land him in jail, but he is increasingly skeptical of Damon's guilt. He takes matters into his own hands and investigates, but doing so means keeping Damon's whereabouts a secret from Nathan and the police. Meanwhile, Nathan wonders what Sam is hiding and grapples with insecurities of his own. Sam wants to confide in Nathan, and Nathan wants to trust Sam, but they discover that negotiating new love can be as dangerous as solving crime.

# www.dreamspinnerpress.com

MAGGIE KAVANAGH writes gay romances that explore flawed human characters finding love. She went to graduate school for English literature and reads and writes voraciously whenever she can steal a moment alone. You can find her in the wee morning hours typing away with coffee at hand and cat in lap, happily embodying the romance writer cliché.

While she focuses mainly on contemporary romance and mystery, don't be surprised if a historical or supernatural tale slips into the mix, as she's always eager to explore different genres. She lives in Southern California.

Twitter: @maggie_kavanagh
Facebook: www.facebook.com/maggie.kavanagh.33
Website: maggiekavanaghwrites.com

When Hunter decides he wants more from his relationship with Jake, the couple finds themselves at a crossroads. Never home for more than a few weeks at a time, Jake has been running from the pain of a rocky childhood ever since high school, when he first enlisted in the army. The thing is, he always comes back to Hunter's bed. It's not the kind of commitment Hunter wants, but it's the kind he's settled for—that and a dead-end job at the local bookstore in the small Southern town where he grew up. When Jake reveals his plans to make a full-time career in the army, Hunter wonders if he's putting his life on hold for a relationship that will never happen. He needs to say something now before he loses Jake. However, if Jake can't conquer his demons, Hunter's asking for more is sure to drive him away.

# www.dreamspinnerpress.com

Also from Dreamspinner Press

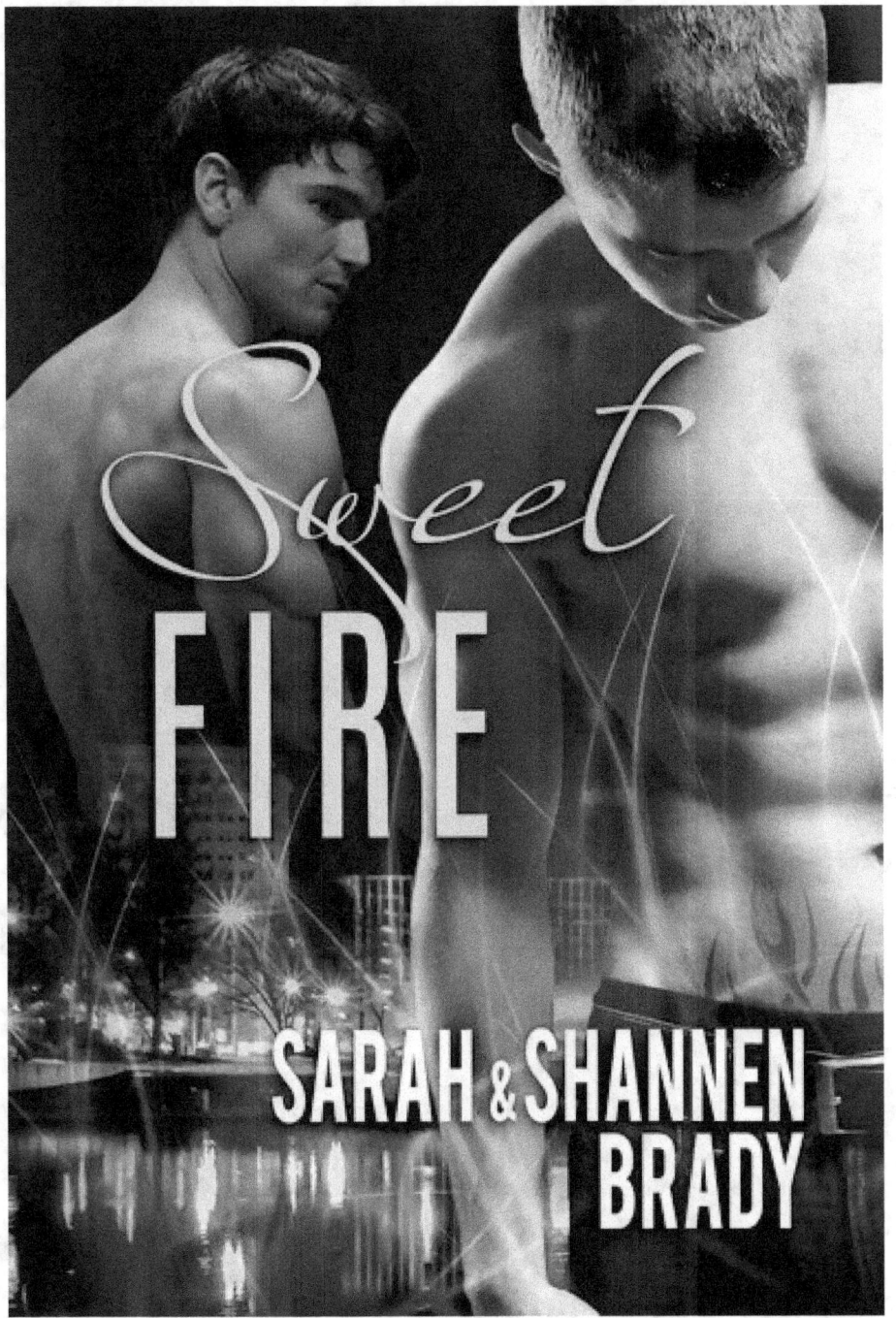

Sweet

FIRE

SARAH & SHANNEN BRADY